D1558702

Texas
Jeopardy

Center Point
Large Print

Also by James J. Griffin and available from
Center Point Large Print:

Death Stalks the Rangers
Death Rides the Rails
Ranger's Revenge

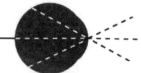

**This Large Print Book carries the
Seal of Approval of N.A.V.H.**

Texas
Jeopardy

A Texas Ranger
James C. Blawcyzk Novel

James J. Griffin

CENTER POINT LARGE PRINT
THORNDIKE, MAINE

The text of this Large Print edition is unabridged.
In other aspects, this book may vary
from the original edition.
Printed in the United States of America
on permanent paper.
Set in 16-point Times New Roman type.

ISBN: 978-1-68324-846-0

Library of Congress Cataloging-in-Publication Data

Names: Griffin, James J., 1949- author.
Title: Texas jeopardy : a Texas Ranger James C. Blawcyzk novel /
    James J. Griffin.
Description: Center Point Large Print edition. | Thorndike, Maine :
    Center Point Large Print, 2018.
Identifiers: LCCN 2018014713 | ISBN 9781683248460
    (hardcover : alk. paper)
Subjects: LCSH: Texas Rangers—Fiction. | Large type books.
Classification: LCC PS3607.R5477 T49 2018 | DDC 813/.6—dc23
LC record available at https://lccn.loc.gov/2018014713

Special thanks to Jim Huggins, Texas Ranger Sergeant, Retired, and Senior Lecturer of Forensics Science, Baylor University, for his invaluable assistance.

———————

Thanks to Karl Rehn and Penny Riggs of KR Training in Mannheim, Texas, for their expertise on weapons.

———————

Thanks to Dr. Keith Souter of Wakefield, United Kingdom, for his assistance on medical questions.

For Jim and Cora Huggins,
and their children, Laura and Dan.

1

Sixth generation Texas Ranger James Charles Blawcyzk lay bellied down at the summit of a forested hill, about ten miles west of the small town of Utopia, where he'd been since before sunrise. He'd removed his hat, on the off chance someone at the isolated ranch down below might spot it sticking above the brush and weeds he was using for cover.

Jim had been working on this investigation for months, and if everything went according to plan, today would be the culmination of his work. Of course, as he well knew, things seldom, if ever, went according to plan in law enforcement. Now was definitely not the time to blow months of painstaking effort by some slight, stupid, mistake.

His horse, Copper, a close coupled overo paint, was picketed below the hilltop, out of sight. Jim had ridden Copper cross-country over the rugged, hilly terrain for more than three miles from where he'd left his dark blue unmarked Chevy Tahoe patrol car and Copper's attached trailer, hidden deep in a draw off Cherry Creek Ranch Road.

"Dang flies," he muttered, as he slapped a horse fly which had landed on the back of his neck and bit. Blood splattered on his neck and hand from the flattened insect. Jim wiped the blood and fly's remains off his hand on a patch of dried grass, then refocused his Nikon D5 camera on the men loading white plastic wrapped bundles onto a silver Ford F350 pickup and flatbed trailer, from a ramshackle barn at the hardscrabble ranch along Cherry Creek. He snapped picture after picture as the men continued loading the bundles, then concealed them under bales of hay. When their job was completed, and they began to cover the load with a blue tarp, he slid back from the top of the hill, put his hat back on, and hurried to where Copper was waiting.

"We'd better move quick, boy," he said to the sorrel and white splotched paint, as he pulled the picket pin. "We've got to be back at the truck before those *hombres* make it to the highway, just in case they fool us, break their pattern, and take a different route today. I won't be able to reach Randy, and let him know our boys are on the move, until we've got cell service again." He coiled up his rope, hung it from the saddlehorn, tightened his cinches, and climbed into the saddle. "Let's move, partner."

Jim kept Copper at a fast walk for the first quarter-mile, until the horse warmed up, then pushed him into a steady lope, urging him into a gallop where the terrain permitted. Once they reached Jim's truck and trailer, he dismounted and loaded Copper, still saddled and bridled.

"Sorry for leavin' the gear on you, Copper, but

we're cuttin' it too close as it is," Jim said, as he slammed the trailer doors shut and secured them. "I'll try'n make this up to you once everything's over. Don't worry, I've got your peppermints." He unlocked the Tahoe, got behind the steering wheel, fired up the engine, threw the truck into gear, and began rolling. Once the vehicle reached the top of a rise, he hit the button on the steering wheel to activate the truck's Chevrolet Mylink and his Bluetooth cell phone connection. He spoke a phone number, and gave a sigh of relief when a connection was made. After two rings, the voice of Ranger Randy Newton from Company D came over the Tahoe's speakers.

"Howdy, Jim. 'Bout time you called. I was startin' to get worried. Where you at?"

"Howdy, Randy," Jim answered. "Workin' my way down Cherry Creek Ranch Road right now. We've gotta talk quick. Dunno how long I'll have service back here," Jim responded. "I'm movin' as fast as I dare, between the bad road and haulin' Copper behind me. Ow! Damn, that hurt," he said, when the truck hit a particularly deep chuckhole.

"I heard that bang clear over my phone," Randy said, laughing. "Hurt your head much?"

"Nah, but the bump smashed my hat on the truck's roof. Gave me a real jolt," Jim answered. "How about you, Randy? What's your position?"

"My position is sittin' down on my butt in the

11

driver's seat of my truck, lookin' at the damned dust devils," Randy answered. "If you want to know my location, I'm in the abandoned sand pit just off Farm 1050 and Cherry Creek Ranch. Those boys headed my way?"

"They should be on top of you any minute, smart mouth," Jim said. "If they hold true to form, they're gonna head east to Utopia, then cut north on 187 to pick up 470 East, toward Tarpley."

"*Bueno*," Randy answered. "I'll keep 'em in sight until you catch up to us."

"Don't get too close," Jim cautioned. "We don't want to spook those *hombres* after all this time."

"Don't worry," Randy answered. "The only things I like to get too close to are a nice, cold, long neck Lone Star, and my wife. Those boys won't see me."

"*Bueno*," Jim answered. "I'm gonna hang up, so I can concentrate on this poor excuse of a road. Even by Texas gravel backroad standards, this one's real bad. Ouch!"

"Another chuckhole?" Randy said, laughing once more. "Try drivin' a little faster. Maybe with any luck the jouncin'll send your brains from your butt back up to your head, where they belong."

"Funny, Randy. Real funny," Jim said. "I'll see you down the road."

"Later."

• • •

Jim had just reached the intersection with Farm to Market Road 1050 when his phone came back to life.

"Yeah, Randy?"

"You get out of the back country yet?" Randy said, as soon as he heard Jim's voice.

"Just got to 1050," Jim answered. "Our boys headed east?"

"They sure enough are," Randy said. "I reckon we're about eight miles ahead of you. I'm keepin' well back, but I won't lose those *hombres*, neither. I've never yet lost a man I was trailin'."

"What about that woman you were followin' out of Sabinal, the one who killed her husband and boyfriend both?" Jim asked.

"Hey, I never said I hadn't lost a *woman,* just a *man,*" Randy retorted. "Besides, she was drivin' a big honkin' Mercedes, while I was in this here damned Dakota. There was no way I could keep up with her. Good thing the county boys managed to set up a roadblock in time to stop her."

"She ain't the only woman you lost, as I recollect, until you somehow talked Susanne into marryin' you," Jim answered. "Good thing those deputies jumped outta the way in time, too, if I remember right. From the pictures, that woman sure made a wreck of their cars."

"She sure did," Randy agreed. "Our plan still the same, Jim? I'll follow these boys until they cross back into Company F territory, then you'll take it from there?"

"Unless they do somethin' to make us change it," Jim answered. "In that case, all bets are off."

"All right. Tell you what. I'll stick with our boys as far as Utopia, then drop off. I'll pull up in front of the general store, and you can take over from there. It doesn't matter none for that little bit until you're back in Bandera County."

"Sounds reasonable to me."

"Of course, that all depends on whether that Chevy you've got can move fast enough to stay with us, especially with you haulin' that cussed spotted hay burner around."

"Don't you worry about that. We'll be on your back bumper before you know it. I'm sure glad I got lucky and the state gave me this vehicle— heavy duty, dependable . . . it's one of the best around. Besides, I told you we'd never be able to collect the evidence we needed without me goin' through the malpais on horseback, to where I could sneak up on that ranch without bein' spotted."

Most Texas Rangers, especially those not stationed in west Texas or the Panhandle, no longer owned their own horses, instead borrowing one when needed, usually from the Texas Department of Corrections, or else a rancher or farmer. However, Jim was one who still did—his paint gelding. He'd named the horse Copper because

14

his mostly sorrel coat shone like a newly minted penny.

"All right, I'll give you that much," Randy conceded. "We did need your horse. Besides, whoever's drivin' that Ford is goin' nice and slow. He sure ain't takin' any chances on gettin' pulled over for speedin' or some such. You won't have to push too hard to find me."

"Okay. Talk to you in a bit, Randy."

Jim hung up, then called out another number, which was quickly answered.

"Ranger Garcia."

"Rudy, Jim Blawcyzk. You'll be lookin' for a silver Ford F350 pullin' a flatbed trailer, loaded with hay, goin' east on 470. I don't have the plates. I'm gonna pull it over at 470 and South Little Creek Road, then back off. I figure you can pick it back up at South Seco Creek, and stick with it until they roll into my county. I'll take over from there."

"How long do you figure it'll be until they're in my sight, Jim?" Rudy asked.

"Probably about forty-five minutes or so," Jim answered. "I'll call you soon as I stop them, then once I've let them go."

"That sounds just fine. I reckon I won't need to follow those *hombres* too close."

"Not at all. You can stay as far back as you'd like. We sure don't want to scare those boys off. Not this far along."

15

"No, we sure don't," Rudy agreed. "I'll be in position in about twenty minutes. That should be plenty of time. Lemme know once you've turned 'em loose."

"Will do."

Rudy hung up. Jim grabbed a handful of cashew nuts from an open bag in his truck's console, gulped them down, then popped open a warm can of Dr Pepper and took two swallows. He pushed down on the accelerator, until the Tahoe settled at a steady seventy-five mph.

Jim drove at high speed until he saw Randy's Dakota up ahead, then slowed down and remained about a quarter-mile behind. He dropped back to the speed limit, keeping Randy in his sight until they reached the small town of Utopia. The limit dropped to thirty within the town proper, and apparently the Ford's driver wasn't taking the least chance of being pulled over for a traffic violation, for Randy's truck fell exactly to thirty. Jim drew a little closer, and watched Randy pull over in front of the Utopia General Store. He could see the pickup and trailer they were following a little way ahead. Two minutes after he rolled past Randy, his phone rang.

"They're all yours, Jim," Randy said. "Good luck."

"Same to you, Randy. Too bad you can't join in on the fun at the other end."

"Sure wish I could, but I've already contacted Rhonda to let her know it's time for us to move in on that ranch. She's waitin' for me back at Cherry Creek Ranch Road, so we can go in there and clean out the snakes at our end."

"Understood. Although Rhonda Johnston could handle that all by herself."

"I won't deny that, but better to be safe than sorry."

"You've got that right. Thanks again for all your help, Randy. I appreciate your lettin' me work in your county. Tell Major Dolan again for me that I appreciate him lettin' me come into D's territory, too. I'm obliged to you both."

Texas Rangers were assigned to a company, and then stationed in a centrally located town, from which they had several counties to cover. It was a major violation of protocol to go into another Ranger's territory, without notifying the Ranger whose territory you needed to enter, and getting permission from him or her, or their commanding officer. The only exception was a direct order from Headquarters itself.

"Not a problem at all, Jim. After all, this whole thing started in your area. Once it's all over, we'll have to get together for a few beers."

"Sounds good to me. Good luck to you and Rhonda, too. Be careful."

"You know it. *Adios.*"

"*Adios*, Randy."

Once they left the Utopia town limits, Jim picked up his speed a bit and drew a little nearer the Ford and trailer. He watched the rig turn right as expected, heading east on Ranch Road 470. When they neared South Little Creek Road, Jim called Rudy to let him know he was about to make the stop, then flipped on the red and blue strobe lights hidden behind the Tahoe's grille, and hit his siren. He drew in a deep breath as he waited to see what the driver of the Ford would do.

"Damn! We've got company!" Bobby Lee Meredith exclaimed, when he spotted the vehicle rapidly pulling up behind him, lights flashing. "What're we gonna do?"

"Keep goin' a little ways, until we can see if he just wants to get around us," Brady Keyes, one of his partners, advised.

"I warned you to be careful, Bobby Lee, and not do any speedin'," Jasper Coates, the third man, said. "Now we could be in one helluva fix."

"I wasn't speedin', Jasper, damn it, and you know damn well I wasn't," Meredith said. "I'm gonna pull over right here. We just need to keep cool, until we see what that cop wants. Here's hopin' he only wants us to move over so he can get by. Or maybe he's just lookin' for illegal Mexes or somethin'."

18

He pulled into a wide spot on the shoulder of the road.

"Damn it. He pulled in right behind us," Meredith said.

"We could just kill him, soon as he gets out of his car," Coates said. "Gun him down when he opens the door and steps out."

"Don't be a damn fool, Jasper," Keyes said. "Out here on a main road, in full daylight? We don't kill this cop unless we have to. I'd rather we try and outrun him, if things turn sour. He's pullin' a horse trailer, so he won't be able to go all that fast."

"Neither will we, with what we're haulin'," Coates said. "I don't want to take that chance."

"Especially since that ain't just any cop," Meredith said, as he watched the peace officer get out of his truck, and place his hand on the butt of the pistol hanging at his left hip. "He's wearin' a Ranger badge. That's a damn Texas Ranger. I sure as hell don't want to tangle with the damn Rangers. We'd just better be real polite, and keep our hands where he can see 'em. Maybe he's just lookin' for another truck like this one, or only wants to ask us if we've seen anythin'. We'll wait and find out."

"But not too long," Coates said. "He makes one wrong move, and I'm goin' for my gun. There's three of us and one of him. He don't stand a chance."

"Just make certain you get him before he pulls his gun, if it comes to that," Meredith said. "I don't feel like takin' a damn bullet. You two keep quiet, now."

He rolled down his window.

"Howdy, Ranger," he said. "What seems to be the problem? I wasn't speedin' or anything, was I?"

"No, there's no real problem," Jim answered. "I just happened to notice a couple of the tie downs on your load are comin' loose. I pulled you over just to warn you, so you could tighten 'em up before you lose some of your load, and maybe cause an accident. We'd sure hate to see that happen, wouldn't we?"

Meredith let out an audible sigh of relief.

"No. No, we sure wouldn't want that to happen, Ranger. Thanks."

"No problem at all. I'll just stay behind you while you secure that hay. It'd be a shame if some drunk, or a texting teenager, crashed into the back of your rig while you were getting things fixed."

"Appreciate that, Ranger. We're obliged. Brady, Jasper, go check those straps."

"Sure, Bobby Lee," Keyes said. "C'mon, Jasper."

He and Coates got out of the truck.

"Which ones are loose, Ranger?" Keyes asked.

"A couple of 'em on the left side of the trailer," Jim answered. "But if I were you boys, I'd check all of 'em, just to make certain."

"That's good advice, Ranger. We'll take it,"

Coates said. "C'mon, Brady, let's get at 'em."

Several of the tie downs had, indeed, come somewhat loose, as usually happened if they weren't checked within a few miles after the start of a run. Of course, the three men hadn't noticed Jim help two straps at the back of the trailer's load loosen a bit more, when he pretended to inspect them while they worked on the side tie downs. He casually leaned against the front of his Tahoe while Keyes and Coates checked and tightened every strap.

"Everything seems to be fine now, Ranger," Coates said. "Most of 'em weren't too loose, but we appreciate your noticin' those that were, and lettin' us know."

"Glad to have been of help. Where're y'all headed?" Jim asked.

"Austin," Keyes said. "This hay's for a horse farm just north of town."

"Then it's a good thing I stopped you," Jim said. "You'd never have made it that far. If you'd ever lost all that hay on I-35, you boys would have been in a real fix. It could have been a very expensive ticket."

"I guess we would have been, at that," Keyes said. "Well, I reckon we'll be on our way. Thanks again, Ranger."

"You're welcome. Drive careful, now."

"Bobby Lee always does, Ranger," Keyes said.

Jim waited until the two men were back in their

pickup, and watched them pull away. He made a U-turn, parked a quarter-mile down the road, then called Rudy Garcia. While waiting for Rudy to answer, he removed his badge and slipped it into his shirt pocket.

"Rudy, it's Jim. I just turned 'em loose. They're headed your way. The pickup's bearing Farm Truck plate Paul 1 David 226. Plate on the trailer is Farm Trailer George Henry Mary Robert 79."

"Great. I should spot that rig in a few minutes," Rudy said. "You figure they're gonna head through Bandera?"

"That's what I'm countin' on."

"All right, that means I'll stay with 'em to Bandera, then let you know which way they go from there."

"It'll most likely be through Pipe Creek. Then they'll pick up 46 to Boerne. If that's the route they take, I'd appreciate you stayin' with 'em until the Kendall County line."

"Okay, I'll do just that. Soon as they make the turn on 46, I'll give you a holler, Jim."

"If they keep on 16 toward San Antonio instead, then you'll have to keep with 'em, since they'll be staying in your county."

"If they do, I'm liable to lose them in city traffic."

"Maybe you will, but I won't. Not now," Jim said. "If they do head for San Antonio, I'll be right behind you."

"Well, we should know shortly. I see that truck comin' now," Rudy said. "Talk to you when we reach Bandera."

Once Rudy was off the phone, Jim made some minor adjustments to the monitor on his laptop, and the transponder connected to it.

"It's workin' just fine," he said to himself, as a series of pings sounded, as well as a small green rectangle moving steadily eastward along the black line which indicated Farm to Market Road 470. "Those boys have no idea I stuck a tracking device underneath their trailer. Unless somethin' goes real wrong, they're gonna lead me right straight to the delivery point. They're sure gonna be surprised when they find out this is their last run."

Thirty-five minutes later, Jim's cell phone rang.

"Yeah, Rudy?" he said, as soon as he answered.

"They took 46 all right, Jim." Rudy answered. "It seems like your hunch was right on target. It appears they're headed for Boerne."

"Yeah, the tracking device is workin' perfectly, at least so far," Jim answered. "It showed them take the turn. You still got 'em in sight?"

"Just," Rudy answered. "I'm keeping far enough back they won't spot me and get suspicious. There's a couple of cars and a trash hauler between us right now."

"That's good," Jim said. "Stay with 'em until I tell you to back off."

"Do you still want me to drop out soon as we cross into Kendall County?"

"Nah, unless you'd rather. If you could stick with 'em until they reach Boerne, I'd really appreciate it."

"I don't have a problem with that."

"Thanks. Let me know when they get close to Boerne. It'll be interesting to see whether they get on I-10 or stay on 46."

"Sure thing, Jim. Soon as they hit I-10 I'll let you know. Or if I happen to lose 'em."

"Okay. Talk to you in a bit."

Jim hung up, and settled to following a couple of miles behind Rudy, while keeping track of their quarry's progress on his computer monitor. Fifteen minutes later, his phone rang.

"Yeah, Rudy?"

"You still got 'em on the screen, Jim?"

"Plain as day."

"Then you know they went over the interstate and are stayin' on 46. Wait a minute. What the hell are they doin'?"

"I dunno, but keep 'em in sight until I get closer," Jim said. "The information I was given said they might be headin' for another delivery point, rather than the usual one. It looks like they could be doin' just that."

The Ford had made a sharp left turn, then a quick right, to head north on South School Street. It crossed over Frederick and Cibolo Creeks, where South School changed to North School, and continued north.

"Seems like they're gonna stay on 51, Jim. After that, either they're gonna take Business 87, or else pick up the Sisterdale Cutoff to Ranch Road 1376. I'll know in a minute."

Jim's phone went silent, until Rudy spoke again.

"They've caught a red light at 87 and the cutoff, Jim, and are waiting for it to change. They ain't gonna turn off, seems like. They're not in the left turn lane, and don't have a turn signal flashing. I'm gonna pull into the lot for the Lung Fung Chinese place and let you take over, before they spot me. You want me to pick you up some Chinese while I'm there? I could sure go for some General Tso's chicken."

"No, I can't stomach Chinese grub," Jim answered, laughing. "However, I wouldn't mind a pizza from Broken Stone. That's in the same strip mall. Besides, shouldn't you be orderin' Mexican? You'll look pretty funny in a Chinese restaurant."

"No funnier than you would goin' into a soul food place, white as you are, with those blue eyes and blonde hair, paleface. I'll see what I can do about the pizza," Rudy said, also laughing. "And a couple of beers from the Boerne Brewery. Hold on. The light just changed. Yep, they're staying north on the cutoff. Dollars to doughnuts those boys are gonna pick up Ranch 1376 north. It'd be damn stupid to cut back toward town from here."

"Unless, somehow, they've realized they're being followed, and are tryin' to throw us off."

"I doubt it, Jim. I stayed well back until just now."

"All right, I'll be on their tail in a minute. Thanks for the help."

"Anytime. I just pulled into the lot. I can see you rollin' up on me now. Listen, I don't have anythin' doin' that can't wait until tomorrow. Could you use an extra man for backup? After all, since they've apparently already changed plans, you don't know what you might be facin' when they do finally stop."

"Ya know, that's not a bad idea," Jim agreed. "As long as you can clear it with the major, I'd sure appreciate havin' someone else to watch my back."

"I'll contact him now, and get right back to you."

"*Bueno.* Our boys just got onto Ranch 1376. While you're callin' the major, I'll radio in and have the other two units repositioned. They were waiting over in New Braunfels, since that's where the delivery was supposed to be made, but it doesn't look like it now. I'll have 'em swing over to Spring Branch and wait there. That way, they'll be in location to head in any direction."

"Okay. I'll get back to you soon as I have the okay from the major."

Once Rudy hung up, Jim flicked on his two-way radio and picked up the mic. Most Rangers no longer left their radios on now, unless they absolutely needed to use them. The background static, and chatter from the various county sheriff's departments, state troopers, and local law enforcement agencies could be extremely distracting.

In addition, the chances were far greater that a criminal would intercept a police radio transmission than a cell phone conversation. The advent of cell phones, and wider coverage over the years, had made the use of radios far less efficient or necessary.

"Ranger Unit 810 to dispatch."

"Ranger Unit 810."

"Dispatch, I need you to contact Ranger Units 873 and 942 for me. I'd like them to move from their present locations to Spring Branch. I'll also need you to confirm that they've received my instructions."

"10-4, Ranger Unit 810. Contacting them now."

Jim kept about a mile behind the Ford, which was still heading north on Ranch 1376. Unless the delivery was going to be made somewhere along that road, the next chance for the pickup's occupants to turn would be when they reached Sisterdale. A few minutes later, his radio crackled back to life.

"Dispatch to Ranger Unit 810."

Jim keyed the mic.

"Ranger Unit 810."

"Confirming Ranger Units 873 and 942 are repositioning to Spring Branch. They will be at Farm to Market Road 311 and U.S. 287."

"10-4, Dispatch. Tell them to stay on the road behind the Spring Branch store. That should keep 'em out of sight."

"Will do, Ranger 810."

"10-4. Ranger 810, out."

Jim hung the mic back in its bracket, but left the radio on. He closed to within half-a-mile of the Ford. When the truck reached Farm to Market Road 473, it turned right, heading east. Jim's phone rang before he also made the turn.

"Jim, it's Rudy. Sorry it took me a few minutes to get back to you, but Major Voitek had stepped out of the office, so Mary had to track him down. I'm cleared to assist you until this is over."

"Thanks, Rudy. I'm obliged. Our boys just turned east on Farm 473. I'm about a half-mile behind."

"Where the hell are they headed?" Rudy asked. "There ain't nothing much out here. Of course, that might be exactly what they're countin' on."

"I dunno. It sure beats the hell out of me," Jim answered. "I reckon we're about to find out, though."

"Here's hoping," Rudy answered. "I'm on my

way again. I should catch up with you shortly. How about the other units?"

"All set. They'll be waitin' down at Spring Branch, until we figure out for certain where these *hombres* are headed."

"That sounds about right," Rudy answered. "Once I see your rig, I'll stay a couple of hundred yards behind."

"Okay, Rudy. I'll keep you posted which way they're goin'."

Jim reached Farm 473 and turned right. Ahead, the Ford picked up speed slightly.

"Sure hope they reach wherever they're headed soon," Jim muttered. He stepped on the Tahoe's accelerator, to match the pace of the Ford, which was now visible a few hundred yards ahead. Several miles later, he called Rudy.

"Rudy."

"Yeah, Jim?"

"They just went by the junction with Farm 474, and seem to be slowing down. It appears like they could be lookin' for a turnoff. Stay on your phone."

"Okay, Jim."

A minute later, Jim spoke again.

"We're goin' past Samson Road. They're slowin' down a bit more. The next turn they could take would be Old Blanco Road. Let's see."

About thirty seconds went by.

"Yep, they just put their left turn signal on, and

are slowin' down. There they go onto Old Blanco. I'm gonna stay on 473 for a couple hundred yards, then pull over. Don't want to chance them seein' me. Why don't you pull over right where you are? Once they reach the intersection with Crabapple and Blanco-Kendalia, we'll take up their trail again."

"All right."

Jim drove past the Old Blanco Road junction, then pulled into a small, long-abandoned sand and gravel pit on the left side of the road. The green rectangle on his monitor continued for slightly more than a mile, then turned left. It only went about a hundred yards before it stopped moving, and the pings went silent.

"Rudy, they've stopped. I'm gonna drive up Old Blanco and see where they've pulled into. You stay on 473 to Crabapple, then meet me at the intersection of Crabapple and Old Blanco."

"You've got it, Jim."

Jim put his Tahoe back into gear, then turned onto Old Blanco Road. The rectangle on his monitor never moved, but the pings resumed, getting louder and more frequent as he neared the place where the Ford had stopped. Jim drove slowly past a dirt road on the left, where a haze of dust indicated a vehicle had just passed. One man, who apparently had gotten out to close and lock the gate, was walking up the road. A sign at the road's edge read "Thunder Ridge Nursery—

Plants and Garden Supplies. Wholesale Only."

"Got ya!" he exclaimed, when he spotted the Ford and trailer, backing into a large corrugated metal barn or storage building.

"Rudy, we've got 'em," he said into his phone. "They're at a place called Thunder Ridge Nursery. I'll be with you in a couple of minutes. I'm gonna look things over first."

"I'm just getting to Crabapple and Old Blanco," Rudy answered. "I'll see you there."

"All right."

Jim hung up, then dialed another number.

"Ranger Thornton."

"Jerry, it's Jim Blawcyzk. The *hombres* I've been following have stopped. I need you and Mason to meet me and Rudy Garcia at Old Blanco and Crabapple Roads, just outside of Kendalia."

"Sure thing, Jim. I'll come in from 281 and 473, and have Mason take Sattler Road. I don't want to take a chance on having someone spottin' us travelin' together, and getting curious. We'll be there in twenty minutes."

"That's fine. It'll give me some time to finish scoutin' out the situation. In fact, I might even stop at the little general store in the center of Kendalia, to grab a couple of Dr Peppers before I meet up with you boys. If those *hombres* did see me, and got a bit suspicious, stoppin' at the store should throw 'em off. My badge's in my shirt pocket, and I sure ain't dressed like a Ranger, so anybody in the store'll just take me for a rancher or cowboy passin' through. If someone at the store does ask, that's what I'll tell 'em. See you soon."

"See ya, Jim."

Rudy reached the meeting spot shortly before Jim arrived. Jim pulled up a few yards past him, then both men got out of their vehicles, Rudy walking up to join his fellow Ranger. Jim, who as usual was munching on cashews and holding a can of Dr Pepper, opened the left front door of his horse trailer to check on Copper.

The horse stuck his head out to sniff the air, look around, and nuzzle Jim's shoulder. Jim gave him a pat on the nose and a peppermint. Copper took the treat, then went back to munching his hay. Seeing Jim and Rudy standing there in conversation, any passersby would just assume they were two cowboys or ranch hands, who'd stopped to exchange howdies, or perhaps talk horses and cattle.

"Did you get ahold of Jerry and Mason?" Rudy asked.

"Yeah. They'll be here in about ten minutes now, I'd say."

"What're we gonna be up against?"

Jim pushed back his white Stetson and ran a hand through his hair before answering.

"I can't be certain, but I've seen worse," he said. "There's only two buildings, and the one nearer the road didn't seem to be much more than a one room office. There didn't appear to be anyone in it. The building our boys went into is a big metal warehouse type structure. There's a garage door and an entrance door in the front, and I'd bet my hat there's one each in the rear, too. There's another dirt road that circles around the back. Both of 'em are gated. There's security cameras at all four corners of the warehouse, and a couple on the smaller building, so we'll have to hit 'em hard and fast."

"Do you have a specific plan in mind, Jim?"

"Yeah. Not one I like, but with those gates and cameras, it's the only chance we have of gettin' the drop on however many men are in there before they're ready for us. Me'n you are gonna go in the front. I'll take the lead, smash down the gate, then bust through the garage door. I'll have Jerry and Mason take the back and do the same. With any luck, we'll get those *hombres* between us, and they won't put up much of a fight."

"And I just saw a pig fly overhead, too," Rudy said, dryly.

"Yeah, well if you've got any better ideas, Rudy, now's the time to come up with 'em."

"I wish I did, but your plan is the same one I'd use."

33

"Then let's get ready while we're waitin' for our partners."

Rudy went back to his gray Dodge Dakota, while Jim opened the tailgate of the Tahoe. He took his badge from his shirt pocket and pinned it on, then removed a bulletproof vest and slipped that on, as well as a Remington shotgun, which he placed on the front seat of his truck. A moment later, two more Ranger SUVs pulled up, a black Tahoe and a dark green Dakota. Ranger Jerry Thornton got out of the Dakota, and Mason Kennedy from the Tahoe. They exchanged howdies with Jim and Rudy, then Jim explained his plans to them.

"Jerry, I'll give you and Mason a couple of minutes to work your way around the back. The road you're lookin' for is a quarter-mile before the main entrance. This is it right here."

Jim indicated the road on his cell phone's map.

"Seems like there's at least halfway decent cover, until we get close to the buildin'," Mason noted. "Quite a few live oaks planted around the place. Of course, once we bust in there, cover ain't really gonna matter."

"No, it sure won't," Jim agreed. He checked his watch. "Let's go in at one ten."

At precisely ten minutes after one, Jim smashed through the gate at the main entrance to Thunder Ridge Nursery. The gate flew open at the impact of the Tahoe's push bar, the right side of the gate falling off its hinges, the left sagging, bent and twisted. With Rudy right behind him, Jim tore up the dirt road, then crashed through the warehouse's fiberglass overhead door, shattering it and sending panels sailing in every direction. He braked to a hard stop, with Rudy turning his Dakota sideways to block the door. At the rear of the building, Jerry slammed his Dakota through the door, with Mason skidding his Tahoe to a stop behind him.

Jim leapt from his truck, shotgun in hand.

"Texas Rangers!" he shouted. "Nobody move. Down on the floor, now!"

He fired one round from his Remington into a shelf of empty glass bottles for emphasis. One man toward the back started for his pistol, but a bullet between his feet from Jerry's pistol quickly discouraged him. He dropped to his belly, and put his hands behind his head.

"Next one who tries somethin' like that will wind up dead," Jim warned. "Get down on your bellies, hands behind your necks, and stay there. Don't even wiggle."

The door to the bathroom was flung open. The man in its doorway fired one hasty shot, which hit Rudy in his left arm. Before he could pull the trigger again, Jim turned his shotgun and fired another round. The lead shot took the shooter in his chest and stomach. He staggered backward.

35

When the back of his knees hit the edge of the lid up toilet, he collapsed to a sitting position, his butt jammed in the porcelain throne. His chin dropped to his lead riddled chest.

"Anybody else?" Jim asked. "Rudy, how bad are you hit?"

"I dunno," Rudy answered, from where he had slumped against a pile of bundled wood shavings. He still had his gun pointed at two of the men on the floor. "I'm bleedin' like a stuck hog, though. Dammit. Wearin' a bulletproof vest, but I still took a slug. What kind of luck is that?"

"All bad, I'd say, but it could've been a lot worse," Jerry said. "You could have been shot in the head."

"Which would have ruined a perfectly good hat," Mason added.

"Or the face, which might have improved his looks," Jim added.

"Real funny," Rudy said, through teeth gritted against the pain. "Just what I needed. I get shot, and instead of a doc I've got two damn comedians to deal with."

"Mason, get your first aid kit," Jim ordered. "Call for an ambulance, too. The nearest one will be from the Kendalia Volunteer Fire Department. Also let the Kendall County Sheriff know we'll need some assistance out here to close this road, guard our perimeter, and keep people away. Hang on, Rudy. Jerry, let's secure these prisoners."

"I'll notify Headquarters what went down, too."

"I appreciate that, Mason."

There were nine men in the warehouse, plus the dead one in the bathroom.

"How about that son of a bitch who shot Rudy, although I already know your answer, Jim?" Jerry asked. "It looks like you pretty much made mincemeat of him."

"He's halfway to Hell by now," Jim answered. Bobby Lee Meredith heard him and recognized his voice. He looked up from where he was lying, and stared at Jim.

"Damn! You're the Ranger who pulled us over just outside Utopia," he said. "I should have known you wanted more than to have us secure our load."

"I told you we should've killed him on the spot, Bobby Lee," Jasper Coates said. "Just so you know, Ranger, if it had been up to me, I would have."

"That might not have been as easy as you think," Jim answered. "But I purely do appreciate you boys leadin' us straight here. I'm obliged."

"The bastard stuck a damn trackin' device on our rig, damn him," Brady Keyes exclaimed.

"That's right," Jim said.

"We don't have to worry," one of the other prisoners said. "These bastards didn't show us a warrant, or read us our rights. We'll be set loose in a couple of days, at most."

"We didn't need a warrant, since we had probable cause," Jim said. "I watched that truck bein' loaded, got plenty of pictures, and followed it right here. As far as your rights, you haven't been charged with anything . . . yet. As soon as we make certain you're gonna behave, we'll read you the charges, and the Miranda."

Mason hurried back inside, carrying his first aid kit. He went over to Rudy to begin treating his bullet wound.

"The ambulance is on its way," he said. "Company Headquarters has Lieutenant Stoker comin' up from San Antonio, too. You know there'll be an inquiry into the shootin', Jim, so he'll be takin' over once he gets here. I was told none of us were to talk to the media until he arrives. You'll probably be placed on leave."

"I'm not worried about that; at least, for right now," Jim answered. "Let's just get to work here."

Once the prisoners were secured, Jim walked over to the Ford pickup. He rolled back a corner of the tarp, cut one of the tie downs, pulled off four bales of hay, then reached between two others and pulled out a brick sized, plastic wrapped bundle.

"Well, well, look what we have here," he said. "I do believe it's time to tell you boys what charges you're facin'."

38

• • •

After securing the prisoners, giving them the charges against them, and reading them their rights, Jim, Jerry, and Mason began searching the warehouse, while Rudy waited for medical transport. Twenty minutes later, the ambulance from Kendalia arrived. The two volunteer EMTs, both women, quickly took over where Mason had left off.

"You did a good job, Ranger," one told him. "It appears the bullet hit an artery. Your friend would have bled to death if you hadn't bandaged his arm so well." To Rudy, she said, "Ranger, we'll load you up, pump some I.V. antibiotics and fluids into you once we're rollin', and stabilize your arm. Would you rather go to St. Luke's Baptist in Boerne or Baptist Emergency in San Antonio? They're both about the same distance."

"Baptist Emergency. It's closer to home."

"Baptist Emergency it is."

Rudy was loaded on a gurney. His fellow Rangers wished him luck, then once he was in the ambulance, they went back to combing through the warehouse.

2

The captives had been transported to the Kendall County jail by three county deputies. Jim was taking more photographs of the man he'd killed as Jerry and Mason still collected evidence from the interior of the warehouse. A white Dodge Charger pulled up in front. A moment later, Texas Ranger Lieutenant Jameson Stoker walked in. Stoker was known throughout the Department of Public Safety as a brusque, no nonsense officer. He nodded to Jerry and Mason, then went over to Jim.

"Jim."

"Howdy, Lieutenant."

"Before we start, I see all the Austin and San Antonio television stations have satellite trucks outside, plus there's reporters from most of the area papers. None of you said anything to them, did you?"

"I had to tell 'em there's an active investigation going on here, and that there'd be no information forthcoming," Jim said. "That's it. The deputies have kept 'em at bay since then."

"How'd they get this close?"

"One of the damn deputies let 'em past the roadblock. I'm certain Sheriff Martin's gonna give him a real dressing down for that. Luckily, the deputy at the end of the road stopped them from getting any closer, or they would have been right up our butts."

"Good. One more quick question. I realize why, in this situation, you're not wearing clothes that meet the dress standard, but what the hell happened to your hat? I need to know just in case anyone asks, since I'm certain those media people must've taken your picture."

"I banged my head on the roof of my truck when it hit a bad chuckhole. I haven't had the chance to punch it back into shape yet."

"Your head, or your hat?" Stoker said. He managed a rare smile.

"Both," Jim answered. "I can probably straighten out the hat, but most folks seem to think my head's too far gone to fix. Although, there are plenty who would *love* to try'n punch it back into shape for me."

Stoker managed another smile before he spoke again.

"That's fine. Now, is this the only shooter?"

"Yeah. He's the son of a bitch who got Rudy. I couldn't give him the chance to finish what he started. We haven't moved the body to ID him yet. We're still waiting on the M.E. Any word on Rudy?"

"He was in surgery, that's all I know. Are you saying the county medical examiner hasn't shown up yet?"

"We're still waitin' on him, yeah."

"What's takin' him so damn long?"

"I've got no idea, Lieutenant. I'm gonna ask him the same thing when he does finally show up."

"You let me handle the medical examiner, Jim. What've you got here?"

"An awful lot of heroin and marijuana," Jim answered. "It's gonna take some time to total up exactly how much. It was shipped up from a ranch outside of Utopia. That's where they were manufacturing and packaging the stuff. Randy Newton and Rhonda Johnston have cleaned up at that end. In addition, it appears there might be a Mexican connection. I'm certain the boys from the DEA will be interested in that. We've got quite a bit of cash, and a good number of weapons, too."

"How many were involved?"

"Ten, here: this *hombre*, and nine we took prisoner. We're gonna be on scene for some time collecting evidence yet. I don't know how many Newton and Johnston picked up at the ranch."

"I'll be here, Thornton and Kennedy will be here, but you won't be, Ranger," Jameson answered. "You're on administrative leave, as of right now."

"What do you mean, I'm 'on leave as of right now'?" Jim asked.

"This is a Ranger-involved shooting, Jim.

You know the procedure. Any Ranger involved in a shooting, particularly one that results in a death, either is placed on office duty or administrative leave until the investigation into the circumstances of the aforesaid shooting is completed and adjudicated."

"But not usually immediately," Jim protested. "Unless it's a case where it really appears a Ranger might've made a mistake, or was in the wrong, he or she isn't taken off duty right away. They at least have a chance to explain what happened, and finish up the case they're workin' on. Besides, this was a clear-cut situation of defending ourselves. The *hombre* I shot had already put a bullet in Rudy. He would have kept on shootin' if I, or Jerry, or Mason hadn't stopped him. That would have given his partners a chance to get in on the act. If one of us hadn't shot him, you might very well have had three dead Rangers on your hands."

"I'm sorry, Jim, but that's the way it has to be," Stoker answered. "You can go on home and write your report, but that's it."

"Lieutenant, you sure as hell can't take me off this case. I'm the one who started this investigation. It was my informant who gave me the lead that took us to these *hombres*. I've been workin' this case for over two months now, in addition to all the other ones I've got. It's my case."

"The hell I can't, Ranger." Most officers used first names when talking with the men under their command. Calling Jim "Ranger" instead indicated Stoker was rapidly losing patience with him. "We've only barely gotten things calmed down after the last shooting you were involved in. You're well aware there were protests for weeks after you shot those two men. You're starting to build quite a track record for yourself. This isn't the old days, when your grandpas could just pretty much take the law into their own hands. We've got to be more responsible now, because we've got to answer for all of our actions. You're also well aware there are who knows how many lawyers out there willing to sue the police at the drop of a hat. Any excuse will do for them to sue a law officer, the department he works for, and anyone even remotely connected."

"You mean I should've just let that *hombre* still sittin' with his butt in the toilet gettin' stiff—while you lecture me—shoot Rudy again?"

"That's not what I'm saying at all."

"Well, it sure as hell sounds like it," Jim said. "As far as those two men who killed my pa, they were ISIS recruited terrorists, as you damn well know. If my pa hadn't stopped that bunch, givin' his life in the process, they and their partners would have blown up the Alamo, and killed who knows how many folks. My pa got four of those *hombres* before he was gunned down, and

I got the two who killed him. We'd do it again in a minute. Those protesters were just stirrin' up trouble. Hell, most of 'em weren't even Muslims. They'd have done the same no matter who happened to run across those men, or else would've found some other reason to raise a ruckus. I don't think you should be talkin' about my pa, nor my grandpas, as if they were some sort of rogue cops, or gunslingers shootin' up everyone and everything in sight."

"I'm not saying that, and I apologize if that's what you think I meant, but your family members have been Rangers for so long I just feel there might be some of the old days still left in your thinking, Jim. It's not just those terrorists, either. Every ethnic, racial, religious, immigrant, gay rights, or you name it group in the state is willing to pin the blame for a shooting on the police, especially the Rangers. They blame us for everything the organization did wrong in the past."

Jim's face was red with rage now. He barely kept himself in check, visibly shaking as he answered.

"Now, you've gone from the absurd to the ridiculous, Lieutenant. There's no minorities involved here at all. The guy I shot is white, or I guess I should say *was* white, and I'm sure as hell white, unless I've been wearing the best disguise ever concocted since the day I was born.

In fact, Rudy's Hispanic, so in this case, *he's* the minority. His family's been in Texas since it was still part of Mexico. Maybe once he gets out of the hospital he can start his own protest, against the damn drug runners who shoot law officers. I can't believe you're more worried about what folks think than your own men."

"You're bordering on insubordination, Ranger. I'm walking a fine line here. All of us are. You've been involved in two fatal shootings, that have left three men dead. I'm ordering you to leave, *right now*. You might want to begin writing your report as soon as possible. Make certain you get the facts straight."

"Rudy will tell you what happened, once he's well enough," Jim said. "In fact, Jerry and Mason can tell you right now."

"I'll be taking their statements, too, as well as Newton's and Johnston's," Stoker said. "Once all the evidence is gathered, there will be a hearing. Once that is held, if you are exonerated of any wrongdoing, then perhaps you will be allowed to return to this case. Notice I said *if,* and *perhaps*."

"Your meaning was plain, Lieutenant. Real plain."

"Jim, I don't mean to be so rough on you," Stoker said, his tone conciliatory now. "I really don't. However, I'm just as much stuck in the middle as you are. I also just *knew* you'd argue with me, which is why I came on so strong. I hope you'll come to understand that. I know you won't believe this, at least not right now, but I am on your side. I'm attempting to watch your back, in a difficult situation for all of us."

"I'm tryin', Lieutenant," Jim said. "But right now, I feel like I've been kicked in the gut. It hurts like hell, bein' taken off a case I've worked on for so long, and so hard."

"Hell, you think I don't know it does? I'm gonna do my best to make certain everything is cleared up real quick, and that you'll be back on full duty as quickly as possible."

Knowing he had no choice, Jim reluctantly gave in.

"All right, I reckon I can go along with that, but what do I do in the meantime?"

"Hell, I don't know," Stoker answered. "Spend some time with that new boy of yours. Have more sex with your wife, maybe in the middle of the day. I know I never have enough time for that with mine. Ride your horse more often. Get in some fishing or hunting. Go up to the Ranger Museum in Waco and do some P. R. work. You know the tourists love to see a real, live, genuine Texas Ranger in person, and we're generally too busy to have men there most of the time, even though it is Company F's Headquarters. You clean up good enough so the folks visiting the Museum, particularly the kids, will love seeing

47

you and talking with you, especially if you bring your horse along.

"As for what you should do right now, I'd suggest you head on home, let your wife know you're all right, then have a few drinks and unwind. The sooner you do that, the sooner we can wrap things up here. Don't worry, I'll personally make certain the integrity of the evidence, and your case, isn't compromised. I promise you that. I'll be in touch with you sometime tomorrow."

"All right, Lieutenant. There is one thing before I leave. You'll need to obtain a search warrant for Hangar Three at the New Braunfels airport. That's where this delivery was originally supposed to be made. That hangar needs to be searched for evidence, too."

"Okay, Jim. That'll be done. Now, get on home. I won't call too early, so you can get some rest. If I were you, I'd just write a quick summary of the facts tonight, while they're still fresh in your mind, then finish a complete report after you've had a good night's sleep. If you'll forgive my saying so, you look like hell."

"I kind of feel like it, too. I'll talk to you tomorrow. Jerry, Mason, see you later."

"Take it easy, Jim," Jerry advised. "We've got things handled here. Just don't scare the visitors at the Museum *too* much, if you do go up to Waco."

"Yeah, you get on home, and don't worry," Mason added. "We're not gonna screw this case up on you. Not on your life."

"I appreciate that," Jim said. He walked out of the warehouse, got a bucket of water from the tack compartment in the front of his horse trailer, pulled off the lid, and gave Copper a drink. He removed the saddle and bridle from his horse, and put those in the tack compartment. After that, he punched his Stetson back into shape, got into his truck, and started the drive home.

Stoker watched him drive off. He shook his head when he saw Jim tip another can of Dr Pepper to his lips.

"I sure hope you don't get drunk and crash, Jim, drinkin' that hard stuff," he muttered, then sighed. "Time to try and keep this pot from boilin' over."

3

Jim heaved a sigh of relief when he turned right off Farm to Market Road 1626 onto Tunnel Trail, at the San Leanna/Manchaca town line. He shook his head in disgust at the mansion at Tunnel Trail's entrance, then continued down the single lane dirt road.

Jim's home was at the end of the road, on land which had been in his family for generations, ever since his namesake, the first James Blawcyzk to join the Rangers, had settled there and built a small horse ranch, way back in the 1870s. San Leanna had been a prosperous community then, but had faded away over the years, until it was reorganized and made a comeback in the early 1960s.

The Blawcyzk family had nearly lost their land, shortly after Jim's father was killed fighting the terrorists who were attempting to destroy Texas's most sacred shrine, the Alamo. Two corrupt county commissioners had attempted to swindle Jim's mother out of the property, and they'd nearly succeeded. They were in jail now. If they hadn't been stopped, the Blawcyzk family land would have been covered with McMansions just like the one at Tunnel Trail's entrance.

After reclaiming the land, then making certain

legally that it could never be sold or traded again, except for a park, Jim had cleaned up the old family cemetery, moved the remains of all his paternal grandparents there, cleared the brush which had taken over most of the property, then had a home built for himself and his wife, Kimberly, and a smaller one for his widowed mother. It always felt good to get home to the four-bedroom, one-story brick house, with its wide front porch always beckoning a welcome, and the screened back patio which looked over the horse barn, corrals, and pasture. A wing off the back contained Kim's office.

Jim had called Kim to let her know about when he'd be home, so, as usual when he was hauling Copper, he drove straight past the houses and came to a stop at the barn. When he did, Frostie, the family's tan Wheaten/Cairn terrier mix, came bounding up. Jim got out of the truck.

"Howdy, Frostie, you goober," he said to the dog, patting him on the head. "How many varmints did you round up today? I got me a few, myself. Looks like you're gonna be the only one in the family doin' any more varmint huntin' for a spell, though."

Frostie tagged along, his tail wagging wildly, while Jim lowered the ramp of the horse trailer, opened the back doors, and unloaded Copper. The dog disappeared into the stable, hoping to find one of the barn cats to chase.

"C'mon out, boy. You've been standin' in there long enough," he said to the horse. Copper backed out of the trailer, and whinnied a greeting to the two horses in the corral, Jim's mother's blaze-faced chestnut quarter horse gelding, Slacker, and Kim's bay Morgan, Freedom. They returned the greeting, then went back to working on their hay.

"I'm gonna feed and brush you, then turn you out, Copper," Jim said. "Sorry about bouncin' you around so much today. Good thing I installed the extra padding in your trailer. I knew it'd come in handy. I'll worry about cleaning out your trailer tomorrow. It's not like I'll have anything else to do, except finish some paperwork."

Copper followed him into the barn, and went straight to his own stall. Jim poured a full measure of grain into his manger, then brushed him out and cleaned out his hooves while the horse ate. Once Copper was finished with his grain, Jim turned him out with the other two horses, and threw several flakes of hay over the fence. Copper rolled in the sand to scratch his back, got up, shook himself off, and began chomping on the nearest hay.

"I'll see you before I turn in," Jim promised his horse. "C'mon, Frostie. It's gettin' close to suppertime. I haven't had anything but cashews and Dr Pepper since this mornin', and I'm plumb starved."

• • •

Jim entered his house through the back door, which opened directly into the kitchen.

"Kim, I'm home," he called.

"We're in the living room," his wife called back.

Jim walked through the dining room, then into the living room, with its cathedral ceiling, the room dominated by one wall of gray granite and a large fireplace. A bay window in the front wall overlooked the horse pastures. Two ceiling fans circulating the air helped keep the room cool. The house did have central air conditioning, but both Jim and his wife preferred to use that only on the hottest, most humid days. Kim was sitting in her favorite rocker, holding her laptop and working on some files, with Josh sleeping in his cradle alongside her. Jim wasn't surprised to see his mother, Elizabeth, whom everyone called Betty, also in the room. She was reading the day's copy of the Austin *American-Statesman*. He walked up to Kim and gave her a kiss on the cheek, then his infant son, and his mother.

"I'm sorry that I couldn't get home in time for supper," he said. "Things got a little complicated."

"Don't worry about it," Kim answered. "I've gotten used to that by now. Yours is keeping warm in the oven. You don't need to tell me or your mother how your day was, either. We already know."

She picked up the remote, then clicked on the television and DVR. The five o'clock news from KEYE, the CBS station in Austin, came on the screen. After the introductory logo and music were finished, the two anchors appeared on the monitor.

"Good evening, I'm Blake Carlson."

"And I'm Jane Humphries. We have breaking news tonight. Our lead story involves the wounding of a Texas Ranger, and the fatal shooting of the alleged suspect by another Ranger. This evening, we are following that developing story out of the small settlement of Kendalia, where the Texas Rangers are apparently involved in a major investigation. Sources tell us that one Ranger has been wounded in a gunfight, one suspect killed, and several more taken into custody."

On the monitor behind them, a still photograph of Jim's horse trailer could be clearly seen, along with the rear of his Tahoe, with the rest of the truck resting half inside the warehouse, amidst the debris of the smashed door.

"Our Doris Monroe is live at the scene," Humphries continued. "Doris, do you have any new developments for us?"

The camera moved from the anchors to the monitor, which was now showing the reporter.

She was standing at the main entrance to the Thunder Ridge Nursery crime scene.

"Good evening, Jane, Blake. Right now, I don't have a lot of information that I can give our viewers. The Rangers are being really tight-lipped about whatever or whoever they are investigating here. What we do know is there is some kind of search still going on. One Ranger has been wounded, and taken to Baptist Emergency Hospital in San Antonio. There has been no word on the seriousness of his injuries. At least one suspect has been shot and killed. We've had no late word as to any other injuries, nor as to what led to the gunfire.

"We understand from a source at the Kendall County Sheriff's Department, who spoke on condition of anonymity, that several arrests have been made. Other than that, the only statement we've had at all, until a short while ago, was a brief one, made earlier."

A clip of Jim appeared on the screen.

"There will be no questions answered at this time," he said. "All I can tell you is this is part of a longstanding investigation. The Rangers will be releasing more information at the appropriate time." He turned away, with the reporters shouting questions at his back.

The camera returned to the reporter.

"We have had one more statement since then, which provided a bit more information. The next clip is the only other briefing we've received."

Lieutenant Jameson Stoker's image appeared on the screen.

"Good evening. My name is Lieutenant Jameson Stoker, of Texas Ranger Company F, based out of San Antonio. I am going to issue a brief statement. I will not be answering any questions at this time.

"Earlier today, several Rangers raided the building you see behind me. In conjunction with this raid, Rangers from Company D conducted another, at a ranch outside of Utopia. In the course of the raid here, one suspect resisted arrest. He shot and wounded one of our men. Another Ranger then returned his fire, killing the suspect. Nine others have been taken into custody at this site. I do not, as of yet, know how many persons were arrested at the other location. I am not going to release any information at this time about why this business was being investigated, nor how long we will be on scene.

"In addition, I will not be revealing the identity of the wounded Ranger, nor the deceased suspect, at this time. I also will not be naming the Ranger who shot and killed the suspect, who has been placed on administrative leave, which is standard policy whenever a member of the Department of Public Safety, including a Ranger, is involved in a shooting, particularly one that results in a fatality.

"I can tell you the wounded Ranger is undergoing surgery. His injuries are serious, but I don't believe they are life threatening. My expectation is we will remain on scene here for several more hours. Once all the evidence has been gathered, I will hold a briefing at nine o'clock tomorrow morning, at which time I will be free to release many more details, and will take questions then. That will take place at Company F's headquarters in Waco. I thank you for your patience."

"That's all I have at this time," the reporter said. "I'll be staying here to await further developments. Blake, Jane, back to you."

"Thank you, Doris," Carlson said. "In other news . . ."

Kim clicked off the television.

"Jim, you don't know how worried I was about you, until you called. There was a bulletin earlier today about a Ranger being shot, and I was so afraid it was you. I wish you had called me sooner."

"I called the first chance I had," Jim answered. "I knew you'd be frantic, but I was right in the middle of that raid. If anything had happened to me, someone from Headquarters would have let you know. There would have been a couple of other Rangers at the door."

"I can't tell you how many times I heard your father say the exact same thing, Jim," Betty said. "It never made me feel any better when he said it, and it doesn't help hearing *you* say it, either."

"I'm sorry, Ma, but there was nothing I could do until I called," Jim answered. "At least neither of you will have to worry about me for a while."

"What do you mean?" Kim asked.

"I'm on administrative leave, indefinitely. You see, *I'm* the one who had to shoot the suspect they were talkin' about on the news."

"It was you? I knew it, as soon as I saw your truck in that picture on the news!" Kim exclaimed. "Why?"

"Because he'd shot one of my partners, Rudy Garcia. If I hadn't taken him out, he would have shot Rudy again. If he'd been able to keep shootin', that might've given his partners a chance to go for their guns, which would have led to a real bloodbath. We were outnumbered two to one, so the odds are me'n the other men with me would most likely have all been killed."

"Is your partner going to be all right?" Kim asked.

"He should be. He was hit in the arm, but the bullet clipped an artery. He was still in surgery the last I knew. I'll take a drive down to San Antonio to see him sometime tomorrow. I've got to finish my report before I can do anything else, though. Lieutenant Stoker wants it ready as soon as possible. He needs it for the inquiry."

"You're not in trouble, are you, honey?" Kim asked.

"No, I shouldn't be. An inquiry is merely routine after any police officer involved shooting. This will be just like the one I had to face after killing the men who killed my father. I'll have to write a report and be questioned, evidence will be gathered and witnesses interviewed. After that, there will be a hearing, and once that's done, I'll be back to work."

"How about you? Are you all right, Jim?" Betty asked.

"I will be. It's never easy havin' to shoot somebody, no matter what the circumstances. Right now, I'm more tired and hungry than anything else. I'll get my supper, then I'm gonna have a couple of beers and unwind on the back patio before I tackle that report. Luckily, I won't have to write the entire thing tonight, just the bare bones."

"I'll get your supper for you," Kim offered.

"No, you don't have to. I can get it myself," Jim answered. "I know you've got a lot on your plate right now . . . so I'll put a lot on mine."

"Jim . . ." Kim said.

"What?"

"I put up with a lot from you, but your bad jokes are too much. I could easily get a divorce on grounds of extreme cruelty. All I'd have to do is give the judge a list of those jokes, and I'd get everything."

"But then you wouldn't have me."

"That's the point."

"And I know when it's time to leave."

Jim headed into the kitchen.

"Don't let him fool you, Kim," his mother said, once he was out of earshot. "Those jokes, and his acting like nothing is wrong, is just his way to attempt to keep you from worrying. What happened today is really eating him up inside, but he's trying not to show it. He's just like his father was that way. He'll keep everything locked up, rather than bringing his feelings out in the open. He'd rather kill himself than admit he's emotionally a mess. It's part of a lawman's code. Never show your emotions, or admit you have feelings."

"I know," Kim answered. "I wish he would open up, and I'll try to get him to talk to me, but he'll probably close up like a clam. All I can do is be there for him."

"And that's all he wants," Betty answered. "Even though he'll never admit it."

Jim turned off the oven, then opened it to find half a meat loaf, a baked potato, and pork and beans waiting for him. He removed those and set them on the kitchen table, then opened the refrigerator to get a can of beer and bottle of ketchup. Ketchup was something he put on almost everything he ate, except dessert. Frostie sat next to the table, eyeing Jim expectantly, his tail wagging.

"It figures," Jim muttered, as he popped open the beer, took a swallow, then sat down to his supper. "Kim makes one of my favorites, meat loaf, and I'm not here to eat with her. Well, I'm still in one piece, unlike poor Rudy. I hope the lieutenant calls me tonight if he has any news on how he came through surgery."

Ravenously hungry, Jim devoured his meal quickly, although Frostie got almost as much meatloaf as he did. Jim again opened the refrigerator, to find both pecan and buttermilk pies on the lower shelf.

"Which one should I have?" he said to himself. "Ah, the hell with it. I'll have some of both."

He removed both pies from the refrigerator, along with a can of spray whipped cream. He cut two large slabs from each pie, loaded them up with the whipped cream, gave a squirt of it to Frostie, then took a large one for himself, filling his mouth with the cream until he looked like a rabid dog, and replaced what was left of the pies and whipped cream back in the fridge.

Once he finished his dessert, he put the dishes in the dishwasher and turned it on. He then took two more cans of beer from the fridge, went out on the screened back patio, settled into his wooden rocking chair, and popped open one of the beers.

Frostie settled alongside him, his head resting on Jim's feet. Jim sat lost in thought as the full moon worked its way across the sky. After more than three hours, Kim came out to join him.

"Jim, your mother's gone home, and I'm more than ready for some sleep. Are you going to come to bed?"

"Not quite yet," Jim answered. "You go ahead. I'll be there in a little while. I just want to stay out here a bit longer, then I've got to at least start my report for the lieutenant."

"Are you certain you'll be all right?"

"Sure." Jim gave her a smile. "I'll be fine. You go ahead and get your rest. Is Josh still sleeping?"

"I fed him and put him in his crib half-an-hour ago," Kim answered. "He'll sleep for at least two more."

"Good. I'll be in before then, so when he does wake up, I'll take care of him," Jim said. "That way, your sleep won't be interrupted."

"All right, but if you need me, you come get me," Kim said. "Good night, Jim."

She leaned over and kissed him.

"I'll do that," Jim assured her. "And don't worry. I won't be out here much longer. Good night, honey."

Jim remained outside for another hour, still lost in thought. He finally drained the last of his beer, then pushed himself to his feet and went back inside.

Kim was fast asleep, so he undressed without waking her, then took a quick shower, having decided to wait until morning to start his report, and the hell with Lieutenant Stoker.

Right now, he was too damned tired to do anything but clean up and get some much-needed sleep. After he toweled off, he pulled on a pair of briefs, knelt to say his nighttime prayers, then crawled into bed. Kim gave a soft sigh when he settled against her. Frostie, as usual, was curled up in his dog bed, surrounded by his toys and blankets.

Jim slept for an hour, before Josh's cries from his nursery awakened both he and his wife.

Jim stirred, and swung his legs over the edge of the mattress.

"Are you certain you don't want me to take care of Josh?" Kim asked him, her voice heavy with sleep. "I'm awake, anyway."

"No, you go back to sleep," Jim said. "I never did start my report, so I'll work on that while I'm feeding him."

"All right, honey."

Kim burrowed more deeply under the sheets, while Jim pulled on a pair of jeans, then padded barefoot down the hall to Josh's room.

Kim was awakened by the first rays of the rising sun streaming in the bedroom window. She reached over for Jim, then noticed he wasn't there. Still half asleep, for a moment, she thought he'd already gotten up and was out feeding the horses. Then, she realized she hadn't heard him come back from feeding Josh. She threw back the sheets and hurried to Josh's room, fearful that Jim might have fed the baby, then gone off to do something foolish.

She put that thought out of her mind. Jim might be upset over being placed on leave, but that didn't mean he'd make a drastic mistake. That just wasn't in him . . . she hoped.

The door to Josh's room was slightly ajar. Kim pushed it open. She put her hand to her mouth in surprise, then smiled.

Jim was lying on the floor, holding Josh, who was wearing only a diaper. The baby was lying face down on his father's chest, his head snuggled up against Jim's throat. Frostie was lying next to them, with his head on Jim's stomach. All three were peacefully sleeping.

Frostie lifted his head, looked at Kim, waved his tail slowly, then closed his eyes and went back to sleep. Kim smiled, thought briefly of waking them, then changed her mind. The look on Jim's face was the most rested she'd seen him in weeks.

She went back to their bedroom, got her cell phone, then went back to the nursery and took several pictures of her son, husband, and dog. All three slumbered on, blissfully unaware of her presence. She left them as they were, and went to take her shower.

Jim was awakened by Josh nuzzling at his breast, in a futile attempt to nurse. He lifted the baby up in the air to arms' length, then smiled at him.

"I'm plumb sorry, little pard, but you're workin' on a dry hole, there. That well ain't ever gonna fill. Let's find your mom, so she can feed you."

Jim got up and carried the baby back to the bedroom, with Frostie following. Kim had just finished dressing.

"Jim, there you are," she said. "I see you're both awake. I was beginning to think you'd sleep all morning."

"No, but Josh is hungry," Jim answered.

"Let me have him."

"Here you go, pal. Back to Mom," Jim said, as he passed the baby over to Kim. "If you want, Kim, I'll get breakfast ready, soon as I've fed the horses. Is there anything particular you'd like?"

"Not especially," Kim answered. "You know I'm not big on breakfast. Coffee and cereal will do just fine. I'm glad to see you're hungry, though. I thought perhaps after everything that happened yesterday you wouldn't have much of an appetite. I should have known better."

"I'm not really all that hungry," Jim said. "I'm just gonna make some bacon, eggs, and pancakes. See you in a little while."

Jim kissed her, after she sat down and began nursing Josh, then he pulled on a T-shirt, socks, and boots. He grabbed a Texas Ranger Company F cap from its wall peg alongside the kitchen door, and put that on.

"C'mon, Frostie, time for you to have a run."

Man and dog headed outside, Frostie racing across the horse pasture and disappearing into the brush, no doubt looking for a squirrel or rabbit. He loved to roam, and would be gone most of the day, but somehow seemed to know his boundaries. He never went off the Blawcyzk land.

Jim fed the horses, promising Copper that he'd give him a good bath later, then washed his hands and face at the sink in the barn. He headed back inside.

"Do you want me to turn the morning news on?" Kim asked, from where she was changing Josh's diaper.

"No, that can wait, since they won't be able to say much more than they did last night," Jim said. "I *am* gonna be interested in what Lieutenant Stoker has to say. He said he'd have a press conference at nine this morning, and I'm pretty certain at least one of the Austin or San Antonio stations will cover that live, probably all of 'em. I'll get breakfast started."

Since Kim didn't eat much for breakfast, and his mother hadn't put in an appearance yet, Jim was cooking mostly for himself. He prepared half-a-pound of bacon, four eggs sunny-side up, and four large pancakes, as well as a pot of coffee. While they were cooking, he filled a bowl with cereal for Kim, and put that on the table, along with a quarter pound of butter and a quart jug of maple syrup for his pancakes.

One thing he couldn't tolerate was artificially flavored maple syrup, which to him was just sugar water. It had to be the real thing, from New Hampshire or Vermont. Even that couldn't be the light, delicate syrup from the first sap run of the sugaring season. He wanted to *taste* the rich maple flavor, so the syrup had to be Amber or Dark grade from the second or later runs. Once everything was ready, he called for Kim. She came into the kitchen, holding Josh.

"Do you want me to take him while you eat?" Jim asked.

"No, I'll just put him in his seat," Kim answered. "It's hard to believe how big he's gotten already, and he's only six months old."

"He's gonna have the size to be a Ranger, that's for certain," Jim said. "But thank goodness he got your looks, rather than my ugly mug. I still don't know how I convinced you to even go out on a date with me, let alone marry me."

"It was your charm, not your looks," Kim answered.

"Kim, you might be a beautiful woman, and

a wonderful wife and mother, not to mention a terrific lover, but you're a terrible liar. What charm?"

"I meant your personality? No, that can't be why," Kim retorted. "It must have been a case of temporary insanity. That *has* to be it. Although you really aren't all that bad looking, Jim."

Jim had met his future wife, Kimberly Maria Tavares, coming out of the Kendall County courthouse. He had just finished testifying in a trial, and was on his way out of the building, when Kim, rushing to meet a filing deadline with the county clerk, literally ran into him. When she attempted to apologize, he assured her he wasn't hurt, except that his heart would be broken if she refused an invitation to have supper with him. The line was corny, to say the least, but it worked.

Looking into those deep blue eyes, somehow intrigued by this tall, blond Texas Ranger with the crooked smile, Kim tried to say "no", but for some reason it came out "yes". Less than a year later, they were married. While neither one was strikingly good-looking enough to turn heads, they did make an attractive couple, the six-foot-four, one-hundred-eighty-five-pound lean Texas Ranger, and the five-foot-eight, slim, tan-skinned and dark-eyed businesswoman.

Kim was of Mexican Spanish ancestry, from a family which had been living in Texas for several generations before the revolution that would eventually lead to its becoming a republic, then a state. Her deep brown eyes and jet black hair contrasted nicely with her husband's fair features. She had obtained her Master's Degree in Business Administration from St. Edward's University in Austin, worked for several companies in the area, then began her own business, Tavares Consulting, which helped minorities and women start their own enterprises.

In addition, she assisted business owners in navigating the pitfalls of establishing trade between the United States and Mexico. The business had struggled at first, but now had grown large enough that Jim's widowed mother, Betty, agreed to become Kim's assistant. They worked out of an office at home, an arrangement which always left one of them available to care for Josh.

Betty also created and sold stained glass windows and suncatchers in a little studio behind her house.

Jim, of course, had followed in his family's tradition. He was the latest in a long line of Blawcyzk males who had gone into law enforcement, and the Texas Rangers, dating back to the 1870s. His Polish ancestors had settled in Texas even before the Civil War, joining a colony of Polish immigrants who worked in the cedar shingle mills of Bandera.

"That's just because nobody even notices me when I'm standing next to you," Jim answered. "Let's eat."

Josh gurgled and smiled in his baby seat through most of the meal.

"I'm gonna put you on Copper today or tomorrow," Jim said to his son.

"You will do no such thing," Kim said. "He's barely six months old. He doesn't even know what you're saying."

"He might not, but he knows what a horse is," Jim answered. "He smiles at the horses every time he's with me at the barn, and he loves to grab Copper's nose. Copper likes to nuzzle at him, too. It's never too soon to teach a future Ranger how to ride."

"Jim, perhaps Josh won't *want* to be a Ranger when he grows up. Did that ever occur to you?"

"Of course he's gonna want to be a Ranger," Jim said. "It's in his blood. But if for some reason he doesn't, I'll adjust. I'll be disappointed, but it'll be his decision. Once he's old enough to understand what it means to be a Ranger, and especially for this family, he'll want to be one. I'd bet my hat on it."

"Jim, let's not talk about this now. We have years ahead of us before Josh is even in high school, let alone college. But let me ask you one question. What if our baby boy had been a girl?"

"Then she'd be the first female Blawcyzk to become a Texas Ranger," Jim answered, without hesitation. "That could still happen, if we give Josh a little sister."

There was a soft knock on the back door, then Betty came into the kitchen.

"Did I just hear talk of another grandchild?" she asked.

" 'Mornin', Ma," Jim said. "We were just talkin', is all. Kim wanted to know what would have happened if Josh had been a Jessica. I told her she would've been the first Blawcyzk woman to join up with the Rangers."

"And I told him perhaps *none* of our children will want to follow in his footsteps," Kim said.

"Bootsteps," Jim corrected.

"Whatever," Kim said.

"You're fighting a losing battle, Kim," Betty said. "I had the same argument with his father when Jim was born. He said Jim would be a Ranger, and sure enough, he is. Nothing could change his mind, and Jim proved him right. He never wanted to be anything but a Ranger, like his dad, from the time he was old enough to walk. I don't know what it is, whether it's in the blood, or it's Texas, or maybe just the tradition of the Rangers and this family, but I'd be very surprised, no, I'd be shocked if Joshua doesn't want to become one, too."

"If he does, that's fine, but I just don't want

to see Jim push him into doing something he doesn't want," Kim answered.

"I won't," Jim assured her, then downed the last of his coffee. "I'd better get started on my report. I didn't do one damn word of it last night."

"All right, honey. Betty, you're here a bit early this morning," Kim said.

"I know, we have a full day ahead of us," Betty answered. "But mostly, I want to watch Lieutenant Stoker's briefing along with you two, that is, if neither of you minds."

"Why would we mind?" Kim said. "In fact, I'll be glad to have you with me. It might be a bit of comfort, in case the lieutenant says something to make me worry . . . or upset Jim."

"I told you there's nothing to worry about," Jim tried to reassure her. "Being put on office duty or administrative leave after an officer involved shooting is standard procedure. Everything will be cleared up within a few weeks, and I'll be back at work. Maybe this is a blessing in disguise. You've both been after me to take things easier, and I've got some work that needs doing around here. Now's my chance. But right now, I've got to get started on my report, so when the lieutenant calls later I won't be lyin' when I tell him I'm putting it together. I'll see both of you in a little while."

"Jim, wait," Kim said. "Before you go, I want to show you and Betty the pictures I took of you and Josh this morning, while you were both still sleeping. I've already posted them on social media. You were so tired you never even heard me come into Josh's room to check on you."

Kim clicked on her cell phone and opened the camera.

"Look, Betty. Isn't this just precious? Jim must have fallen asleep after he fed Josh. And look at Frostie."

"These are just adorable," Betty said. "They're so cute. What do you think, Jim?"

"I like them, but I wish I'd been lying on my belly, so you'd have gotten my good side." He chuckled.

"Oh, go on with you, Jim," Kim said. "You're hopeless. Get out of here, so your mother and I can have some coffee before we start work."

"All right. I can take a hint."

Jim headed down the hall and into the room he used as a combination den and office. When he and Kim did have their next baby, this would become that child's room, but for now, it was his. It was equipped with a large screen television, DVR, computer, and CD player, as well as shelves of reference books, DVDs of Western movies and television series, and Western novels.

The room was decorated with southwestern tribes' and Sioux Native American Indian pottery, a Navajo rug, and several Western prints on the wall, a number of those by well-known artist

Andy Thomas. Several bronze cowboy and horse sculptures were placed strategically on the table tops and windowsills. He sat down, opened his laptop, and began typing.

Forty minutes later, Jim returned to the living room, where his wife and mother were already seated in front of the television. Josh, his feeding and diapering needs having been met, was sleeping peacefully in his cradle.

Just as Jim took a seat on the couch, the KEYE Breaking News logo appeared on the television screen, followed by the morning news anchor, Caitlin Cobourn.

"Good morning, I'm Caitlin Cobourn. We have a special report on a developing story which we have been following since yesterday. Any moment now, we are expecting a briefing from the Texas Rangers about a raid which they conducted yesterday on a plant nursery business outside of the small town of Kendalia. During the course of the operation, one Ranger was wounded, and one of the suspects shot and killed.

"None of us in the media have received any further information since a short statement made last night, by Lieutenant Jameson Stoker of Ranger Company F. Our reporter, Doris Monroe, is standing by outside of the headquarters of Company F, on the grounds of the Texas Ranger Hall of Fame and Museum complex in Waco.

Doris, while we are waiting for the briefing to begin, do you have anything more for us?"

"Caitlin, I have to say no. There has been no information whatsoever forthcoming from the Texas Rangers or any local law enforcement, except for the two brief statements given at the scene last night. Our sources at the Department of Public Safety have also refused to release any information, even on condition of anonymity. The Rangers are being really tight-lipped about this entire event."

"So, you have been able to uncover nothing at all, Doris?"

"Not one thing, Caitlin." She glanced away for a moment, then said, "Wait, here comes Lieutenant Stoker now. It appears as if Major Arthur Voitek, who is the commanding officer of Company F, is with him. Let's hear what they have to say."

The two officers walked up to the waiting reporters. Lieutenant Stoker held a cordless amplified microphone in one hand, a sheaf of papers in the other.

"Good morning. For those of you who may not know me, I am Lieutenant Jameson Stoker of Texas Ranger Company F. With me is Major Arthur Voitek, the commanding officer of Company F. We thank all of you for your patience while we gathered the information we needed before we could hold this briefing. I will be reading a statement, and will take your questions afterward. I also have more information in this news release, which will be handed out at the conclusion of this briefing. I do have to advise y'all, any questions which might interfere with, hinder, or compromise the integrity of our ongoing investigation, will be answered with a 'no comment'.

"Yesterday afternoon, in the culmination of a several months' long investigation, Texas Rangers from Company F staged a raid at a wholesale garden supply house called Thunder Ridge Nursery, just outside Kendalia. At the same time, a simultaneous raid took place at the Double Dot H Ranch near Concan, in Uvalde County. That operation was handled by Rangers out of Company D.

"Two of our men have been observing apparent illegal drug activity at the ranch. Yesterday, one of the men, Ranger James C. Blawcyzk of Company F, who had initiated the investigation based on a credible tip from an informant, gathered evidence and photographs which showed what appeared to be packages of illegal drugs being loaded onto a pickup truck and trailer at the Double Dot H Ranch. In coordination with other Rangers, from both Company D and Company F, Ranger Blawcyzk followed the vehicle to the Thunder Ridge Nursery.

"In the events that followed, shots were

exchanged, and one of the participating Rangers, Rudy Garcia of Company F, was shot in the left arm, and seriously wounded. I am happy to report that Ranger Garcia has undergone successful surgery at Baptist Emergency Hospital in San Antonio, including a procedure to repair an artery which was severed by the bullet, and is expected to make a full recovery. He should be able to return to active duty within a few weeks.

"Seeing his fellow Ranger shot, Ranger Blawcyzk returned the alleged shooter's fire, killing him. That person has been identified as Dale Robert Bohannon, aged twenty-six, from San Marcos, Texas. Nine other suspects surrendered without resistance, and were taken into custody. Their names and cities are on the press release I will be handing out at the end of this briefing.

"At the Double Dot H Ranch, six additional suspects were taken into custody. Their names and cities are also in the release. Based on information Ranger Blawcyzk had developed, we also obtained a search warrant for a hangar at the New Braunfels Regional Airport. That warrant was executed last night, resulting in the gathering of significant additional evidence.

"At the Thunder Ridge Nursery, a considerable amount of illegal drugs, specifically heroin and marijuana, was confiscated, along with a number of weapons, and a good amount of cash.

We are still inventorying the drugs; however, I can say their street value would be well over a million dollars. I can also state we obtained more evidence of alleged illegal drug manufacturing and distribution, at both the Double Dot H Ranch and the New Braunfels Airport. This operation has resulted in a large amount of drugs being intercepted before they could reach the streets for distribution. It is a significant step in the never-ending fight to stop illegal drug trafficking.

"Ranger Blawcyzk, per Department of Public Safety standard operating procedure, has been placed on administrative leave, until the shooting of Mr. Bohannon has been completely investigated. That investigation will be conducted by myself, Major Voitek, and Marilee Hudson, Inspector General for the DPS.

"I would like to say, based on the preliminary information we have gathered so far, it appears that Ranger Blawcyzk followed all normal police procedures, and his fatal shooting of Mr. Bohannon, while unfortunate, was justified. The evidence we have indicates that Ranger Blawcyzk, fearing for the life of his already wounded fellow Ranger, Ranger Garcia, as well as his own life and those of the other Rangers on scene, acted prudently and well within the law to protect both himself and his fellow Rangers. I have every confidence he will be vindicated at the conclusion of the hearing.

"Now, I am prepared to take a few, brief questions, as is Major Voitek. Yes, Peter?" The lieutenant pointed to one of the reporters.

"Lieutenant Stoker, can you divulge who fired the first shot, and how many shots were fired altogether?"

"From the evidence we have gathered so far, it appears two warning shots were fired first, one each by two of the Rangers. The deceased was apparently hiding in a bathroom, and shot Ranger Garcia from ambush before the building could be searched. After the suspect shot Garcia, Ranger Blawcyzk fired one round from his shotgun in return, which struck the assailant, killing him. All this happened within a few minutes after the raid began."

"So, there was a total of four shots, three from the Rangers, and one from the suspects?"

"That is correct. However, I want to emphasize that only one shot was fired by the Rangers on scene at anyone, and that shot was fired in apparent self-defense. Next? George?"

"Lieutenant, can you provide us the names of the other Rangers involved in this operation?"

"Those are in the news release y'all will be receiving when we're finished. Next? Doris?"

"Lieutenant, you stated the Ranger who allegedly fired the fatal shot is James . . . Bluh-zhick?"

"That is correct."

"Could you possibly spell that last name?"

"Sure. It's B-L-A-W-C-Y-Z-K." Stoker smiled. "It's Polish, like the major's. Kind of hard to pronounce, until you get used to it."

"Would that be the same James Blawcyzk whose Ranger father died when he foiled a terrorist attempt to blow up the Alamo? The same man who also tracked down and killed the other two men involved in the attempt, who eluded capture for several weeks after their plot failed?"

"Yes, it is the same man. As you know, the Blawcyzk family has had members serving the people of Texas as Rangers for several generations. It is not merely a coincidence, nor surprising, that Ranger Blawcyzk would be involved in what occurred yesterday, and also after the unsuccessful attempt to destroy one of Texas's most sacred shrines.

"The Blawcyzks have been sacrificing their time, their families, and sometimes their lives to help keep the citizens of Texas safe for many, many years. There is no question as to Ranger Blawcyzk's integrity, his devotion to duty, and to performing his job according to proper, established police procedures, and the law." Jameson's voice snapped as he concluded. "Any inference otherwise is an insult, and an affront to the Texas Rangers in general, and to Ranger Blawcyzk, and his family, in particular. Next! Yes, Reynaldo?"

"Do you have any evidence which would lead you to believe the apparent drug activity which was uncovered, has any connection to international drug trafficking, particularly any connection to the Mexican drug cartels? Also, were the DEA and FBI involved, or was this strictly a Ranger operation?"

"It's far too early in the investigation, and I wouldn't be able to comment on that aspect in any case, nor as to the involvement of any other law enforcement organizations, local, state, or federal. Last question. Yes, Monica?"

"I would just like to ask Major Voitek if he has a comment."

"Yes, I do. Thank you for asking, Monica. As Lieutenant Stoker just said, we are very early into our investigation of recent events. However, we have seen nothing to indicate Ranger Blawcyzk, or the other Rangers involved, acted with anything but the highest degree of professionalism. Except for the two warning shots, they fired only after being fired upon. They risked their lives to keep a huge amount of drugs from ever reaching the streets. I have every confidence in each and every one of the men and women under my command, and am certain the results of our inquiry will bear me out."

"Begging your pardon, Major, it sounds to me as if you have already come to a conclusion, and your investigation into the death of Mr.

Bohannon at the hands of one of your Rangers is a mere formality. Could we be looking at a cover-up here?"

"Monica, I won't even dignify that question with a response. And that concludes this briefing."

"Anyone who wants a news release, I have them right here," Stoker said.

"You've heard what the Rangers just said, Caitlin," Monroe said, as the camera returned to her. "Apparently, yesterday's events, including the fatal shooting of a suspect, were part of a very long, and very large, investigation into illegal drug activity. Hopefully, we'll find out more in the coming days. Back to you."

"Thank you, Doris. You have been watching a special report from KEYE News, a short briefing by Lieutenant Jameson Stoker and Major Arthur Voitek of Texas Ranger Company F concerning the fatal shooting of a suspect during a raid yesterday. We hope to have more information as we follow this developing story, on our noon broadcast, then on the evening news. We now return to our regular programming."

Jim clicked the off button on the remote and turned off the set.

"Well, I reckon I'd better get working on my report again. It wouldn't do not to have it ready when the lieutenant calls."

"Your mother and I have plenty of work to get

done too," Kim said. "If you need us, just let us know."

"Will do," Jim said. He got up and headed back to his office.

Jim's cell phone rang about an hour after the briefing ended. Lieutenant Stoker was on the other end.

"Howdy, Lieutenant. I figured it wouldn't take you too long to call."

"Good mornin', Jim," Stoker answered. "I assume you saw the briefing this morning."

"I sure did. I appreciated you and Major Voitek stickin' up for me, and the rest of us."

"I hope you didn't think we wouldn't."

"No, not at all. I just was glad to see you did. You can never be certain when pressure might come down from some politician or bureaucrat in Austin, and force you to hedge, or make some mealy-mouthed, meaningless statement."

"Nope, that hasn't happened. So far, the only things we've heard are mainly support for us Rangers, for doing a tough, thankless job, and a few calls from legislators, as well as the governor's office, making certain we will be doing a thorough and impartial investigation. I assured them we would."

"I wouldn't expect anything less," Jim said. "I didn't do anything wrong, so I've got nothin' to hide."

"And, of course, we *have* received a few calls from folks who want to blame you, without even waiting for the results of the investigation. You know there's always a few of those, whenever a cop is involved in a shooting."

"Of course there are."

"Jim, how's your report coming along? Is it finished yet?"

"Just about, Lieutenant. I've got a few more things to add, then I want to read through it once more, and make certain I've dotted every I and crossed every T. I'll have it done before noon."

"That's good. As soon as it's completed, email it right over to me. We want to get started right away."

"You mean I won't get to take a nice, long vacation?"

"Sorry, Jim. First, knowing you as well as I do, you don't want a vacation. Second, we need to get this investigation over with so we can get you back on duty as quickly as possible. With Rudy laid up, and three unfilled vacancies in the company, we're really short on manpower, so we can't afford to dawdle around for a month or more. We have enough of a backlog in our case load already. Major Voitek and I have already spoken with Inspector General Hudson, and she agrees we'd like to have this thing wrapped up in two weeks at the most. To that end, can you meet with us at Company Headquarters tomorrow morning, at ten o'clock? We'll do our questioning of you then."

"I think I can just barely squeeze that in, with my *very* full schedule," Jim answered, the sarcasm plain in his voice. "Do you want me to just bring my report with me, rather'n sending it today?"

"No, send it as soon as you're done with it," Stoker answered. "That way I can get copies to the major and Ms. Hudson, so we can go over the report today."

"Sure, that's not a problem," Jim said. "How's Rudy doin'? I plan on takin' a drive down to San Antonio and see him later today."

"I'd like you to wait a couple of days before you do that, Jim. First, he's doin' real well, but his surgeon doesn't want him to have any visitors except for family until tomorrow at the earliest.

"Second, I don't want you talking to Rudy until after I've had my chance to meet with him, and get his version of what happened. It might look bad if you went to see him right away, like maybe you were both trying to get your stories straight. I know," Stoker said, when Jim started to object. "You could do the exact same thing by telephone. The difference is, telephone calls can be traced, there are records, and someone could even overhear the conversation. A personal face-to-face is different. You'd have to sign in, of course, plus the hospital's security cameras would show you were there. We don't want to give any do-gooder or sharp lawyer the chance to say there was collusion. As soon as I interview Rudy, I'll give you a call and let you know you can visit. In the meantime, just be patient, all right? And try not to worry. I'm not."

"You don't have to. It's not your butt that's on the line," Jim retorted. "Okay, I can see your point, Lieutenant. Just do me a favor and tell Rudy I was askin' about him, will you?"

"Of course, Jim. I'll see you tomorrow. Oh, before I forget, do you want me to ask for a local officer to stand watch at your place for a few days, just to keep the media folks off your back?"

"No, that won't be necessary. I can handle them all right. You've been here, so you know they can't just drive up to my place. Besides, if they give me too much trouble, I'll sic Kim and my ma on them. Those reporters sure don't want to tangle with those two."

"You're right about that," Stoker said. He managed a soft laugh. "They're both lovely ladies, but awful tough when they need to be. Tomorrow, Jim."

"See you then, Lieutenant."

"Oh, well, back to work on this damn report," Jim muttered, hanging up the phone and returning to his computer.

4

It was usually just about a two-hour drive from Jim's home to Company F's Headquarters in Waco, but he was out the door and on the road before six-thirty, even though he didn't have to be at Company F until ten. If he didn't beat the horrific Austin morning rush hour traffic, or if an accident or construction caused major delays on the highway, he might very well be late for his preliminary hearing. There was no way in hell he was going to let that happen.

He made a quick stop at a donut shop for some hot glazed doughnuts and a Dr Pepper, then was back on I-35 northbound five minutes later. He pulled into the Texas Ranger Hall of Fame and Museum complex just before nine o'clock, and drove around the back to Company F's Headquarters. With time to kill, he thought about going into the Museum, which he always enjoyed, but decided against it. This wasn't the right time.

He'd wait until at least after this morning's hearing, or, as he thought of it, more of a Spanish Inquisition, with Lieutenant Jameson Stoker in the role of the Grand Inquisitor, Tomas de Torquemada. He knew being placed on leave was mandatory, and the lieutenant was merely doing his job. However, despite Stoker's reassurances, along with his and Major Voitek's defense of the men and women of the Texas Rangers during yesterday's media briefing, being investigated for possible wrongdoing after seeing Rudy Garcia take a drug runner's bullet was eating him up inside. He knew dang well if he'd made the least little mistake, he'd be hung out to dry, left to twist slowly in the wind, despite his family's years of service and his own dedication to the state of Texas, and the Rangers. Try as he might not to, he could just picture himself becoming a scapegoat to satisfy the wolves sure to be howling at Ranger Headquarters' doors.

He stayed in his Tahoe until twenty to ten, then checked his appearance in the rearview mirror one last time. He'd donned a clean white shirt, crisply pressed tan trousers, and a carefully knotted hunter green tie with a paint horse design.

He'd brushed all the dust off his white Stetson—which he'd reshaped—and polished his tan Western boots, as well as his custom-made tooled leather belt, to a high shine. He'd also polished the belt's buckle, which was of engraved sterling silver, over which was a brass representation of a Ranger badge, and the belt's two silver and brass keepers, with his initials "J" on one and "B" on the other. That belt, as were most of the Rangers', was made by inmates at the Huntsville State Prison.

As he'd buckled the belt on earlier, all Jim could think was that he hoped *he* wasn't about to become one of those prisoners. The thought of himself making Ranger belts from behind bars was too ironic to contemplate. His silver star on silver circle badge, which had been passed down in his family from generation to generation, was pinned above his left breast pocket.

Since he hadn't been ordered to turn in his gun, his Ruger SR1911 hung in the holster on his left hip. Rangers could choose any sidearm they preferred, as long as it met requirements, but as far as Jim knew, he was the only man, or woman, in the Rangers who carried a Sturm, Ruger pistol. Most of them preferred Colts or Glocks.

Of course, given his choice, Jim would be wearing his great-great-great grandfather's Colt .45 Peacemaker, which, like his badge, had been passed down through the generations. The antique revolver had been maintained, and also restored, so that it still worked perfectly. It fit Jim's hand as if it had been molded to his palm. He'd fought long and hard to be allowed to carry the Peacemaker, without success. He hadn't been satisfied with any other gun until he tried the Ruger. Even now, he still wasn't certain whether he'd chosen the SR1911 because he truly felt it was a superior weapon, or because wearing it was a slight act of defiance.

My grandpas sure had it easier, Jim thought, as

he straightened his tie and knotted it even tighter. *They could wear whatever they wanted, and carry whatever weapons they chose. No dress codes, no nit-picking rules coming out of Austin. And for certain nobody questioning 'em if they had to shoot a bad guy, particularly one who was shootin' at them. Still, this is the only job I've ever wanted, and I damn sure ain't givin' it up without a fight.* He sighed. *Time to get this over with.*

Jim stepped out of his truck, put on his light brown sport coat, and picked up his copy of his report from the front passenger seat. He locked the truck, trudged across the parking lot, and entered his code in the keypad that allowed access to Company F—and went inside.

Mary Huggins, one of F's three administrative assistants, along with Margie Montgomery and Stacy Hadlock, was seated at her desk. She looked up when she heard Jim come into the reception area.

"Good morning, Ranger Blawcyzk," she said, her warm smile brightening Jim's mood, at least a bit.

"Good mornin', Mary," Jim answered. "You're looking nice, as always. Where's Stacy and Margie?"

"Margie's in with Major Voitek. Stacy's on a personal day. Her daughter had a doctor's appointment, so Stacy took the day off."

"Patty's not ill, I hope."

"No, she just had to take a physical in order to play softball for her school."

"That's good to hear. Tell Stacy I said howdy."

"I'll do just that," Mary promised.

"Mary, I realize I'm a couple of minutes early. Are Lieutenant Stoker and the others ready for me yet?"

"Let me check with Major Voitek. I know the Lieutenant and Ms. Hudson are in his office."

She picked up the phone and dialed an extension, which was answered after two rings.

"Major? Ranger Blawcyzk is here. Are you ready for him?" There was a pause, then Mary said. "Thank you. I'll send him right in."

She hung up the phone.

"Major Voitek said they're ready. They'll be in Conference Room B. Go right ahead. And Jim, good luck. I know you'll be cleared of any wrongdoing."

"Thanks, Mary. I wish I could be as confident as you are. I'm gonna stop and use the men's room, then walk into the lion's den."

Lieutenant Stoker, Major Voitek, and Inspector General Hudson were already seated at one end of the conference table when Jim entered the room. Each had an open manila file folder in front of them. Also on the table was a digital video camera and recorder. Marjorie Montgomery, one of Company F's other administrative assistants, was at a smaller table, with a digital tape recorder, computer, and legal pad in front of her. The lieutenant waved Jim to a chair at the opposite end of the table.

"Good morning, Ranger Blawcyzk," Stoker said. "Are you prepared to begin?"

"Yes, sir, Lieutenant," Jim answered.

"Fine. Before we get started, there are two questions which must be answered. First, even though this is an internal investigation, you do have the right to have an attorney present throughout this hearing. You also have the right to call a halt to these proceedings at any time. Do you wish to have an attorney?"

"No, Lieutenant. That won't be necessary."

"All right. Second, do you have any objection to these proceedings being video and audio recorded?"

"No, Lieutenant."

"Then let's begin."

The recorders were turned on.

"This hearing today is part of the DPS Internal Affairs investigation of the fatal shooting of Dale Robert Bohannon by Texas Ranger James Charles Blawcyzk, during an attempt to arrest several suspects allegedly engaged in the manufacturing of illegal drugs with intent to distribute," Stoker began. "The investigating officers are myself, Lieutenant Jameson Stoker of Texas Ranger

Company F, acting as lead investigator; Major Arthur Voitek, Commanding Officer of Company F; and Marilee Hudson, Inspector General for the Texas Department of Public Safety. Also present to create a transcript of the testimony today is Marjorie Montgomery, Administrative Assistant for Company F. Ranger Blawcyzk has waived his right to have an attorney present, and has agreed to have his testimony recorded. He has also been advised he may stop these proceedings at any time he deems it necessary. Would you please confirm that, Ranger Blawcyzk?"

"That is correct," Jim answered.

"Thank you. For the record, would you please state your full name and rank?"

"James Charles Blawcyzk, Texas Ranger, currently assigned to Company F out of Waco, Texas, and stationed at Buda. My assigned territory includes the counties of Hays, Blanco, Comal, and Kendall. I have been a Texas Ranger for slightly more than three years. Prior to that I was a state trooper for five years."

"Ranger Blawcyzk, we have all read your written statement concerning the events of May 10th of this year, 2017, which led to the fatal shooting of Dale Robert Bohannon. We would now ask you give an oral account of what exactly took place at the Thunder Ridge Nursery warehouse that led to Mr. Bohannon's death."

"Certainly. Would you like the information

which brought myself and several other Rangers to the site of the confrontation with Mr. Bohannon and his associates, or just the events which took place that day?"

"I believe I would like to hear simply an abbreviated version of your actions prior to and including May 10th," Hudson said. "It appears your complete rendition of the days prior is already in your written report, am I not correct?"

"Yes, ma'am, you are, Inspector General."

"Then please reiterate the main points of what is in your report."

"Yes, ma'am. Approximately two months ago, one of my informants provided me a tip that large quantities of drugs were being transported to, and were also being manufactured at, a ranch in Uvalde County, the Double Dot H, then moved for distribution throughout the larger cities of Texas and beyond. My informant also told me much of the product was being transported to the New Braunfels Regional Airport, for trans-shipment by small private plane.

"After doing a preliminary investigation, I came to the conclusion the information I received was, in fact, credible, and actionable. Since the ranch in question, the Double Dot H, is located in Uvalde County, which is part of Company D's area, I reported to Major Voitek that I would be following up in that county. I then contacted both Major John Dolan, commanding officer of

Company D, and Ranger Randy Newton, who covers Uvalde County, to ask their permission to operate in their area, per protocol. They both readily agreed.

"For the past several weeks, either myself or Ranger Newton have been maintaining almost constant surveillance on the Double Dot H Ranch, in conjunction with updated information my informant was able to provide. Most of that surveillance was done by Ranger Newton. He would observe the only road into and out of the ranch, Cherry Creek Ranch Road, for any activity, particularly vehicles arriving or departing.

"Due to the remote location, he could not maintain direct surveillance of the ranch without being discovered, but could only watch the entrance to Cherry Creek Ranch road from a place of concealment.

"One week ago, my informant told me the date a large amount of product was to be transported, which was two days ago. He also mentioned the shipment would possibly not be taken to the New Braunfels airport, as usual, but to a different destination. Therefore, I decided to stake out the Double Dot H Ranch, along with Ranger Newton.

"To make certain I was unobserved, I approached the ranch under cover of darkness, concealed my truck and horse trailer, and rode horseback to a spot where I could watch the ranch without being discovered. Ranger Newton positioned himself in an old sand pit at the junction of Farm to Market Road 1050 and Cherry Creek Ranch Road, where he could observe any vehicles leaving or entering. Cherry Creek Ranch Road has no outlet, so anyone entering or leaving it would have to pass by Ranger Newton's observation post.

"From my location at a ridge above the Double Dot H, I observed several individuals removing plastic-wrapped packages from a barn at the ranch, loading them onto a pickup truck and trailer, then concealing them under bales of hay. I photographed this activity, and those photos are now part of the evidence in this case.

"Once the load was covered with tarps, three individuals got into the truck and departed the ranch. I rode my horse back to where I could receive a cell phone signal, and proceeded to call Ranger Newton to advise him the suspects were moving. I returned to my vehicle, and proceeded back to Farm 1050. Ranger Newton and I followed the suspects' vehicle to Utopia, where Ranger Newton left the surveillance. I then notified Ranger Rudy Garcia of Company F, who is responsible for Bandera County.

"After the suspects entered Bandera County, I stopped them, using a ruse that some of the tie downs on their load had come loose, and was able to attach a tracking device to their trailer. Ranger Garcia then took up following the suspects, with myself staying a good distance back. When the suspects crossed into Kendall County, I took over the surveillance, at which time Ranger Garcia volunteered to remain as backup.

"As my informant had stated might occur, the suspects did indeed change their destination, stopping at the Thunder Ridge Nursery, just outside of Kendalia. I observed their vehicle being driven into a structure at that business. I contacted Ranger Garcia, as well as Rangers Jerry Thornton and Mason Kennedy, who were standing by to assist.

"I then reconnoitered the situation at the nursery. Once that was done, I rendezvoused with the other three Rangers. Due to the circumstances at the nursery, namely there being security cameras covering the entire property, and no cover within fifty feet of the structure the suspects had entered, the decision was reached that any raid would have to be made quickly, without warning.

"Therefore, I used my vehicle to break down the locked gates to the facility, as well as the front overhead door of the building. Ranger Thornton used his to break down the back door, with Rangers Garcia and Kennedy right behind us.

"Once inside, I exited my vehicle, holding my shotgun. I announced, "Texas Rangers", and ordered the persons inside to submit to arrest. To make certain my orders were understood, I fired one round into a shelf of glass bottles. One of the suspects then reached for a gun. Ranger Thornton put a warning shot between his feet, and ordered the suspect to drop his weapon and lie face down. The suspect complied, as did the others.

"Before we had a chance to secure the prisoners and search the building, an individual who was in the bathroom emerged and fired one shot, striking Sergeant Garcia in his left arm. I returned the shooter's fire. My shot struck him in the chest and upper abdomen, killing him instantly, or almost so. The remaining suspects submitted to arrest without resisting."

"Thank you, Ranger Blawcyzk," Hudson said. "I apologize for making you recite your recollection of the events; however, I wanted to hear them in your own words."

"It was no trouble, Inspector General," Jim answered.

"Ranger Blawcyzk, are you prepared to answer our questions at this time?" Stoker asked.

"I am, Lieutenant."

"Fine. Inspector General Hudson, would you care to start?"

"I would. Thank you, Lieutenant."

"Ranger Blawcyzk," Hudson then said. "We are only concerned with the actual events which took place at the Thunder Ridge Nursery. Your recitation of what took place prior to the confrontation at that site corroborates what is in your written report. Therefore, I will be directing my questions specifically to what took place in the nursery warehouse. Do both of you agree with me, Major Voitek, Lieutenant Stoker?"

"Yes," Voitek said.

"The same for me," Stoker answered. "This inquiry is strictly concerned only with the events that led to the fatal shooting of Mr. Bohannon, and nothing else."

"Very well. Ranger Blawcyzk, you have indicated that you entered the warehouse by driving your vehicle through the front overhead door, while Ranger Thornton did the same to the rear door. Are you absolutely certain there was no other method you could have used to approach the building without being discovered?"

"Absolutely none. While I was waiting for Ranger Garcia, Ranger Thornton, and Ranger Kennedy to arrive, I looked over all possible approaches to the warehouse. While there was good cover up to within about fifty feet of the building, there was none beyond that. In addition, as in my report, there were security cameras covering the entire property. Using the element of surprise by breaking down the doors with our vehicles was the safest method, both for ourselves, and the suspects."

"Except for Mr. Bohannon," Stoker pointed out.

"I suppose I can't argue with you there, Lieutenant," Jim said.

"Please continue with your testimony, Ranger Blawcyzk," Hudson said. "When you came under fire, you returned it immediately?"

"Yes, ma'am."

"I see. Now, when you had to fire upon the deceased, could you not have aimed so as not to cause a fatal wound?"

"I have two responses to that question, Inspector General. First, one of my fellow Rangers had already been shot by the deceased, Mr. Bohannon. I had to make a split-second decision. With my partner already wounded—and, of course, I had no idea how badly—and my other partners' lives, as well as my own, threatened, I had to make certain Mr. Bohannon could not fire his weapon again.

"Second, as you are aware, police officers are trained to shoot to render a shooter incapacitated, both to protect their own lives, and the lives of others. That means aiming for the largest target, the center of the body, either the chest or abdomen. Trying to aim for an arm or leg would very likely mean the shooter would be able to keep up his attack, or that the officer's shot could very possibly miss. Even a head shot, except one by an expert marksman, is riskier than a shot to the body.

"Unfortunately, real life shooting situations

are not like an old Roy Rogers or Gene Autry television show or movie, where the good guy shoots the bad guy's gun out of his hand, or at worst, shoots him in the arm. When we aim at a shooter, we aim to incapacitate or kill."

"I am indeed well aware of that, Ranger Blawcyzk. I didn't mean to be impertinent. However, that is the kind of question the media or private citizens will ask, so I wanted to make certain we had a clear response from you. Thank you. I do have one more question. Could you not have used a smaller weapon, so the chance of Mr. Bohannon receiving a fatal wound would have been lessened?"

"Inspector General, we had no idea what we would be facing when we entered that warehouse. No clue as to how many persons were inside, what kind of weapons they had, or perhaps even whether there were booby-traps set up. As you know, drug dealers and human traffickers often have superior firepower compared to what is available to law enforcement. I chose to prepare myself with my Remington shotgun, due to its charge being able to cover a wider area. It is also a more intimidating weapon than my pistol. Not that any drug runner is likely to be intimidated by any weapon."

"You could not have dropped the shotgun and unholstered your pistol to use that instead?"

"No, ma'am. There wasn't time. Mr. Bohannon

had already shot Ranger Garcia once, and was preparing to shoot him again. If I, or any of my partners, took the time to switch weapons, Mr. Bohannon would have most likely shot Ranger Garcia again, probably fatally. If he had been able to continue shooting, the odds are one or more of his partners would have also had the chance to use their weapons. Since we were outnumbered two-and-one-half to one, and the suspects were more heavily armed, it is highly probable my partners and I would all have been gunned down."

"Do you mean *all* of you, Ranger Blawcyzk?"

"That's what I said, Inspector General. Criminals don't generally believe that old apocryphal legend about 'One riot, one Ranger'. I had no choice other than to use my shotgun to drop Mr. Bohannon as quickly as possible. I repeat, *no* choice. None. Nada. Ninguna. Zaden. Keiner. Hnkto. Geen."

"That's enough, Ranger," Stoker warned. "You've made your point."

"Indeed you have, Ranger Blawcyzk, and I do have to say I'm impressed by your apparent knowledge of several languages," Hudson said. "I have no further questions at this time. Thank you."

"You're welcome, Inspector General."

"Major Voitek," Stoker said.

"Thank you, Lieutenant. Ranger Blawcyzk,

I am sure you are aware, as part of this investigation, all radio transmissions during the entire time these events were taking place will be examined, as well as all your cell phone records, and those of the other men involved."

"And woman," Jim reminded him. "Ranger Rhonda Johnston took part in the action at the Double Dot H."

"Thank you for reminding me of that, Ranger. We will also be interviewing every other Ranger who took part in this operation. I have just one question for you, which I hope you will answer honestly, to the best of your knowledge. Did you follow proper procedure at all times? There was no violation of those procedures, even the slightest, even in error, at any time?"

"No, Major, to the best of my knowledge, there was not. I'm not saying some error might not have occurred, but if there were any mistakes made, they were minor."

"And you would testify to that under oath, if necessary?"

"Yes, I would."

"Thank you, Ranger Blawcyzk. Lieutenant Stoker, I have no more questions. You may start your questioning."

"Thank you, Major. I do have several questions for you, Ranger Blawcyzk," Stoker said. "First, it would appear, both from your answers here and your written report, that you intended to go into that building on your own, except that Ranger Garcia volunteered to back you up. Is that correct, and if so, why would you even think about getting involved in such a dangerous situation without backup?"

"That is not correct, Lieutenant. Rangers Thornton and Kennedy were standing by to assist me at the New Braunfels Airport, where I was informed the delivery was originally supposed to take place. However, since I had also been told the delivery point could possibly change, they were also prepared to move as quickly as possible to a new location.

"Once it became obvious that the drugs were being taken to a different destination, I contacted dispatch and had them tell Thornton and Kennedy to move to Spring Branch, from which location they would be able to move in any direction.

"Once the drugs reached the new destination, I had Rangers Garcia, Kennedy, and Thornton meet me at a nearby spot, where we finalized our plans. At no time did I ever consider attempting to go in single-handedly. This was always intended to be a multi-person operation. However, to be completely candid, if it had been necessary, I would have gone in alone, since if the arrests had not been made that day, the drugs would most likely have been moved before we had time to return."

"Thank you for clearing that up. Second, did

you have any alternative plan, in case your first attempt to apprehend the suspects failed?"

"Nothing in particular. However, we knew going in that we would most likely be facing a fluid situation, as the wounding of Ranger Garcia bears out. Despite wearing a bulletproof vest, as we all were, Rudy was still hit by a bullet in his left arm. We were ready for almost any eventuality. When we raided the warehouse, we positioned our vehicles to make it virtually impossible for the suspects to reach any of theirs. The truck and trailer used to transport the drugs were blocked inside the building by our vehicles, and for any of the suspects to reach their vehicles outside the warehouse, they would have had to attempt getting past us. Obviously, that would have been nearly impossible."

"Even with Ranger Garcia wounded, and out of action?"

"Rudy was wounded, but far from out of action. Despite his wound, he still managed to keep two of the suspects covered until we were able to secure all of them."

"One final question. Do you feel there is anything you could have, or should have, done differently?"

"I don't believe so, no, Lieutenant. Of course, hindsight is always perfect, and when I have more time to reflect, it's conceivable that I might come up with a thing or two I could have done differently. However, I don't believe I would have made any major changes in procedure. The way the raid, arrests, and recovery of drugs, cash, and weapons were executed was the most feasible plan under the particular circumstances. I would like to point out that, despite there being ten heavily armed suspects in the building, we were able to take them by surprise, except for Mr. Bohannon, the single shooter, who just happened to be using the bathroom when we struck. Had he been in the main part of the building with the others, his shooting would most likely have never occurred. As it is, he is the person most responsible for his own death, by opening fire on us.

"We were able to make the arrests with only one injury to any of us. And, if Mr. Bohannon had surrendered without resistance, he would still be alive today. My actions, and those of my partners, were completely justified, both from a procedural perspective, and from the principle of self-defense. In the same situation, under the same circumstances, I would perform my job in the exact same way."

"Thank you, Lieutenant. Inspector General Hudson, Major Voitek, do you have any further questions?"

"No," Hudson said.

"I don't," Voitek also said.

"Then, unless you wish to make a final statement,

Ranger Blawcyzk, this hearing is concluded."

"No, I've got nothing to add," Jim said.

"Fine. This concludes the oral interview of Ranger James Blawcyzk, Company F, in the fatal shooting of Mr. David Bohannon during an interdiction of illegal drugs. This interview will be part of the investigating committee's final report. Thank you for your cooperation, Ranger Blawcyzk."

"You're welcome."

The recorders were turned off.

"Jim, I'm sorry we had to put you though this," Voitek said, "but you know it was necessary."

"I understand, Major. How's Rudy doing?"

"He's doing much better," Stoker answered instead. "I'm leaving straight from here to conduct my interview with him. You'll be able to visit him tomorrow if you'd like."

"I'll do just that. Thanks, Lieutenant. Will he still be in the hospital, or back home?"

"No, he'll be at Baptist Emergency for at least another four or five days," Stoker said.

"Ranger Blawcyzk, this is off the record of course, but unless we turn up something unexpected, our investigation should be completed very quickly," Hudson said. "We haven't had time to thoroughly review all the evidence, of course, but so far, it appears you acted properly at all times. We'd like to have you back on duty as soon as possible."

"Thank you, Inspector General. I appreciate your candor, and your confidence in me."

"Jim, what are your plans for the rest of the day?" Stoker asked.

"I thought I'd visit the Museum for awhile, then head on back home and spend some time with my family. Maybe I'll cook supper so Kim doesn't have to."

"That sounds like a fine idea," Stoker answered. "Try and relax, and not worry."

"I'll do my best," Jim said. "I'll wait to hear from you or the Major."

"It won't be long," Voitek reassured him. "Now, I've got to get back to my office. You take care, Jim."

Jim spent the next few hours at the Ranger Museum, enjoying the exhibits, as he always did, mingling with the visitors, posing for photographs with some, and signing a stack of Junior Texas Ranger membership certificates that were ready for mailing. Someday in the near future, his father, having died in the line of duty, would be inducted into the Ranger Hall of Fame. He left just after three-thirty, and arrived home shortly before five-thirty, driving even more quickly than usual. Once he got home, he parked the Tahoe and headed into the house. Frostie came bounding out of the barn, and followed Jim inside.

Kim was in the kitchen, getting ready to give Josh his bath. Jim kissed her on the cheek, and chucked Josh under his chin.

"How are my two favorite people in the world doing?" he asked.

"We're both just fine," Kim answered. "Your mother already fed the horses, before she went out for dinner with some friends. How did the hearing go?"

"About as I expected," Jim said. "Things should be cleared up in a couple of weeks. If you're ready for supper, I'll get the steaks on the grill. I'm starved."

"So am I," Kim answered, "but I've got some contracts to sign and send off. That will only take me a little while. Since you got home earlier than I expected, would you mind giving Josh his bath before you start supper?"

"Not at all. I'd love to give my little pard his bath," Jim answered. "C'mon, pal, time for a swim."

He took Josh from Kim, who then sat at the kitchen table and opened her laptop.

"I still can't get used to electronic signatures being legal," Jim said. "Give me old fashioned paper documents any day."

"You're just an old dinosaur, and always will be," Kim said, laughing. "Will you please get Josh in his tub before the water cools off?"

"Sure."

Jim put Josh on a soft towel, next to the baby's tub on the kitchen counter. He took off Josh's polo shirt, shorts, and diaper, and blew a raspberry on his boy's belly. He then gently lowered him into the tub. As babies, particularly boys, are wont to do, once Josh was in the warm water, he had to pee. The stream caught Jim squarely in the face.

"You little son of a gun," Jim said, spluttering, grabbing a dish towel to wipe his face. "You did that on purpose."

"No, he did not," Kim said, rushing over to help, laughing hysterically. "How many times have I warned you, Jim, babies will pee when they're put in the tub? Did you ever listen to me, and put a washcloth over his little wee-wee, just to be safe? *Nooo.* This was bound to happen. Hold on to him, now. You know how slippery he can be in the tub."

Jim finished wiping off his face, then looked down at Josh and chuckled.

"Kim, you were right," he said. "What we talked about the day before last."

"What was that?"

"Remember you said he might not want to become a Texas Ranger? You were right. He ain't gonna be a Ranger. This dang kid's gonna be a fireman. He's already practicin'."

"Jim . . ."

"What?"

"Never mind. You're hopeless. Please, just

finish giving Josh his bath while I send off the last of these contracts."

"All right. Y'know, now that I think about it, maybe Josh *is* gonna be a Ranger. He dang for certain already has good aim. He got me right between the eyes."

Kim glared at her husband.

"Jim, just finish bathing him, dry him off, get him dressed, and give him to me, then get supper started, before I take the dish sprayer and give you a good dousing myself."

"All right, all right, I can take a hint," Jim said. He hurriedly bathed Josh, dried and dressed him, then gave him to Kim. Once she had the baby, he went to the refrigerator, took out two T-bone steaks from the freezer, two ears of corn from the refrigerator to roast, along with lettuce, tomatoes, radishes, broccoli, an onion, and carrots to make a salad, and a can of cashews from the cabinet. He always liked to add a few nuts to a salad, to give it some added texture. Lastly, he took two potatoes from the cupboard, then called to Frostie.

"C'mon, boy, you can come outside with me while I make supper," he said. "Kim, do you want wine with your meal, beer, or just soda?"

"I think I'll just have ginger ale," she answered. "There's ice cream in the freezer for dessert, along with a jar of hot fudge topping and whipped cream in the fridge to top it off."

"That's fine. I reckon I'll stick with Dr Pepper then," Jim answered. "Supper will be ready in about forty-five minutes."

"That will give me just enough time to feed Josh."

"Perfect. It's a nice evening to eat on the deck. The humidity's down, and there's a soft breeze cooling things off. I'll see you out there."

With Frostie tagging along, knowing he was bound to get some steak trimmings, Jim headed for the deck.

After they ate, Kim went to check on Josh, while Jim made certain the mesquite coals in the grill were extinguished, then cleaned up the dishes. He turned on the dishwasher and went back outside. After stopping to say good night to Copper and the other horses, he walked to the far corner of his land, to the Blawcyzk family cemetery, which was shaded by two enormous trees, a sycamore and a live oak, and overlooked the pond Jim had dug. The waning gibbous moon cast an eerie light on the tombstones. Jim stopped for a moment at each of his grandparents' graves, then sat down by his father's, whose headstone had just recently been installed. The stone was simply inscribed "Michael J. Blawcyzk, Texas Ranger", underneath which were his dates of birth and death, "March 18, 1965 – October 16, 2016". There was a space where a ceramic picture of Jim's father would be fastened to the stone, once it had been completed. The grass had still not completely filled back in over the grave.

Jim's father, and his namesake, his great-great-great-grandfather James J. Blawcyzk, the first of his ancestors to join the Rangers, had both died in the line of duty. The others had all served Texas heroically, but survived to die peacefully of old age.

"Pa, I hope you're restin' easy," Jim said, softly. "I sure ain't. I had to kill a man a couple days back, an *hombre* who had shot one of my partners, and was gonna keep on shootin'—which means I didn't have any choice. So, now I'm in trouble, and might get kicked outta the Rangers.

"Things sure have changed, Pa, and not for the better, even in the short time you've been gone. Major Voitek and Lieutenant Stoker keep telling me not to worry, that everything'll turn out all right, but I can't help it. Seems more'n more like the good guys are the bad guys and the bad guys are the good guys these days. I sure wish you were here to talk with me, Pa. I still wish you'd gotten to meet your grandson before you got killed, too.

"Little Josh is growin' like a weed. I swear he even looks a bit like you. I'm certain he'll grow up to be a Ranger, like you'n me . . . unless he becomes a fireman. When I was giving him his

113

bath tonight, he peed and gave me a good squirt plumb square in my face. I sure miss you, Pa. So do Ma and Kim. Anyway, I just wanted to visit with you for a little while. I know you're up there, listening. I'm gonna say good night, and get some sleep. I'll see you again tomorrow."

Jim headed back to the house, said his prayers, undressed, and crawled into bed. By the time Kim joined him, he was already sleeping.

5

Logan Daniels took a final puff on his cigarette, then tossed the butt onto the pavement. He swallowed hard before he entered a nondescript office building on the outskirts of San Marcos. He took the elevator to the third floor, and went through an unmarked door into an office at the end of the hall.

A matronly receptionist, her graying hair dyed silver, with glasses hanging from a cord around her neck, looked up when he walked in. On the wall behind her was a small sign that read "XMD Logistics and Distribution". Other than that, except for a few sorry looking, neglected plants, struggling for life, and a photograph of the receptionist's grandchildren on her desk, there were no other decorations. The paint was drab, the carpeting shabby and worn.

"Good morning, Mr. Daniels," she said. "Mr. Prescott is waiting for you. He said for you to go right on in as soon as you got here."

"Thanks, Deidre," Daniels answered. "You're looking younger every day. What kind of mood is he in this morning?"

"Why, thank you, Mr. Daniels. I'll bet you say that to all the ladies, but I'll be happy to take the compliment. The usual, I'm afraid. I swear, if I weren't paid so well, I'd look for another job."

"That's what I expected, although I was hoping not to hear that," Daniels said. "Well, I might as well get this over with."

Daniels walked past the receptionist's station, knocked on a door marked "Private", and entered that office without waiting for an answer. He shut the door behind him.

"Logan, you were supposed to be here half-an-hour ago," David Prescott said, without a hello or handshake. "We've got a major problem, and you show up late?"

"I'm sorry, Mr. Prescott, but there was a semi rolled over on the Interstate. It even had the frontage roads tied up. And I couldn't call because when I dropped my phone last night the screen shattered. As soon as our meeting is over, I'm going to get another one."

"If you can't solve the problem you've created, you may not need another one," Prescott threatened. "Do you realize how much product we lost? How much money?"

"I'm well aware of it, yes, Mr. Prescott."

"What happened, Logan? How the hell did the damn Texas Rangers get onto us?"

"I have no idea, Mr. Prescott. I'm sorry," Daniels said. "Everything was secure, as far as any of us knew. You know where the ranch is located. There should have been no way anyone could have spied on it without us knowing about it. That's why it was chosen."

"But the Rangers surely did," Prescott retorted. "Even worse, the idiots you hired who were transporting the load allowed the Rangers to follow them right to the drop-off. Apologizing doesn't mean a damn thing, Logan. Now, I realize that this shipment is lost, so we'll just have to write it off as part of the cost of doing business. However, I want to make certain nothing like this ever happens again. Do you understand?"

"Yes, sir, I do, Mr. Prescott."

"Good. Now first, I want to make certain none of the men the Rangers arrested will talk, to try and make a deal."

"None of them will, Mr. Prescott. You have my assurance on that. Even if they did, they have no knowledge of who they were working for. They were hired through an intermediary, who is utterly reliable, so there is no possibility the Rangers could obtain any information that would lead them back to us."

"You'd better be right. Mr. Kenney is extremely displeased. He wanted you terminated immediately; however, I was able to convince him to give you another chance. That means I stuck my neck out for you. On reflection, he realized I was right, that up until this incident, you have been a valued employee of our firm, one who has contributed immensely to our success. However, there is one condition. Mr. Kenney wants one issue solved. If that is not done successfully, then you *will* be terminated, and I'm certain you're aware that doesn't refer merely to your employment."

"That's pretty plain, Mr. Prescott. What does Mr. Kenney want done?"

"Just this."

Prescott clicked on a remote. A screen shot of Jim from the KEYE news appeared on the wall-mounted television.

"He wants this man eliminated. James Blawcyzk, the Ranger who apparently was the one that ferreted out our Concan operation. He'd like all the Rangers involved taken out, of course, but realizes that would be impossible. Getting rid of just this one will be problem enough. Are you up to the task?"

"I'll make certain it happens," Daniels answered. "I assume you want his death to look like an accident?"

"We'd rather have him just disappear without a trace if at all possible. However, if that can't happen, or his death can't be made to appear an accident, then any method used to kill him is fine, as long as it can't be traced back to us. Of course, it would be preferable if you could get the name of his source, or how he discovered our operation, out of him before he died. Obviously, we want that person eliminated, too."

"Understood, Mr. Prescott. Shall I take care of it personally, or use a third party?"

"Either way will do. If you have a reliable third party, that would probably be preferable. There would be less chance of Ranger Blawcyzk's untimely and unfortunate demise being traced back to this firm."

"I know several. How soon would you like this taken care of?"

"Let's wait and see what the hearing into your man's shooting comes up with. Perhaps we'll be fortunate, and Blawcyzk will be kicked out of the Rangers, or even better, arrested for murder or manslaughter. If he goes to prison, that will make your job easier. I'm certain there would be no end of inmates who would be happy to eliminate him, without us having to be involved at all. In the meantime, let's allow him to sweat until the investigation into his actions is closed. If, as I'm almost certain will happen, he's let off the hook, then his death should take place immediately."

"He won't be found guilty of anything, the way things went down. I'm certain of that, Mr. Prescott. Not from what the men who were there tell me."

"I'm in agreement with you on that, Logan. However, sometimes patience pays off in big dividends. We'll wait. But, if Blawcyzk does get reinstated to active duty, Mr. Kenney and I will expect him dead within a week. If he isn't, you will be, because if you aren't terminated, then I will be, and there's damn sure no way I'd allow that to happen. Now, get out of here. Send Deidre in on your way out."

Deliberately, Prescott picked up a letter from his desk, and resumed reading it. Knowing there was nothing more to be said, Logan Daniels departed.

6

Rudy Garcia was lying in his hospital bed, watching a rerun of a Dallas Cowboys game, when Jim walked in.

"It's about high time you got back to work, instead of lying around doin' nothin' all day long, Ranger," Jim said in greeting.

"Jim, you old son of a bitch," Rudy answered. "I thought you'd forgotten all about me, lyin' here all lonesome and forlorn."

"I wanted to be here sooner, but had to wait until Lieutenant Stoker gave me the okay," Jim answered. "Besides, from the looks of those two pretty young nurses who left your room as I was coming down the hall, you're not all *that* lonesome. If your wife catches you with them, you'll have more than just a bullet busted arm to worry about."

"What Delores doesn't know won't hurt her," Rudy answered. "Besides, all I do is look. I've seen her watching good-lookin' guys, too, so we're even. Yeah, I heard about your suspension. There's damn sure no reason for it, except us lawmen can't make a move without bein' second-guessed nowadays. I wouldn't worry too much. You'll be back at work before you know it. What's in the box you've got there?"

"Bein' shot hasn't left you short of breath, Rudy, that's for damn certain," Jim said. "As far as what's in the box, it's paperwork from Major Voitek. He figured as long as you had nothing else to do, you might as well finish up some reports."

"You can't be serious," Rudy said.

"I sure am," Jim answered. "Let me get the files out for you."

He opened the box and pulled out two containers. One held a pizza, the other a take out from the Mandarin Blossom Chinese restaurant.

"If those are reports, they're the best damn smelling reports I've ever seen," Rudy exclaimed.

"You're right," Jim said. "I had to put this food in a box and seal it tight to sneak it past the nurses and doctors. Good thing I'm wearing my badge, because I had to talk security out of searching it, too. When we were trailin' those drug runners, you never did get your General Tso's chicken, and I didn't get my pizza. I've got four beers in here to go along with the chuck. Sorry they're not dark ale from the brewery, but I just couldn't get up there."

"Jim, I don't care where this stuff is from. It's not hospital chow, and that's all that matters. Hand it over."

"Sure." Jim handed Rudy the container of chicken, then popped open one of the beers and put it on his bedside table.

"We'd better eat fast, before we're found out," Jim said, as he bit into a slice of mozzarella, bacon, and onion pizza.

"What can they do to me if we are?" Rudy answered. "Throw me out? I'd welcome that. Last they told me I'm gonna be stuck here for at least another week."

"You must've been hit worse than any of us thought," Jim said.

"A bit," Rudy answered. "The bone splintered pretty good, which meant my surgeon had to poke around a lot to make certain she got all the bits of bone out of my arm, so they wouldn't cause me trouble later, or worse, start an infection. But at least, after rehab, I should have full use of the arm again."

"That's good news. You're doin' okay otherwise?"

"Now that you've brought me some decent food I am. I must've lost fifteen pounds since I got here. The food's barely edible. Enough about me. What about you, Jim? It's gotta be rough as hell on you, not bein' able to work. When the lieutenant questioned me about what happened, I made certain he knew you had no other choice but to down the bastard who got me. How's the case against those sons of bitches we rounded up progressing?"

"I dunno," Jim said, with a shrug. "I'm not allowed to even ask about it until after the department finishes their investigation into the shooting. And you're right, it's damn rough. At least I'm getting a lot of paperwork caught up, and goin' back over some of my older open cases, to see if I can come up with more on those. I'm working almost as hard as if I hadn't been put on leave at all, except mostly with my computer, from home. And, of course, I get to spend a bit more time with Kim and Josh, which is always good. Enough talk about work. How's your wife and girls doing?"

"They're just fine. Worried about me, of course, but they've held up through this whole thing pretty well."

For the next half-hour, Jim and Rudy watched the game and made small talk, until one of Rudy's nurses came into the room, holding a needle. She stopped short when she spotted the empty food containers and beer bottles.

"Ranger Garcia! You know you're on a restricted diet," she exclaimed. "Who said you could have that . . . that pizza! Chinese! And beer!"

"He did, Carmen," Rudy said, pointing directly at Jim.

"And just who are you?"

"Ranger Jim Blawcyzk. I was with Rudy when he got shot," Jim answered.

"That doesn't give you the right to bring him food that's not on his menu," the nurse answered.

"I didn't," Jim said. "I ate all the Chinese and pizza, and drank the beers. Rudy's had nothing but saltines and water all the while I've been here."

"I don't believe one word of that."

"Jim's telling you the truth, Carmen," Randy said. He gestured at the empty pizza box, Mandarin Blossom containers, and beer bottles. "If you don't believe him, there's not a helluva lot you can do about it, anyway. He ate and drank all the evidence."

"I suppose I am too late," the nurse said, disgustedly. "If you get sick, Ranger Garcia, it's your fault, not mine. However, Ranger Blawcyzk, you'll have to leave now. It's time for Ranger Garcia to get his shot. It has to go into his buttocks. I'm certain you'd rather not see that."

"I've seen Rudy's butt before, and you're right, nurse," Jim said, laughing. "It's not a pretty sight. I'll be leaving now. Rudy, you take it easy."

"You too, Jim. Call me as soon as you get cleared for full duty. And *muchas gracias* for the, uh, bread and water."

"Any time, Rudy," Jim said. "I'll bring more next visit."

"There won't be a next visit," the nurse said. "I'm going to make certain of that."

"Don't worry, Jim," Rudy said. "You come visit anytime you want. It's driving me plumb loco just layin' around. Carmen, lighten up. It was just a little food, that's all."

"It was more than . . ."

"*Vaya con Dios*, Rudy," Jim broke in, before the nurse could continue her tirade.

"*Adios*, Jim."

Ten days later, at eight-thirty in the morning, Lieutenant Stoker showed up at Jim's front door. When he rang the bell, Kim answered.

"Lieutenant Stoker, hello," she said. "This is certainly an unexpected surprise. I trust it will be a pleasant one."

"Good morning, Mrs. Blawcyzk. I'm certain it will be. May I come in?"

"Of course."

Kim held the door open for him.

"Is Jim home?" Stoker asked, once he was inside.

"He is, but he's not here at the house," Kim answered. "I hope you're bringing good news."

"I am—at least, I think it is," Stoker answered. "There are still a few details to wrap up, but Jim's been conditionally cleared to go back to work, before the final decision from his hearing is actually issued. That's the good news. The bad news is, I need him to come back on duty immediately."

"That's not bad news at all, especially for me," Kim said. "He's been underfoot and driving me crazy for the past week. Don't let him know I told you, but he's been doing nothing but stewing and fretting for days now."

"I knew he would be. I'll be more than happy to get him out of the house for you," Stoker said. "Where can I find him?"

"He's out by the pond, watching the fish play volleyball, or perhaps water polo."

"I'm almost afraid to ask, but what does that mean?"

"I'm going to let Jim explain that to you, if you don't mind, Lieutenant," Kim said, smiling. "You wouldn't believe me if I tried. Do you know how to find him?"

"As a matter of fact, yes," Stoker answered. "He showed me the pond after he first dug it. I'll find him."

"Great. And thank you. You've taken a big load off my mind."

"It's a big load off *all* of our minds," Stoker said. "I'd better go find Jim and tell him the news before he sees my car, or gets the word on his phone. It hasn't been released to the media yet, but you know how these things can somehow get out."

"He'll be happy to see you. Make certain to stop for a cup of coffee before you leave."

"Thank you, Mrs. Blawcyzk. I'll do just that."

Stoker walked to where he knew Jim would be, the pond he'd dug after he reclaimed his family's land. The pond was fed by springs and a small branch of Onion Creek, so it had quickly become home to bass, bluegill and pumpkinseed sunfish, and crappies. Jim enjoyed fishing, but never fished in that pond, though. He considered all its inhabitants his pets. Most of his friends wondered how he would treat an alligator if one ever turned up in his pond. The general consensus was he'd probably shoot it, so it wouldn't eat any of the fish, but a few thought he might try and tame it.

Stoker stopped for a moment when he first caught sight of Jim, who was shirtless and sitting at the edge of the pond, tossing something into the water. He was concentrating so hard on what he was doing he never even heard Stoker approach.

"Hey, Jim, are you gonna talk to me, or just keep doing whatever the hell you're doing all morning?" Stoker called.

Startled, Jim jumped to his feet and spun around.

"Lieutenant. I'm sorry, I never heard you. I sure wasn't expectin' you. I'm not certain I'm happy to see you, either."

"Well, you should be," Stoker answered. "You're going back to work."

"I'm *what?*" Jim said. "I'm sorry, Lieutenant, but I could have sworn I just heard you say I'm goin' back to work."

"I did, and I'll explain everything in just a

minute . . . after *you* tell *me* exactly what you're up to. Your wife told me you're watching the fish play volleyball."

"That's right, I am," Jim answered. "You see, I go down to the doughnut shop and buy a box of doughnut holes. I bring them back here and throw 'em to the fish. When they take a bite, the doughnut hole bounces back and forth like a volleyball, or mebbe like in water polo. Watch."

Jim bent over, reached into the box at his feet, pulled out a handful of doughnut holes, and tossed them into the pond. Instantly, the surface of the water began swirling, and as the fish nipped at the food from underneath, the doughnut holes began bouncing back and forth along the pond's surface, much like volleyballs being hit over a net, as Jim had claimed would happen.

"See? Fish volleyball. But enough about the dang fish. You're serious, Lieutenant? I'm going back on duty? When? How?"

"Well, I thought you were going back to work, but after seeing this little display right now, I'm thinking perhaps you should be placed on medical leave for a thorough psychiatric examination. Fish volleyball? Really, Jim? Have you been drinking, Ranger, or are you just plumb loco?"

"Neither. I'm training my bass for the fish Olympic games."

"Enough. It's time for you to get up off your

bass and back to work. No, to answer your next question, the results of the investigation aren't quite ready. So far, we have found nothing to indicate you violated procedure, so you are being allowed back on full duty, as I said, effective immediately.

"As to the how, Major Voitek and I just happened to be on a conference call with Inspector General Hudson, preparing the first draft of our report, when a call came in from the Hays County Sheriff's Office. There's been a murder a few miles outside Wimberly. They need Ranger help, and you're the only man who's available—plus, of course, Hays is one of your counties. So the decision was made to put you back on full duty, conditionally, pending the release of the final report. Major Voitek, the Inspector General, and I anticipate that should be within the week. Unless we turn up something, which none of us expects to happen, the conditional part of your return will be lifted within ten days.

"Listen, Jim, we've wasted enough time here already. Get back to the house, get yourself dressed, and start heading for Wimberly. Contact the sheriff's office en route, and they'll give you the address and what details they have."

"Yes, sir, Lieutenant. I'm on my way."

Jim tossed the remaining doughnut holes into the pond, grabbed his T-shirt, and headed for his house on the run.

• • •

Less than an hour later, Jim was rolling up to 11033 Mount Sharp Road, in an unincorporated area of Hays County. This remote stretch of Mount Sharp was dirt and gravel, and isolated County Road 219 departed from Mount Sharp onto Longhorn Trail. Hays County Deputy George Lennon was leaning against the hood of his patrol car, which was blocking the dirt drive to 11033. He waved to Jim when he saw him approach, and lifted the yellow crime scene tape also blocking access. Jim waved back and drove under the tape, then another quarter-mile to the house, a one-story wooden structure with peeling paint, sagging porch, and a patched roof.

Another deputy, Duane Malquit, was waiting for him, sitting in the shade of a pin oak. Sitting alongside the deputy was another man, in his mid- to late twenties, dressed in faded jeans, a dirty blue T-shirt so full of holes it appeared it had been riddled with buckshot, and a battered Dallas Cowboys cap. He was puffing nervously on a cigarette.

Next to the house was an older model gray Nissan Sentra with expired plates, and a beat up red Toyota Tacoma pickup parked behind it. Jim would hazard the Nissan belonged to the victim, and the pickup to the man with the deputy. The two men got up while Jim parked his Tahoe, got out, and opened the tailgate.

"Howdy, Jim," Malquit said. "Glad to see you're back on the job."

"Howdy, Duane. Not as happy as I am," Jim answered. "What've we got here?"

"One elderly female victim. Pamela Sue Dearing, age 76. This is her grandson, Mason Palmer. He's the one who found the body. He says she was shot. I've already gotten a search warrant run up here."

"I'm sorry about your grandmother, Mr. Palmer. I'm Texas Ranger James Blawcyzk from Company F. I'll be heading the investigation into her death. I'll need to ask you some questions, of course."

"Thank you, Ranger. I'll help you any way I can. I want to see whoever killed my grandma rot in jail for a long time before he gets the needle," Mason said.

"We'll do our best to find whoever's responsible," Jim answered. "Duane, have you been inside yet?"

"Not yet," Malquit said. "I only looked through the front door. I figured it'd be better to leave everything undisturbed until you got here, Jim. I did dust the doorknob and frame for prints, though. I have those for you."

"Fine. Let's get started," Jim said. "Mr. Palmer, did you touch anything in the house, move anything, or remove anything?"

"Only the telephone, Ranger," Palmer answered.

"There's no cell service way out here, so I had to use grandma's land line to call the sheriff. Once I got ahold of him, I went straight back outside. I couldn't stay in the house, not with my grandma lyin' dead on the floor."

"I understand completely," Jim said. "Mr. Palmer, I'm going to have to ask you to remain outside while Deputy Malquit and I gather evidence. You're not a suspect at this time, but I am requesting you stay here until we're finished with the preliminaries. I promise I won't keep you any longer than necessary, but I do need to question you before I'm able to allow you to leave. I'd also like to fingerprint you, if you have no objections."

"That's all right with me," Palmer answered. His eyes were moist with tears. "I guess . . . I guess I'll have to let my mom know, and my sisters. And start to make the arrangements."

"You'll have to wait a couple of days for the arrangements," Jim said. "The county medical examiner will need to perform an autopsy. Has he been notified yet, Duane?"

"He has. He should be here shortly," Malquit answered.

"Good. Then let's get to work."

Jim took his camera from his truck, along with an evidence collection kit containing, among other items, medicine droppers, plastic collection bags, scrapers, tweezers, a magnifying glass, small bottles, collection tubes, fingerprint dusting powder, stain marking liquid, and cloths. He took a pair of nitrile booties from a box and pulled them over his boots, then donned two pairs of nitrile gloves. He handed booties and gloves to Malquit, ordering him to put them on.

"Let's go inside."

He, with Malquit following, opened the door and went into the house. First glance showed the interior of the small house was the complete opposite of the exterior. It was well-kept and freshly painted, with new rugs on the floor, new furniture in the living room, new appliances and tile in the kitchen, and decorated with landscapes and family portraits, as well as knick-knacks precisely placed on tables.

Jim turned on his digital recorder.

"Texas Ranger James Blawcyzk of Company F, assisted by Hays County Deputy Sheriff Duane Malquit, investigating the apparent homicide of Pamela Sue Dearing, a seventy-six-year-old white female, in her residence at 11033 Mount Sharp Road in Hays County."

He turned to the deputy sheriff and said, "Duane, take a look around to see if there's any sign of a struggle, anything missing, or anything that doesn't seem quite right while I photograph the body, but don't touch anything, of course."

"Do you mind if I watch you before I do that?"

Malquit asked. "I'd like to learn more about how you Rangers process a crime scene."

"No, that'll be fine. You can observe while I work," Jim answered. He began taking photographs of the body, dictating his observations into the recorder as he went.

"The victim was found by her grandson, Mason Palmer, earlier today. Her body is lying face up on the kitchen floor. A bullet wound to the forehead is obvious. On initial observation, it would appear the bullet did not exit the skull, as there is no pooling of blood, nor spattering which would indicate the presence of an exit wound. There are some blood stains on the floor and victim's blouse, consistent with the entry wound. The victim's eyes are open, pupils dilated."

Jim took photographs of the body and room from every angle, then took a stick of chalk from his evidence kit and drew an outline around the body. He took a pencil from his shirt pocket and inserted it into the bullet hole.

"The angle of the wound indicates the victim was shot by a person who was taller than she, from fairly close range. It appears to follow a slightly downward trajectory. There are no powder burns around the wound. The bullet is indeed still in the victim's head, stopping after penetrating several inches into the brain."

Jim removed the pencil, which was now

135

covered with blood and brain matter. Malquit promptly ran to the sink and vomited.

"Sorry, Jim," he said, once he could speak.

"Don't touch the faucet to rinse that puke down until we've had a chance to dust it for prints," Jim answered. "You need to go outside for some air?"

"No, I'll be okay," Malquit answered. "I just wasn't expectin' something like that. Keep goin'."

"Okay." Jim put the pencil in a plastic bag, which he sealed, for later disposal. He lifted Dearing's right arm, then left leg. "Rigor Mortis is still present. The stage it is at, along with decomposition not yet having begun, would place the time of death sometime within the past eight to twelve hours."

He lifted Dearing's blouse, then lowered her slacks and panties.

"There are no obvious signs of a struggle, nor of sexual assault. Preliminary observation indicates no flesh from the perpetrator under the victim's fingernails, as well as no evidence of sexual penetration. Scrapings from under the victim's fingernails, and the vagina, will be taken for lab analysis to confirm that."

He next rolled Dearing's body onto its stomach.

"Livor Mortis is present and set. Pooling of the blood is almost completely on the back side of the victim, indicating she died very quickly."

He pulled the clothes back in place, then rolled Dearing back over.

"There are no other wounds to the body besides the bullet wound to the forehead. No abrasions, contusions, or other injuries. From what the evidence indicates so far, either the victim was taken completely by surprise, or knew her assailant.

"The house also shows no signs of a struggle. All the furniture is in place, nothing is broken, glass knick-knacks have not been knocked to the floor, rugs show no sign of a scuffle, nor are there any fresh marks or bloodstains on the floors or walls of the room where the victim was discovered, except in the immediate vicinity of the victim, nor the adjacent living room. I am turning off this recorder while I take evidence samples from the victim, and while Deputy Malquit and I search the house for more potential evidence. We are awaiting the arrival of the Hays County Medical Examiner to remove the body for a forensic autopsy, which will include recovery of the bullet so its caliber can be determined."

Jim switched off the recorder.

"You can watch me take the samples, Duane, or you can start going through the house, whichever you'd rather."

"I think I've seen enough," Malquit answered. "I'll start looking around. You want me to dust any likely spots for fingerprints, too?"

"That'd help save some time," Jim agreed. "Sure. I've worked with you often enough that I know you know what to do. Just call me if you discover anything. After I'm done collecting evidence from the body, I'll look through the kitchen."

"Will do," Malquit said. He headed down the hallway, while Jim opened his collection kit to begin gathering evidence.

It was nearly two hours later before Jim had gathered all the samples he needed, then gone through the kitchen and living room checking for the slightest bit of evidence, a tiny scrap of cloth, a thread, a strand of hair, or speck of blood that might have come from a minor injury to Pamela Sue Dearing's killer. The Hays County Medical Examiner had arrived almost an hour earlier. Jim kept him waiting until he was finished with his work.

"Duane, I'm just about done in this part of the house," he said to Malquit, who was now dusting the kitchen faucets, countertops, and appliances for fingerprints. "I'm gonna go outside, let the M.E. know he can remove the body, then question Palmer. Can you tell me anything about him and his family?"

"There's nothin' much to tell, Jim," Malquit said, with a shrug. "It's a typical hard-scrabble Texas family, land poor and struggling just to survive from one week to the next. Pamela Sue was a widow. Johnny Joe, her husband, died in a tractor accident about six or seven years back. She's been tryin' to hang onto this old place ever since. If whoever killed her was lookin' for money, they sure didn't find any here."

"What about this house?" Jim asked. "Yeah, it's a mess on the outside, but inside it looks like it was recently all spruced up."

"It was," Malquit answered. "Pamela Sue would take a trip to the casinos in Mississippi whenever she could scrape up enough extra *dinero*. Last year, she hit it big down in Gulfport, and fixed the place up with her winnings, at least the inside. She didn't win enough to take care of the outside, so she said."

"But someone might've figured she still had some money stashed around here somewhere," Jim answered. "That'd be reason enough to kill her, for lots of *hombres*."

"Except this sure doesn't look like a robbery," Malquit pointed out.

"No, it sure doesn't," Jim agreed. "What about the rest of the family, particularly Palmer?"

"None of them ever got into nothin' more than minor trouble. "Johnny Joe and Pamela Sue had three kids. Two of them moved away years back. They'll need to be notified, of course. Jenny's the only one who stayed. She married a no-good drunk name of Tommy Palmer, who was Mason's dad. He killed himself in a car wreck when Mason was only about two, from what I understand. DUI, of course. That was way before I joined the sheriff's department. I was probably only about ten or eleven at the time. Jenny never remarried. She worked days at Drislane's Discount Store in San Marcos, and evenings at the Heart O' Texas Café in Wimberly, waitin' tables. Pamela Sue took care of Mason all that time. Jenny still works at Drislane's, but the café's been closed for a few years now.

"As far as Mason goes, he adored his grandma. He checked on her at least once a week. He's only got a couple minor arrests on his record, one for drunk and disorderly, another for disturbing the peace. If I was a betting man, I'd give you ten to one Mason didn't have a thing to do with Pamela Sue's killin'."

"I reckon we'll find out," Jim answered. "I'll send the M.E. in. Give him a hand if he needs help. I'll be back soon as I finish talking with Palmer. It looks like we've still got at least a couple of hours ahead of us here."

"Sure thing, Jim. I'll keep working in here."

Mason Palmer was again under the shade of the pin oak, still waiting when Jim came back outside.

"No, just stay there," Jim told him, when he started to stand up. "It's real stuffy in the house,

140

and hot as blazes out here, so I'd rather be in the shade. Just let me put this stuff in my truck and I'll be right with you."

Once Jim had put the items he'd gathered inside his Tahoe, placing them in an ice chest so the heat wouldn't deteriorate the samples, he joined Palmer under the tree.

"Were you able to reach your mom?" Jim asked.

"Yes, sir, I was. I let her know I'd be here a while, and that she shouldn't rush up here. I didn't want her to see her mother like that. She knows I won't be home for a while, so she's going over to Mary Scott, one of our neighbors, to be with her until I get home. She's taking this real hard, of course."

"That's good she won't be alone. Mason, before we get started, do I have your permission to record this interview?" Jim asked. "Do you mind if I call you Mason?"

"Yes, to the first question, not at all to the second," Palmer answered.

"Fine. I'll turn my recorder on, and we'll get started."

Jim switched on his recorder.

"Ranger James Blawcyzk, interviewing Mason Palmer, grandson of the deceased, who was the person who discovered her body. First, Mr. Palmer, please let me have your full name, date of birth, and home address."

"My name is Mason Llewellyn Palmer, date of birth August 21st, 1991. My address is 237 Dobie Drive, Wimberly, Texas."

"Thank you, Mr. Palmer. Before I continue this interview, I wish to inform you that you are not, at present, a suspect in the apparent homicide of your grandmother, Pamela Dearing. However, you do have the right to an attorney, if you wish, before we continue. You also have the right not to answer any or all questions, and the right to stop this interview at any time. Do you understand these rights, and are you taking part in this interview voluntarily?"

"Yes, sir, I do, and I am."

"Thank you. Do you live alone at 227 Dobie Lane, Wimberly?"

"That's 237 Dobie Drive. No sir. I live with my mom. I moved back with her after I broke up with my girlfriend six months ago."

"I see. What is your occupation?"

"I'm an attendant at the Brookshire Brothers Gas & Go Station on Ranch Road 12 in Wimberly. I work the three to eleven shift, six days a week. Today's my day off, so I came up here to check on my grandma, like I do every week."

"I understand. Mr. Palmer—Mason, I realize this is a difficult time for you, but please tell me, as best you can, what you found when you arrived here."

"Of course. I got here shortly after six in

the morning, as usual. Grandma was an early riser, and liked to get her errands done before lunchtime. Her old car hasn't run for a few months, so I always took her shopping and wherever else she needed to go. She always made me breakfast, then we would spend the morning together." Palmer hesitated, his voice breaking.

"I-I'm sorry, Ranger," he said.

"There's no need to apologize," Jim assured him. "You've had a real shock. Just take your time, and continue when you can."

"Thanks, sir. Grandma never locked her door, so I just walked in and called her name. When she didn't answer, I went into the kitchen, figuring she was on the back porch or out in the yard. As soon as I did, I saw her lyin' there. I knew right off she was dead. I didn't even try to wake her up, just grabbed the phone, called the sheriff's office, and ran right back outside to wait for 'em."

"So, you didn't touch anything in the house at all, besides the phone, and the door when you opened it. Is that correct?"

"That's right, Ranger."

"Did you notice anything out of place, anything missing? Any sign that someone else had been here?"

"No, I sure didn't. Of course, I really didn't look around much, neither."

"I understand that. Now, Deputy Moore told me your grandmother had used winnings from a casino in Biloxi to remodel the interior of her house."

"She did, but it was a casino in Gulfport, not Biloxi."

"That's right, he did say Gulfport. I apologize for the error. Do you know if she had any money left over? If she did, would anyone have known about it?"

"No, she spent it all. If anyone did kill grandma to try and rob her, they wouldn't have gotten anything. She lived on her Social Security, and what little money my mom and I could spare. Pretty much everyone knew she was broke."

"Did she have any savings accounts, or money in the bank? I'm going to have to get permission to see any records and transactions of those accounts, or get a court order allowing me to access them."

"Not that any of the family is aware of. She didn't trust banks, especially after my grandfather nearly lost this place when he couldn't make the mortgage payments. He was able to get an extension, and somehow managed to scrape enough together to pay off the note before it came due."

"I see. Do you know where he got the money?"

"He sold a few acres to the county, so they could use it as a site for a second pumping station, if one ever became needed. The county commissioners had hoped to attract some big developer from back East to talk a Japanese or Korean car company into building an assembly plant here. As you can see, that never happened. It was a pipe dream right from the start. Who the hell would want to build a factory way out here in the middle of damn nowhere?"

"I sure wouldn't, but then I'm a lawman, not a businessman," Jim answered. "I've only got a few more questions for now. Then, with your permission, I'd like to fingerprint you, so your prints can be compared with any we found in the house."

"I'll be happy to let you take my prints, Ranger," Palmer answered.

"I'm obliged. We'll get to that in a few minutes. Next question. Do you own any guns, Mason?"

"Doesn't every Texan?"

"Just about," Jim answered, with a soft chuckle.

"So do I. I've got a Winchester .22 caliber rifle for hunting rabbits and varmints, and a Mossberg twelve-gauge shotgun for bird hunting. I sold my deer rifle a few months back to help pay my mom's electric bill. You can examine them if you think it's necessary."

"It will be. You don't own any handguns?"

"No, I never had a need for any. They're not much good for hunting."

"How about your grandmother?"

"No." Palmer shook his head. "When Grandpa died, she sold his guns to help pay for the funeral."

"One last question. Do you have any idea who might want to kill your grandmother, and why?"

Palmer shook his head.

"I have no idea, sir."

"That's all the questions I have right now," Jim said. "I know Deputy Malquit has already shown you the search warrant he has for the house and property. I'd like to ask permission to search your vehicle, and also to have your grandmother's car taken to the sheriff's impound so it can be processed for evidence."

"You've got it, Ranger."

"This concludes my initial questioning of Mason Palmer," Jim said, then switched off the recorder.

"Mason, come over to my truck, and I'll get the fingerprinting done," Jim said. "Do you mind if I also take a couple of photographs of you?"

"As long as they're not mug shots," Palmer answered.

"Would there be a reason for me to take those?" Jim asked.

"No." Palmer shook his head.

Jim took a set of Palmer's prints, along with a mouth swab for DNA comparison and testing, then the photos. Once that was done, he got the keys for Palmer's truck.

"Are these other keys for your house?" he asked.

"That's right, sir. Also one for this house,

although I never needed to use it. Grandma never would listen to any of us, and lock her doors. You won't need to unlock my truck, either. I never locked it here."

"That's typical of a lot of country folks," Jim said. He pointed to the tire tracks which led to Palmer's pickup.

"Those are the imprints from your tires. The only other ones here are from my truck, and the deputy's vehicle. Whoever killed your grandmother, it doesn't appear they drove up to the house. You stay where I can see you while I search your truck."

He opened to driver's door of Palmer's pickup, and proceeded to go through it. When he opened the glove compartment, a small plastic bag caught his eye. He removed it and showed it to Palmer.

"I assume you knew this was in here," he said.

"Yeah, Ranger. I wasn't tryin' to hide the stuff, because I knew you'd find it."

"You could've gotten rid of it while I was in the house."

"I thought of that, but didn't want to take the chance you or the deputy might see what I was up to. I figured better you found that weed in my truck than on me."

"It looks like less than an ounce. Was this for your own personal use?"

"Yeah, it was. You gonna bust me for possession?"

"I could, but I'm not going to, at least not this time, since you've been cooperative with the investigation, and more importantly, you just lost your grandmother. I'm just gonna get rid of this stuff, and pretend I never saw it. You'd better not get caught with any again, though."

Jim opened the bag, shook out its contents, and let the slight breeze scatter the marijuana. He crumpled the bag and placed it in one of his evidence bags, to dispose of it later.

The only other item of interest Jim found in the truck was a half empty pack of cigarettes. He shook the smokes out of the pack, checked them to make certain they hadn't been emptied of tobacco and refilled with marijuana, then gave them back to Palmer.

"Mason," he said, "I reckon there's nothing more I need from you today." He fished a business card out of his shirt pocket and handed it to him. "If you think of anything at all, or if you need me, give me a call. I've already gotten your number, so if I come up with anything else tonight, I'll contact you. If it's not too much trouble, could you meet me at the sheriff's office in San Marcos tomorrow? I'd like you to take a polygraph test, if you don't have any objections."

"What kind of a test, Ranger?"

"A polygraph. A lie detector test."

"Sure, I'd be willing to do that," Palmer answered. "What time should I be there?"

"Let's say ten o'clock. That will give me time to get most of my initial report done. I'm going to have to speak with your mother, too. Do you think she'd be able to come with you?"

"I don't see why not, unless she can't get off work."

"She'll be taking time off for bereavement, won't she?"

"Oh, yeah. I didn't even think about that," Palmer admitted. "I guess I'm still shook up. And my mom might not take any time off until we know when grandma's funeral will be. She really can't afford to."

"Don't worry about her having to take time off tomorrow, if she's worried about her job. I'll straighten that out with her supervisor if I have to."

"All right, Ranger. I appreciate that. I'll make certain she's with me tomorrow."

"Good. I'll see you then. Go home to your mom. And take care. Once again, I'm sorry for your loss."

"Thank you, sir. I'll see you in San Marcos."

Once Palmer left, Jim called for a tow truck to come remove Pamela Sue Dearing's Nissan and take it to the sheriff's impound. As soon as that was arranged, he went back inside the house, to continue combing though it for evidence.

7

The following Tuesday, Jim was in his office, poring over the evidence in the Pamela Dearing case. The autopsy had confirmed Dearing had died almost instantly, from a nine-millimeter bullet to the brain. Other than the bullet, he and Deputy Malquit had recovered little evidence from the house.

The only fingerprints they'd found belonged to either Dearing or her grandson, Mason. There was no sign at all of anything missing, not the slightest hint that anyone had even looked in a drawer or cabinet. Likewise, Dearing's car had yielded no clues. It was coated with a thick layer of dust, both inside and out, and the Nissan's motor was as dead as its late owner.

The few prints Jim had managed to obtain from the car were smudged and unreadable. Both Palmer and his mother had come in to take polygraph tests, and each had passed. Right now, Jim was completely stumped as to who had murdered the elderly woman, and why. He had just muttered in frustration and leaned back in his chair to stretch and yawn when his phone rang. He glared at it, then picked up the receiver.

"Ranger Blawcyzk."

"Jim, good morning. It's Major Voitek."

"Good mornin', Major."

"I just wanted to let you know that the report into your shooting of Dale Bohannon is finished. You've been completely exonerated, as we all expected. Lieutenant Stoker is on his way to you right now with the report, for your signature. He's also going to bring you something you *don't* want, the files from the Kendalia drug bust. That case is back in your lap now that you've been cleared. I realize the last thing you need is more added to your workload."

"Thanks, Major. That's the best news I've had since the day I signed on with the Rangers. I really appreciate your calling me, and for clearing my name. I'm grateful to get the Kendalia case back, too. I worked a long time on that one."

"I don't think there was ever any real question the shooting was justified, but I know you were worried," Voitek said. "Welcome back to full duty, Jim. Have you made any progress on the Wimberly murder case?"

"Damn little."

"Just keep plugging away, and you'll get to the bottom of it. I've got to go, Jim. I'm already late for a conference. You'll see the lieutenant in about an hour. Bye."

"Good-bye, Major, and thanks."

Jim hung up the phone, then resumed studying the autopsy report on Pamela Sue Dearing.

• • •

Jim was still digging through all the evidence in the Dearing file, looking for some little thing he might have overlooked, when Lieutenant Stoker walked in.

"Good morning, Jim," he said, as he dropped a thick file on his desk. "That's the paperwork on the Kendalia drug case. It's all yours again."

"Good morning, Lieutenant, and thanks. I'm obliged to all of you for working on it while I couldn't," Jim said.

Stoker settled into the wooden chair alongside Jim's desk. He placed a much thinner manila folder in front of him.

"Speaking of which, here's the full and final report on the shooting," he said. "You just need to read it over, note any changes or corrections, and if there aren't any sign all three copies. Once you've done that, the investigation is officially over."

"Thanks." Jim opened the file, took a swallow from a half empty bottle of Dr Pepper, and began reading. While he did, Stoker got up, poured himself a cup of coffee from the ancient coffee maker Jim kept on top of a dorm-sized refrigerator, then sat back down.

He looked around the cramped office, which was in a precinct substation of the Hays County Sheriff's Department. Besides Jim's desk and chair, plus the two chairs for visitors, it was crammed with file cabinets, stacks of file boxes containing still more paperwork, a coat and hat rack, and a small television, along with a police radio and scanner.

A bookcase held a number of books, along with even more files. Jim's desktop was crowded with his telephone, computer, printer, laptop, a cup holding pens and pencils, and even more papers. On one corner of the desk, within easy reach, were two large glass jars, one filled with cashews, the other with chocolate candy. His nameplate was on the desk, along with several pictures of Kim and Josh, Copper and Frostie, and one of his mother and father.

Also on the desk was a small pewter sculpture, *Texas Ranger Trackin'*, by Philip Kraczkowski, who was best known as the designer of the original G.I. Joe action figure. It was one of a series of that piece, which had been cast in 1972, and depicted an 1880s Ranger on horseback, following an outlaw's trail. Next to that that was a small, long-empty Grenadier porcelain liquor decanter, about the same size as the Kraczkowski piece, titled *Texas Ranger 1887*. This one was from 1978, and also depicted an 1880s Ranger on his horse.

On the wall behind Jim's desk was a large wooden replica of a Ranger badge, with Texas Ranger, Jim's name, and Company F burned into the wood. Several landscape scenes from around

Texas, along with several more Andy Thomas prints, and the official photographs of all the Rangers at their annual "In Service" meetings for the past several years, hung on the other walls.

Stoker took a swallow of his coffee, grimaced, cursed, then lunged for the sugar bowl on top of the refrigerator, as well as the quart of milk inside it. He dumped half of the sugar into his cup, and a good dollop of milk.

"Damn, Jim, you make the worst coffee I've ever tasted," he said. "It's so bitter it reminds me of my ex-wife, and so strong you should sell the stuff to the state DOT to tar roads with it. Why don't you get rid of that old coffeemaker? Hell, a new one wouldn't cost you all that much."

"Because that machine makes my coffee just the way I like it," Jim answered. "Black and strong enough to float one of Copper's horseshoes."

"Or eat out your guts before you're thirty-five," Stoker retorted. "Go back to reading the report, while I try and finish this crap."

"I could offer you a Dr Pepper instead," Jim said.

"Not a chance . . . not this early in the day," Stoker answered. "I'll risk the coffee."

Jim went back to his reading, while Stoker got up to study the Andy Thomas prints on his walls. When Stoker gave a sigh of disgust, Jim looked up from his reading.

"Something wrong, Lieutenant?"

"Yeah, but it's nothing you or I can do anything about. It's bad enough the Rangers are badly underpaid, compared to most other law enforcement agencies, but to add insult to injury most of us are stuck in small offices in county buildings, like yours here. You'd think the least the state could do would be provide us with adequate work space."

"I agree with you, but this place works just fine for me. Yeah, it's a bit cluttered, but it's close to home, and near enough to the interstate so I can get to Austin, Waco, or San Antonio real quick when I have to. It's also easy for folks to find. It suits me perfectly."

"Hell, you still deserve something better," Stoker said. "All of us Rangers do. I'll let you finish going over that report, so you can get back to your real work."

"This won't take me long," Jim answered. "As long as I'm back to full duty, that's all that matters."

He quickly skimmed through the report, then signed all three copies.

"There you are, Lieutenant. All signed."

He handed them back to Stoker, who gave one copy back to Jim, then put the others in his briefcase.

"Jim, you might not believe this, but having you cleared is as much a relief for me as it is for you . . . well, perhaps not quite as much, but you know what I'm trying to say."

"I do, and I appreciate it."

"How are you progressing with the Wimberly killing?"

"I'm not, frankly. I'm making about as much progress with it as with finding whoever's behind the drug running outfit we broke up in Kendalia, or at least put a big crimp in their operation. I've gone through the evidence with a fine-toothed comb, more'n once now. I've talked to every one of the Dearing woman's friends and relatives. Not one has any reason why someone would kill her. The slug the M.E. took out of her skull was a nine-millimeter. Hell, half of Texas carries a dang nine-millimeter pistol.

"There was no sign of forced entry into the house, no fingerprints other than the victim's, her grandson's, and her daughter's. Nothing was missing from the house. She had no bank accounts, and lived on her Social Security checks, so it's highly unlikely robbery was the motive. Since she never locked her doors, any drifter could've just walked right in. Right now, I'm not one damn minute closer to solving the case than I was when I first stepped inside that house.

"The only theory I can even come up with is someone did go into the house, intending to grab whatever valuables they could find real quick, then get out. When Dearing surprised 'em, they panicked, shot her, then took off."

"Except that doesn't explain the lack of any evidence," Stoker pointed out.

"No, it damn sure doesn't," Jim agreed. "Which is why I think that theory ain't worth the powder to blow it to Hell. Someone wanted Pamela Sue Dearing dead. The question is who, and why."

Jim stopped when his phone rang.

"Excuse me a minute, Lieutenant," he said, then picked up the receiver.

"Ranger Blawcyzk." He grabbed a pencil and scrap of paper when the person on the other end of the line started to speak.

"What was the address again? How long ago?" Jim hastily scribbled some notes as he asked a few more questions.

"Who made the discovery? Another elderly woman? Also shot in the head?"

"I'll be there in fifteen minutes."

Jim put down the phone.

"That was the Hays County Sheriff's Office," he told Stoker. "There's been another murder, up on Nutty Brown Road. It might be connected to the Wimberly killing."

"Do you mind if I ride along with you?" Stoker asked.

To those not familiar with the relative infor-mality of the Texas Rangers, compared to other law enforcement organizations, it might seem surprising that a superior officer would ask permission to accompany one of his men or women on a case. However, longtime custom and practice dictated any case belonged to the Ranger in whose territory it occurred. That Ranger would only be removed from the case at his or her request, or for justifiable cause.

"Not at all. Let's go."

Jim got up, grabbed his Stetson from its peg, and headed out the door, with Stoker right behind him. A moment later, Jim was pulling onto Jack C. Hays Trail. He took a left on Bluff Street, then pressed hard on the Tahoe's accelerator. It was eighteen miles over two lane, mostly suburban roads from his office to Nutty Brown Road. As he'd told the deputy on the other end of the line, he'd be there in fifteen minutes.

Nutty Brown Road was near the northeasterly boundary of Hays County, hard by the rapidly growing southwest area of Austin and its adjoining suburbs. With its close proximity to the capital city, this section of Hays County had also seen quite a bit of recent development, mostly upscale tract homes, but also some commercial and industrial structures. However, Nutty Brown itself was, for the most part, still relatively undeveloped. Jim fought his way through the traffic on Farm to Market Road 1826, then raced past the entrance to the Rahda Madhav Dham Hindu temple complex.

A short distance after, he slowed for the left turn onto Nutty Brown. Once he made the turn, the cookie cutter developments thinned out, the land, especially on the left side of the road, still mostly undisturbed. He drove for about a mile-and-a-half, until he spotted a Hays County sheriff's car blocking a dirt driveway on the left.

Apparently, this was a new recruit, since Jim didn't recognize her, and had to stop his car before she let him enter the driveway. He rolled down his driver's window.

"Good morning, sir. May I see some identification?" the deputy asked.

Jim tapped on the badge pinned to his shirt, then pointed to Lieutenant Stoker's.

"These should suffice. I'm Texas Ranger Jim Blawcyzk, and this is my Lieutenant, Jameson Stoker."

"Do you have any identification papers?"

"Do you?" Jim retorted, exasperated.

"Easy, Jim," Stoker cautioned. "Show her your papers."

Muttering under his breath, Jim unbuckled his seat belt so he could pull his wallet out of his hip pocket. He took out his driver's license, as well as his Ranger identification card, and handed those to the deputy. She looked them over for a few moments before handing them back to Jim.

"These seem to be in order," she said. "I'll allow you to proceed."

"Just a moment, deputy," Stoker said, before the deputy could go and lift the crime scene tape tied from her car to a post on the other side of the driveway. "Would you please give me your name?"

"Certainly. It's Melinda Daniels."

"Well, Deputy Daniels, I'm assuming you are new to the sheriff's department. Either that badge has gone to your head, or you weren't trained sufficiently about how to interact with other law enforcement personnel. I'm going to give you the benefit of the doubt, and assume it's the latter. In any event, I'm going to be in touch with your department, to make certain you are aware never to delay a fellow officer again. That's all. Now, move that tape so we can get to the scene."

The deputy flushed bright red.

"Yes, sir."

She lifted the tape, averting her gaze as Jim drove under it. He continued for several hundred yards, until he reached an older model single wide mobile home, set well back from the road, and hidden from view of passing motorists by scrub brush, cactus, and mesquites. In the carport alongside the trailer was a still shiny, older model tan Buick Regal. Another Hays County deputy had his Ford Explorer parked in front of the trailer. The SUV's engine was running, apparently so the deputy could keep cool on this blazing hot day. He shut it off and got out when Jim pulled up.

"Howdy, Jim," he said, as soon as Jim got out of his truck.

"Howdy, Tom," Jim answered. "This here's Lieutenant Jameson Stoker I've got ridin' with me. Lieutenant, Deputy Tom Warner."

Warner nodded to Jameson.

"Lieutenant."

"Deputy," Jameson replied.

"What've we got here, Tom?" Jim asked.

"From the quick look around I took, it seems to be the work of whoever killed the old woman over in Wimberly," Warner answered. "One shot to the forehead, elderly woman living alone in the country. The victim in this case is Susan Hollister, a sixty-nine-year-old white female. Divorced for at least thirty years, no children. The mail carrier got worried when she noticed Ms. Hollister hadn't picked up her mail for over a week, so she called in a welfare check. I got the call.

"When I arrived here and no one answered the door, I forced my way in and found the body. It's pretty badly decomposed, so things are really nasty inside. You both will probably want to put on masks before you go in there. The M.E.'s on his way."

"I'll get them," Jim said. He went to the back

of his truck, opened it, and took out his evidence collecting kit, gloves and booties, plus along with those, two surgical masks. He and Stoker donned those at the front of the trailer. Hardy pulled the mask hanging around his neck back over his mouth and nose.

Tom Warner was an experienced deputy, who knew to close the door once he had exited the trailer, so no chance gust of wind might disturb any potential piece of evidence, no matter how small. When he opened the door, the powerful stench from inside was still detectable, but the masks made it at least bearable. He led the Rangers through the cluttered home, to the bedroom.

Susan Hollister was lying on her back at the foot of her bed, her body already in an advanced state of decomposition. Jim took out his camera and recorder to start taking pictures and dictate his findings.

"Texas Ranger James Blawcyzk of Company F, assisted by Hays County Deputy Sheriff Thomas Warner, also Texas Ranger Lieutenant Jameson Stoker of Company F, investigating the apparent homicide of Susan Hollister, a sixty-nine-year-old female, in her residence at 1010 Nutty Brown Road in Hays County. Deputy Warner states his preliminary findings indicate this apparent homicide may be connected to the homicide of Pamela Sue Dearing."

He turned off the recorder while he took his pictures, then switched it back on as he proceeded to examine the corpse.

"The body is in an advanced state of decomposition," he said, "putrefaction has already set in. The flesh is mottled black and green, and body is bloated. The victim was apparently fully dressed at the time of her death; however, the swelling of her body has split open her blouse. There is a bullet hole in the victim's forehead, just over her left eyebrow. Due to the state of decay, it is impossible to make an estimate of the range at which the bullet was fired, nor its angle. However, dried blood spatters around the victim appear to indicate no exit wound."

Jim covered the recorder's microphone while he told Stoker and Warner, "I'm gonna roll this corpse over. It's awfully bloated. Here's hoping it ain't quite ready to bust open and send fluids spewin' out of its nose and mouth. I'm not in the mood to get sprayed with that crap today."

Carefully, saying a silent prayer under his breath that the corpse wouldn't release pent up fluids and spray them over his face and clothes, Jim rolled Hollister onto her stomach.

"There is no exit wound in the back of the skull, indicating the bullet is still in the victim's brain. Due to the poor condition of the body, it is not possible to perform even a perfunctory forensic examination *in situ*. Removal of the bullet and a complete examination and forensic report will have to be prepared after the county medical examiner performs an autopsy. However, the size and location of the entry wound is consistent with the fatal wound to Pamela Sue Dearing.

"Ballistics examination of the bullet, once recovered, will determine if in fact the same weapon was used to kill both women. Also, due to the advanced decomposition, the time of death can only be widely approximated. I would set that within a period of the past seven to ten days, possibly a bit longer. That time frame will also be narrowed down when the autopsy is completed. For now, evidence will be gathered from the victim's residence, automobile, and land."

He turned off the recorder, then opened his evidence collection kit.

"Tom, do you mind helpin' me go through the rest of the house?" he asked.

"Of course not."

"How about me?" Stoker asked. "Do you want me to lend a hand? There's no point in me just standing around and watching you fellas work."

"I'd surely appreciate that, Lieutenant," Jim answered. "Would you mind searching the car?"

"Not at all," Stoker answered.

"I'm obliged," Jim said. "Take what supplies

you need from my kit. I'm gonna concentrate on this room right here."

The three lawmen assembled the materials they would need for gathering evidence, and set to work. Jim began by taking a pair of tweezers and a baggie, to remove a cigarette butt from the ashtray on the nightstand for processing. Each had the same thought on his mind: *Was a serial killer stalking elderly women in the rural sections of Hays County?*

Logan Daniels settled down on his living room couch with a bottle of beer, flicked his lighter to light up a cigarette, then picked up the remote, turned on the television, and tuned to the KXAN ten o'clock newscast. He took a swallow of his beer, then nearly choked when he saw Jim's official Texas Ranger portrait appear on the monitor behind the two anchor persons. He reflexively spit out the beer, which dripped down his chin, splattered down his shirtfront, and sprayed over the glass and chrome coffee table. His discomfiture only grew worse as he listened to the report.

"Good Evening. I'm Beth Jennings."

"And I'm Jason Cardwell. We are following two developing stories tonight, two stories which are interconnected. First, Texas Ranger James C. Blawcyzk, who has been on paid administrative leave while his role in the fatal shooting of an alleged drug courier was being investigated by Texas DPS Internal Affairs, has been completely cleared of all wrongdoing, and has returned to duty.

"Secondly, there has been yet another murder of an elderly woman in a rural area of Hays County, which Ranger Blawcyzk is now investigating. Our Heather Ramirez has more details on both stories. Heather . . ."

Jim's portrait faded, and the reporter appeared on the screen, standing at the still taped off entrance to Susan Hollister's driveway.

"Good evening, Beth and Jason. I'll start with the news about Ranger James Blawcyzk. Here is a clip of Lieutenant Jameson Stoker of Company F, reading a brief statement earlier today, concerning the results of the investigation into the fatal shooting of Dale Bohannon, an alleged drug courier, during a raid at the Thunder Ridge Nursery outside of Kendalia."

Lieutenant Stoker's image appeared on the screen.

"Good morning. I am going to read a brief statement, concerning the fatal shooting of Dale Robert Bohannon by Ranger James C. Blawcyzk, during the culmination of an extensive investigation into the alleged manufacturing and transport of illegal drugs throughout south central Texas and beyond. I will not be taking any questions. I do have copies of the complete report and findings of the DPS Internal Affairs investigating panel, which I will distribute at the conclusion of my statement."

Stoker paused, adjusted his reading glasses, then continued.

"Texas Ranger James C. Blawcyzk has been completely exonerated in the fatal shooting of Dale Robert Bohannon. The facts show that Mr. Bohannon opened fire on Ranger Blawcyzk and his fellow Rangers, seriously wounding Ranger Rudy Garcia. Correctly perceiving himself and his fellow Rangers to be in danger of losing their lives, Ranger Blawcyzk returned Mr. Bohannon's fire. The charge from his shotgun struck Mr. Bohannon in the chest and upper abdomen, killing him instantly, or nearly so.

"Ranger Blawcyzk followed proper police procedures at all times. I wish to emphasize again, *Ranger Blawcyzk followed proper police procedures at all times.* His decisive action, made in a split second, and under extreme duress, most probably saved the life of Ranger Garcia, and possibly also the lives of Ranger Blawcyzk himself, and the other men who participated in the operation.

"In conjunction with the findings, Ranger Blawcyzk, who had already been returned to conditional active duty, was again placed on full duty status, effective this morning. He has already begun investigating a second apparent homicide of an elderly woman in Hays County. I do not have any further information on that at this time. This concludes my statement. Thank you, and I have copies of the report for those who wish."

Stoker's image faded, to be replaced by the reporter's. She held a copy of the Internal Affairs report in her hand.

"I've had a chance to skim through this report, and from what I have seen, this was a thorough, impartial investigation, with a correct outcome. Now, to the second story. The body of sixty-nine-year-old Susan Hollister, whose identity was released only a short time ago, of 1010 Nutty Brown Road in Hays County, which I am standing in front of right now, was discovered earlier today, the apparent victim of a homicide. Ranger Blawcyzk is investigating her death, as well as the apparent homicide of another elderly Hays County resident, Pamela Sue Dearing, earlier this month. While few details have been released on either apparent homicide, Ranger Blawcyzk did issue the following statement earlier today."

Again, the image on the screen changed, this time from the reporter to Jim, who was standing at the entrance to Hollister's driveway. Microphones from all the Austin media were held to his face.

"Good afternoon. I am Texas Ranger James

Blawcyzk of Company F, stationed in Buda. Earlier today, the Texas Rangers received a report of a possible homicide at this address, from the Hays County Sheriff's Office, and requesting our assistance. Myself and Lieutenant Jameson Stoker responded. Upon arrival, we discovered the body of an elderly female.

"Preliminary findings indicate the death is in fact most likely a homicide. The victim, whom I cannot identify until family has been notified, had been dead for quite some time. Due to the advanced decomposition of the body, an approximate time and cause of death will need to be determined by the medical examiner's autopsy, and the DPS forensic laboratory.

"I do need to resume searching the victim's residence for evidence; however, I will take a few brief questions. Yes, Ms. Ramirez?"

"Ranger Blawcyzk, do you have any idea of the cause of death?"

"I do, but I don't wish to reveal that until the medical examiner can confirm my findings. Mr. Meyer?"

"Do you have any idea as to a motive?"

"At this time, no. Any speculation as to why the victim was killed, if this is indeed a homicide, would be just that . . . speculation."

"Do you think it's possible she was killed because someone wanted her land to develop, and she refused to sell?" Meyer continued. "As we all know, developers are eager to purchase large tracts of land in this part of Hays County, and the adjoining Austin suburbs. It would not be far-fetched that an unscrupulous speculator might resort to murder to get his or her hands on a desirable piece of property."

"The answer to that question will have to wait until we are further into the investigation," Jim answered. "Next question. Mr. Randall."

"Is this apparent homicide related to the homicide of Pamela Sue Dearing, Ranger Blawcyzk?"

"There are some similarities," Jim answered. "However, stating that the two cases are connected at this time would be pure conjecture. We will know more once we have finished processing the scene here, and the autopsy, ballistic tests, and forensic reports are completed. We will be happy to provide you as much information as we can once we ourselves have it, with the caveat that of course no findings which might compromise our investigation will be released. Final question. Mr. Thomas."

"Ranger Blawcyzk, do you believe there could be a serial killer on the prowl, one who is seeking out elderly women for his victims?"

"It is too soon to make any kind of consideration for that possibility. The perpetrator, assuming both cases are indeed homicides, could be male, female, or more than one person. We are still working to develop a profile. While, so far, we have no reason to believe the general public is in danger, it would be wise for everyone to take the usual precautions that should be taken every day: keep your doors and windows locked, don't answer your door to any strangers, and report any suspicious activities or persons to your local or county law enforcement agency immediately. Keep your outside lights on at night. Thank you."

Jim's image faded, to be replaced once again by the reporter's.

"We have had no further statements or information since then," Ramirez said. "Several law enforcement personnel from the Rangers and Hays County Sheriff's Office are still on scene. We will remain here to report any updated information once it is released. Beth, Jason, back to you."

"Thank you, Heather," Jennings said. "In other news . . ."

Daniels cursed, then threw the remote across the room. It hit the opposite wall and shattered. His hopes that damn Ranger might be fired, and arrested for homicide or manslaughter, had been dashed. He had to get rid of Blawcyzk before Prescott and Kenney got rid of him. He grabbed his cell phone from the coffee table and hit the number for one of his contacts.

"Tarquin, it's Logan," he said, as soon as the other party answered. "I've got a job for you."

"What've you got?" Tarquin Sarkanian asked.

"My employer wants a problem eliminated."

"You know that's my specialty, taking care of problems for my clients, and their clients," Sarkanian said. "Hold on just a minute."

Daniels could hear Sarkanian speaking to a woman in the background.

"Honey, go take a walk or something. This call's going to take a while." When she objected, Sarkanian said, "Go buy yourself something pretty, or have a late dinner or something," he said. "Just don't come back for at least an hour."

Daniels heard the woman tell Sarkanian what to do with himself and exactly how to do it, then the door slammed, and Sarkanian was back on the phone.

"Okay, it's clear to talk now," he said. "What specific problem do you need solved?"

"Did you happen to see the news today?"

"I did."

"Then you saw the problem. Ranger James Blawcyzk. He's been interfering with my employer's business ventures. He needs to be removed. If you can find and eliminate his source of information, that would also be included."

"I'm not certain," Sarkanian said. "Taking out a Texas Ranger is just asking for trouble. I can do it, but it'll cost you."

"Getting rid of Blawcyzk is your problem.

Money isn't," Daniels said. "You know I always pay well."

"All right. It'll cost you exactly one hundred thousand dollars, half up front, the rest when the job is completed. Plus expenses. That would include some associates I may need to hire. And another fifty thousand for his contact."

"Are you insane?"

"Take it or leave it, Logan. I'm certain you could find someone to do it for less. However, you've always been satisfied with my services in the past. You know I'm reliable, will do the job properly, with no loose ends, and on the off chance that something does go wrong, I'll keep my mouth shut. Do you want to take a chance with some neophyte?"

"I guess you're not leaving me any choice, you money-grubbin' bastard," Daniels said. "All right, you've got a deal. But Blawcyzk's death has to look like an accident. Even better, if you can make him just disappear, my employer would be most grateful. And this has to be done within a week."

"Listen to me carefully, Logan. I can do the job fast, or I can do it right. Or I can not do it at all. Which do you want? If your employer insists on it being done in a week, I'll do it, but that doesn't give me enough time to make certain the Rangers won't figure out one of their own has been taken out. I need to follow Blawcyzk's movements, ascertain his patterns and his daily routine before I can make a move. If you give me a month, then I'll guarantee no one will ever suspect the sudden, tragic, and unfortunate demise of a brave Texas Ranger in the line of duty was in fact an execution. Take it or leave it."

"I'll take it, but if Blawcyzk isn't dead within the month, you will be, Tarquin."

"Don't threaten me, Logan, you son of a bitch. Unless you want to die along with Blawcyzk. In fact, that might be a nice touch, Blawcyzk dying in the attempt to arrest a drug kingpin, whom he shot dead when said drug kingpin resisted arrest, and put a couple of fatal bullets into the Ranger first. Then the heroic, dying Ranger guns down the drug kingpin before they both go to Hell. Very poetic, don't you think? Just imagine the drama, the humanity. Blawcyzk will die a hero, and you'll be vilified for the lowlife scum that you are. I can even see the headlines now. You'll make all the newspapers and television stations. The story would probably even go nationwide. Perhaps even the tabloids would splash it all over their covers. You'd be as famous as Charles Manson."

"All right, Tarquin, enough. You've made your point. We have a deal. Just get the job done."

"Of course, Logan. Only one more thing."

"What's that?"

"The conditions you put on this job. The price

just doubled. Two hundred thousand dollars or forget it. You can deliver the first hundred-and-twenty-five thousand in the usual manner."

"That's impossible," Daniels answered.

"What you're asking me to *do* is impossible," Sarkanian said. "Do I have to remind you I'm probably the only person who *can* pull this off, and do the job right? Do you want to use my services, or not?"

"All right. But if you weren't so damn good at what you do, Tarquin, I'd tell you to go—"

"It's been a pleasure talking with you too, as always, Logan. *Hasta la vista.*"

8

Unless he was called out on a case, Jim had a weekend routine with his family. His mother would go to the 5:00 P.M. Saturday Vigil Mass at their family parish, St. Paul's Roman Catholic Church in Austin, then usually go out for dinner with a few of her friends. The next morning, she would take care of Josh, while Jim and Kim went to the 8:30 Mass at St. Paul's, the first Sunday Mass of the day.

After Mass, they would stop somewhere for a leisurely breakfast, enjoying that as one of the rare moments they had for just the two of them. After breakfast, they would return home. Jim would take Copper and go for a ride, then come back to the house and prepare Sunday dinner, usually barbequing steaks, burgers, or chicken on the grill, while Kim and Betty took their own horses out for a short ride.

Occasionally, Kim would accompany Jim when he rode, but she'd long since accepted the fact that he preferred riding by himself, unwinding from the stress of job and family.

"It's your turn to pick the breakfast place this week," Kim said, as she pulled her cobalt blue Chevy Equinox out of the church parking lot. "Where shall we go?"

"MacPherson's," Jim said, without hesitation. "We haven't been there in months."

"All right, MacPherson's it is," Kim agreed. She turned right onto David Moore Drive, then left onto West Slaughter. After a few blocks, she turned right, into the lot for Jock MacPherson's Scottish Lion Bakery and Gifts. She chose one of the two empty spaces in front of the building and parked. Kim shook her head as she read the slogan written in gold leaf across the window.

" 'Well, I would not feel so all alone, everybody must get sconed.'

"Jim, sometimes I swear you come here just because Jock has the same weird sense of humor as you. He's lucky Bob Dylan never sued him. I mean, really. Using *Rainy Day Women Number 12 and 35* to sell scones?"

"I doubt Dylan's ever heard of this place, and probably never will," Jim said. "Besides, he'd probably appreciate it. Don't forget, Jock was losing money until he put that up there. Now, he has customers standing in line for an hour on busy mornings. If we'd gotten here half-an-hour later, we'd never get a seat. Uh-oh. Is that a crack in the window?"

"Where?" Kim asked.

"Never mind. I can see Jock's patched it for now, with Scotch tape."

"Jim!" Kim slapped him on the arm. "Let's

177

go in, before I stone you myself. And I do mean *stone,* not *scone.*"

"All right."

They got out of the car, locked it, and went inside the shop. Jock MacPherson, the owner, greeted them in a booming voice. He had a thick Scottish burr, which contrasted greatly with the soft drawl of most native Texans.

"Jim and Kimberly Blawcyzk," he shouted. "Aye, and I thought I'd never be seein' you two again. I truly believed you'd forgotten about old Jock. Take the empty table in the window."

"Sorry, Jock, we've both been real busy," Jim said, shaking his head. "As far as the table, we'll take the one in the back corner, if it's all the same to you."

Jim's caution was an inherent part of his lawman's nature. Whenever possible in public places, he always chose a spot where he could see everyone who came in or out, and where no one could come up behind him unseen.

"Of course, lad," MacPherson said. "I've been following your travails in the newspaper. I'm very pleased things worked out. Coffee for the two of you?"

"Coffee for Jim, but tea for me," Kim answered, as she took a seat. Jim also sat down, and placed his Stetson on one of the two empty chairs.

"Aye, lass, so long as you don't add milk to a fine cup of tea, like so many of you ignorant

Colonials do," MacPherson said, laughing. "That's a sin."

"No milk, just the tea," Kim said.

"I'll have Lola bring that right over," MacPherson said. "I've just taken a fresh batch of cinnamon scones from the oven, so they're still piping hot. How do those sound to you?"

"Four of 'em sound just about right, Jock," Jim said. "As long as they don't have any raisins in them."

"They don't," Jock assured him.

"I'll have just one," Kim said. "Blueberry."

"Make certain mine are slathered with plenty of butter, please, Jock," Jim said. "In fact, why don't you cover yourself in butter, too?"

"And just why would I be wantin' to do such a silly thing?" MacPherson demanded to know.

"Because then you'd be a butter Scotch," Jim answered, laughing madly at his own bad joke.

"Jock, if you'd get me one of those Highland mufflers you sell in the gift shop, I'll suffocate him for you," Kim said. "No jury would ever convict me."

"I'd love to let you do just that, but the news of a murder at my shop would probably scare most of my customers away, although not as fast as your husband's so-called jokes," MacPherson answered. "I'll put your order in, before he comes up with another. Lola will be right over with your beverages."

179

• • •

After their breakfast, Jim and Kimberly headed straight home. Jim, of course, had purchased a dozen scones to take with them. After they got back, Jim played with Josh until it was time for Kim to put him down for his nap, then changed from his Sunday shirt, good pair of jeans, and shiny dress boots into a faded red shirt, well-worn jeans, and scuffed boots. He exchanged his good Stetson for a battered and stained older one, and tied a stars and stripes patterned bandanna around his neck.

Lastly, since Rangers always went armed, but because he wasn't on duty, he was able to carry any weapon he chose. He buckled the gunbelt and holster holding the first Jim Blawcyzk's now-antique but still working single action Colt Peacemaker, which had served five generations of Blawcyzks and the Texas Rangers before him, around his waist. Kim stopped him on his way out the back door.

"Where are you planning on riding, Jim?" she asked him, "And how long will you be gone?"

"Just a couple of hours," Jim answered. "I'm gonna head up to Searight Park, since that's got the best trails left around here, nowadays."

"You're not planning on going the back way behind Thoroughbred Drive again, are you? You know how those people in that subdivision always complain whenever you take your horse on their roads."

"Hey, I didn't force them to move there," Jim answered. "If they don't want to see horses, why do they live on streets named Thoroughbred Drive and Pedigree Way? Not to mention Mint Julep. And where there's a park with horse trails right next to 'em?"

"Can't you just go in the park's main entrance?"

"That's a longer way on the road. Copper can handle just about anything that's thrown at him, but you never know when some driver who's not paying attention might run into us. And the motor vehicle regulations are on my side. There were horse trails here long before those houses were built. This *is* Texas, after all. Horses are part of our heritage. Those people'll just have to deal with it."

"Why don't you trailer him over?"

"It's too much trouble to hitch up the trailer, load and unload Copper, then when we got home unhitch the trailer and clean it out for such a short distance," Jim said. "If I was gonna trailer him, I'd make a day of it, and go where there's more riding trails."

"I wish I could change your mind," Kim said. "But since you're so stubborn about where you ride Copper around here, please, just be careful."

"I always am, you know that," Jim said. He

181

gave Kim a quick kiss. "See you in a couple of hours."

Copper trotted up to the corral fence when he saw Jim coming, hung his head over it, and nickered. Jim rubbed his velvety muzzle and gave him a peppermint. The big paint lipped at his shirt pocket, looking for more.

"Oh, no, you don't," Jim said, laughing. "You'll get your cookie once we're in the barn." He opened the corral gate, let his horse out, then shut it. Copper followed him into the barn, and stood patiently while Jim slipped on his halter and fastened him to the cross ties. He gave him his favorite treat, an oatmeal crème pie, then brushed Copper thoroughly, cleaned out his hooves, and saddled and bridled him.

"Let's get goin', boy," he said, as he swung into the saddle. "It's been too long for both of us since we've had a good ride." He put Copper into a slow walk.

Mary Moore Searight Metropolitan Park was just over the city line, in Austin. It had a variety of facilities, from playgrounds and sports fields to picnic pavilions to a radio-controlled model airplane runway, and even a disc golf course. Some of the several miles of trails that wound throughout the park were fairly popular with hikers and bicyclists, others, in the more remote reaches, were used mostly by horseback riders.

Jim cut between two subdivisions and crossed the creek which marked the south boundary of the park to reach the trails. He followed his usual route, first heading for the main parking lot to stop at the ice cream truck to buy two vanilla cones, one for himself and the other for Copper, then looped around the disc golf field and back to the trail system.

He was nearing the edge of the woods at the back of the disc field when he heard someone yell "Heads up!" He turned just in time to see an errantly thrown disc sailing straight for him. He reacted instantly, grabbed the disc, and tossed it back to its owner.

"Thanks, cowboy!" the young man yelled.

"Not a problem," Jim answered. He nodded and continued on his way. He rode for about another hour-and-a-half, allowing Copper to mainly set his own pace, occasionally putting him into a lope, allowing him to splash with his front hooves or dip his muzzle in the water to blow bubbles when they crossed the stream which ran through the park. They'd been out for nearly two hours, and were in the relatively isolated northeast section of the park, when Jim realized it was time to start back.

"C'mon, Copper," he said to the horse. "Time to go home. I'll give you a nice hosin' down and Vetrolin bath to cool you off once we get there."

He turned Copper around and put him into a

trot. They had only gone about a quarter-mile when the distinctive buzzing of a pack of dirt bikes' engines came to Jim's ears. The sound grew louder as the bikes drew nearer. Copper stopped and snorted.

"What the hell are those idiots doing out here?" Jim muttered. "They've gotta know there's no motorized vehicles allowed on the trails in this park. With any luck, one of the park police officers will take care of the problem. Let's keep goin', boy."

He heeled his horse into a slow lope. The bikes kept getting louder, apparently more than one group, coming from different directions. When Jim rounded a bend, four bikers came into view, riding at high speed, their machines' tires spewing up dust and dirt as they dug ruts deep into the trail. Jim reined Copper to a halt when the bikers came straight at them. Behind them, two more bikers roared into view. Jim pulled his Colt out of its holster. He patted Copper's shoulder.

"Steady, pard," he told the horse. He pointed the gun in the air and fired a warning shot. The bikers kept coming. Jim held Copper steady as a rock, then leveled his gun and fired another warning shot, just above the heads of the oncoming bikers. Both groups were on top of him now. Copper tossed his head, snorted, and shifted his feet, but stood in place as the bikers split at the last possible second, swerving to sweep around both sides of Jim and his horse. They spun, regrouped, and came at them again.

This time, Jim aimed lower, not for the closest man, but his machine. His bullet shattered the lead biker's headlight. The rider lost control for a moment, nearly going down, then managed to regain his balance. He signaled to the others, and they scattered in different directions, disappearing into the trees and brush.

Jim thought about following, but decided against it. If he left the trail and cut through the brush, Copper could ride down at least one of the outlaw bikers, but the chances of him being injured during the chase were too great. Sometimes, even a Ranger had to realize when the odds against him were too high.

Instead, Jim pulled out his cell phone and hit speed dial for the Austin Police Department. He pushed zero to skip past the automated voice menu.

"Austin Police," the operator answered. Jim recognized her voice. "How may I direct your call?"

"Ebony, it's Ranger Jim Blawcyzk. I just had a run-in with a bunch of dirt bikers in Searight Park. Can you have a Park Police officer meet me? Also have a couple of city units dispatched to South 1st Street, near the park. to see if they can spot 'em? I believe they left Searight and got on South 1st, headed toward downtown. They'll be looking for six bikes, one of which is a yellow Suzuki with a busted headlight. There's another Suzuki, orange, a green Kawasaki, a black Honda, and two more black bikes, makes unknown. I couldn't get any plates."

"Right away, Ranger. Where should I have the park unit meet you?"

"At the parking lot for the off-leash dog trail. I'll be on my horse."

"I'll have a unit sent right over."

"Thanks, Ebony." Jim hung up the phone and patted Copper's shoulder.

"You did good, pal. Let's go," he said. "With any luck, one of those sons of bitches fell off his bike, or maybe the whole outfit was stupid enough to stop someplace close by."

By the time Jim reached the dog trail parking lot, two members of the Austin Police Department's Park Patrol Unit were waiting for him. Linda Tracy was standing alongside her mountain bike, and Ted Delancey got out of his Ford Explorer when he spotted Jim riding up.

"Hey, Jim," Tracy called out. "I hear you just tangled with the outlaw bikers who've been terrorizing folks in the parks."

"Howdy, Linda, Ted," Jim answered. "Are you tellin' me today isn't the first time this outfit has stirred up trouble?"

186

"Howdy, Jim. It sure isn't," Delancey said. "We've been trying to round up these bikers for close to a month now. They've been harassing walkers, hikers, and bicyclists in parks all over Austin for about a month now. I have to admit, this is the first time I've heard of 'em bothering a horseback rider."

"It's damn lucky they decided to pick on me, rather'n someone else," Jim said. "They came close to runnin' right into Copper. Almost any other horse would have spooked, dumped his rider, and taken off. Someone would have been hurt bad, possibly even killed, in that case. Their horse, too."

"I'm surprised you haven't heard about them before," Tracy said. "We have come close to getting some of them a time or two, but on those dirt bikes they can outrun most of our vehicles, or squeeze between cars and alleys where our squad cars can't, and disappear."

"I might've heard a mention of 'em on the news, but I've had so much on my plate lately I didn't pay all that much attention," Jim admitted.

"Well, they've been raisin' hell for too long already. Let's get all your information. Maybe that will finally help us identify at least a couple of them." Delancey suggested. "Where exactly did this encounter take place?"

"About a half-mile back into the park," Jim answered. "I'd just turned Copper around to start for home when they came after us, four from in front, two from behind."

"Six?" Tracy said. "The most we've heard until today is four. Of course, with the victims scared out of their wits with those bikers chasing them, the numbers could be wrong. You're certain it was six?"

"As certain as I'm standing here. Just as I'm certain they weren't just trying to scare me. They were trying their damnedest to kill me."

"Hold that thought for just a minute," Delancey advised him. "You say there were six bikers. Can you describe any of them?"

"Not very well," Jim admitted. "The riders, not at all. They were all in black jumpsuits, wearin' black helmets with dark facepieces. I'd never be able to identify any of 'em, that's for certain."

"That's been our problem," Delancey said. "How about the machines?"

"I can do a bit better with those," Jim answered. "Three of 'em were black, one of those was a Honda. One was a puke green Kawasaki, another a bright orange Suzuki. The last one was a banana yellow Suzuki. That's the one with the busted headlight."

"I know the bikes' descriptions have already been broadcast," Delancey said, "but I doubt that will do much good. The few times we've had this problem, when a unit has even seen bikes that match the descriptions, they're out of sight before we can manage to get close. And there's thousands of bikes like those in the metro area. We're looking for needles in a haystack."

"Don't mention hay," Jim said. "It's past Copper's lunchtime, and he's hungry."

Delancey glared at Jim, then shook his head in disgust.

"What about the one with the broken head-light?" Tracy asked. "If we can find just that one, it might lead us to the rest."

"Odds are the rider will have his bike repaired before we can find him," Delancey said.

"Am I right, Jim? If we do find that bike, would you be able to identify it as the same one in the group that came after you?"

"I sure would, Linda. Real easily."

"I don't suppose you'd like to tell us exactly *how* that headlight got busted, would you, Jim?" Delancey asked.

"We can let that go for now, Ted," Jim answered. "Let's just say if we do find that bike before it's repaired, there will be no problem proving it's the one we're looking for."

"Uh-huh." Delancey nodded his head, while Tracy said nothing, and just looked down at her handlebars.

"Is there anythin' else you can tell us? Anything at all?" Delancey asked.

"No. I wish I could, but no."

"Then all we can do for now is write up

an incident report, and add it to the others," Delancey said. He shrugged his shoulders and sighed.

"Here comes one of our units," Tracy said. "Maybe we got lucky, and some of those bikers have been found."

Another Austin Police Ford Explorer pulled into the lot. The man in the passenger's seat, Mustafa Hassan, opened his window. His family had fled Iraq several years previously, and settled in Texas. With his military and police background from his home country, Mustafa had easily passed the Austin Police Department's qualification tests. He'd been with them for almost three years now.

"Howdy, Jim," he said, in his heavy Middle Eastern accent. "It's been a few months."

"It has," Jim said, laughing. "Sorry, Mustafa. I still can't get used to hearin' 'howdy' said with your accent. I can't help laughin' when I hear it."

"You think it's tough for you?" Sandra Petrie said, from the driver's seat. "I have to listen to it over and over, every day."

"Any luck finding those bastards on their damn crotch rockets?" Delancey asked.

"None at all," Hassan answered. "We've had all the units in the area looking for them, but they've disappeared, like always. One of our bicycle officers thinks he spotted them, but they were off in the distance, so he couldn't be certain it was the same group. By the time a car arrived, they were too late to try and locate 'em."

"Jim, I'm sorry, but all we can do is file a report, and maybe we'll get lucky," Delancey said. "We don't have a lot to go on."

"Perhaps the one who's got the broken headlight will be stupid enough to try and have it fixed right away," Tracy said.

"Oh, if only he would be that dumb," Jim answered.

"We'll put the word out to all the motorcycle shops in the area to let us know if a yellow Suzuki comes in to have a broken headlight repaired, or if someone comes in for the parts to replace one," Hassan added. "Sooner or later, they've got to make a mistake."

"Just remember, they're wanted for attempted murder," Jim said. "Cruelty to animals, too."

"Jim, you have no way to prove that," Petrie said.

"Sandy's right, Jim," Delancey agreed. "All the previous complaints stated the bikers were only tryin' to scare their victims."

"Maybe before, but not this time," Jim answered. "They just about ran me'n Copper down. When we didn't move, they swerved around us at the last possible second, then turned around and came at us again. Even my first two warning shots didn't stop 'em. The third one finally scared 'em off."

"Should we know where you put that third one, although I think I already have the answer," Hassan said.

"If we come up with that yellow bike, you'll have your answer," Jim said. "I guess there's nothing more we can do. I'd better start back home. Kim will be worried if I'm too late."

"All right, Jim. I'll look around the park, to see if perhaps that pack of renegades might have dropped something that will help us find them," Tracy said.

"And we'll keep looking for 'em," Delancey said.

"I appreciate that. See y'all later."

Jim turned Copper and headed back into the park. Tracy got back on her bike and took another trail, while Delancey started his car and drove slowly along the dog trail. Petrie pulled out of the lot, turned right on South 1st Street, then made a U-turn over the median divider to head back toward downtown Austin. She and Hassan resumed their patrol.

"I don't care what happened before, or whether or not I can prove what those bikers were up to, Copper," Jim told his horse, as he reined the paint off the trail to cut through the woods and shortcut his way home. "Those sons of bitches were bound and determined to kill us both, probably by spookin' you, so it would look like an accident. We're gonna have to be even more

192

careful than usual from here on out, pal, until I can figure out who's after my hide."

Kim, Josh, and Betty were on the back deck when Jim rode into the yard.

"Jim, you're late," Kim said. "We were starting to worry. How was your ride?"

"It was fantastic," Jim answered. There were some things better left unsaid, and the encounter with the rogue bikers was one of them. There was little to be accomplished by telling Kim what had happened, except causing her needless worry. "The park was really busy, though. Lots and lots of people. That's why I'm late, a lot of kids wanted to pet Copper. Give me a few minutes to unsaddle, and give Copper a quick bath, then you and Ma can go for your ride."

"All right. Josh is sleeping, so you'll need to feed and change him when he wakes up. I expressed some milk, and it's in the refrigerator."

"I might just take a nap too, until he does wake up," Jim answered. "I could certainly use one."

When Kim and Betty returned from their ride, Jim and Josh were nowhere in sight. Neither was Frostie. Copper also was missing from his corral.

"He couldn't have," Kim exclaimed. "He wouldn't have dared!"

"You mean taking Josh for a ride?" Betty said. "I shouldn't have to tell you he did just that. He's been waiting for the day when he could get him on his horse. I can tell you where he went, too. It's a hot, muggy afternoon. That means Jim's out at the pond."

"I'll kill him. I swear I'll kill him," Kim exclaimed. She dug her heels into Freedom's side, putting the gelding into a gallop. Betty also put her quarter horse, Slacker, into the same gait, matching Kim's Morgan stride for stride.

"Kim," Betty said, "Why don't you take my advice? Jim will never change, but perhaps what I told you will get him to listen."

"If he's still got his hearing after I'm through blistering his ears," Kim answered.

It only took them a few minutes to reach the pond. Jim had shed his shirt, boots, socks, and hat, which were lying on the grass where he had tossed them, along with the big for his age Josh's nine-month sized T-shirt, shorts, sneakers, socks, and diaper. Jim was standing in water almost halfway deep up his belly, holding Josh in his extended arms, alternately dipping his son into the water, then lifting him high over his head. Josh was squealing with delight. Copper was lying in the shallows at the pond's bank, keeping cool while he nibbled at the lush grass growing along the water's edge. Frostie was bouncing in and out of the water, barking excitedly.

"Jim! What in the world are you doing?" Kim shouted.

"Cooling myself and Josh off," Jim answered. "It was hot, and he was cranky, so I brought him out here to the pond. He loves the water. He'll be swimmin' before you know it."

"Jim, if you don't get him out of the water right now, you'll be swimming . . . with the fishes. *Permanently*. And please don't tell me you rode him with you on your horse."

"All right, I didn't ride him on Copper," Jim answered, giving her a sheepish grin. "He rode Copper all by himself. Not only will he be swimmin' soon, he's already ridin'."

When he emerged from the water, Kim grabbed the soggy bandanna hanging limply around his neck.

"Jim, if I ever catch you putting our son on that horse again, or taking him in the pond, I'll do this to you."

"Do what?" Jim asked.

"This." Kim yanked him against her and kissed him full on the lips.

"That?" Jim said, looking at her in surprise. "That's an awful funny way to show you're mad at me. Aren't you?"

"I certainly am," Kim answered. "But I realized that, no matter what I said, you were going to do exactly what you did, sooner or later. You can't help yourself. It's in your DNA. So, I thought perhaps I'd try this instead."

She whispered something into Jim's left ear,

something that made him blush bright red.

"I thought perhaps doing that regularly will make you think twice about putting Josh on your horse until he's a few years older."

"Kim. My mother's here! You can't say things like that in front of her!"

"Who do you think gave me the idea?" Kim answered. Betty laughed. Jim flushed even redder.

"Ma!"

"How do you think *you* got here?" Betty said. "Do you think a stork brought you? Or you just happened along out of nowhere?"

"See, Jim," Kim said, now also laughing. For a veteran Texas Ranger, sometimes Jim could be easily flustered by the simplest things. He continued to protest.

"The horses will hear. So will Frostie."

"We'll put the horses in the barn, and lock the dog in the house. And before you say Josh might wake up, your mother has already said she'd watch him tonight. We've left you no excuse. So give me Josh, get your clothes back on, get yourself back to the house, and get that grill smokin', cowboy. I'm starved, and we have a date tonight."

Just around ten o'clock that night, Jim was sitting on the patio, watching a nearly-full moon rise, and listening to a light northerly breeze rustling the leaves on the cottonwoods, sycamores, and live oaks. He had just finished a mouthful of cashews and was washing them down with a swallow of Dr Pepper when Kim joined him. She was wearing only a skimpy blue and white striped two-piece bathing suit, over which was a sheer white cover-up. She was carrying an ice bucket holding a chilled bottle of wine, and two wine glasses, which she placed on a wicker and glass topped end table. Jim nearly choked when she slipped her hand inside the back of his T-shirt and ran her fingertips down his spine.

"A glass of wine before we head for the pond, cowboy?"

"That does sound good," Jim said. "A quick one. And just to remind you, the last time we played this game, nine months later we ended up with Josh."

"And your point is?"

"None at all," Jim said.

"That's what I thought. Are you certain you don't want to sip your wine slowly?" Kim asked. "Perhaps have two glasses?"

"If you keep talking I won't want any wine at all."

"That's not a problem. We can take the wine along, and have our drinks after we swim."

"Now you're talking, but I hope swimming isn't the only thing you have planned," Jim said. "Not after what you told me this morning."

"Trust me, cowboy, swimming is the least part of my plans. Let's go."

Jim got up, and they began the short walk to the pond.

"Why are you walking kind of funny?" Kim asked, as they headed across the field.

"I think you know the answer to that," Jim replied.

9

"Honey, what are your plans for today?" Jim asked, as he finished buttoning his light blue dress shirt. Kim was still in the master bath, drying off after her shower.

"I've got a conference call with several clients at ten this morning," Kim answered. "Then just routine work for the remainder of the day. How about you?"

"I'm going into Austin. I've got to drop off my truck at the DPS garage for service, plus they've finally got the time to repair the dents and dings from when I busted down that door with it, during the raid in Kendalia. I've got to pick up a loaner vehicle when I leave mine there. I'm gonna spend the rest of the day at HQ in Austin, going through records to see if I can match up any prior cases or suspects with the two big cases I'm working on now, especially that drug bust."

"Couldn't you just do that at your office in Buda? You must be tired after last night."

Jim finished knotting a Navy-blue tie around his neck before he answered.

"I could, but since I'll be in Austin anyway, the records will be right there, plus there's specialists I can call on if need be, for example the forensics artists. Besides, a fresh look by another pair of eyes might notice something I've overlooked. If anyone's around, I'll have them take a look at what little I've got."

"Are you having breakfast before you leave?"

"Nah, I don't have the time. I'll just swing by and grab a cup of coffee and some doughnuts."

Kim came out of the bathroom, wrapped in a fluffy pink robe.

"You'll be home on time for once, then."

"I sure plan on it," Jim answered. He kissed her on the cheek, then jammed his Stetson on his head. "Gotta run. Love you. See you tonight."

A short while later, Jim pulled up to the Department of Public Safety garage at the department's main complex in Austin. He shut off the Tahoe, got out, and went inside the building. Jake Kearney, the chief mechanic, was behind his desk, writing up a work order on another vehicle.

"Howdy, Jake," Jim said. Jake looked up and nodded.

"Good mornin', Jim. I'll open the garage door. Bring your truck inside, and let's see what we've got."

"Sure thing."

Jim went back out to his truck, waited for Jake to open the overhead door, then drove the Tahoe inside. Before he could even shut off the engine and get out of the truck, Jake was already shaking his head.

"What's the matter?" Jim asked, once he shut off the truck and got out. "Is it in that bad a shape?"

"Let me put it to you this way: All police vehicles take a beatin', we know that. And Ranger vehicles take some of the worst, especially yours. But you've outdone yourself this time. I'm gonna have to get the dents out of the hood and front fenders, replace the busted grille and headlight, and repaint the entire front, hood and both fenders. You need tires, the front end is way out of alignment, and I've no doubt she'll need new struts. I'd imagine the brake pads will need to be replaced too, and the rotors ground down, or even also replaced. That's not even counting what else I might find once I get into it, plus the routine maintenance. Where the hell have you been drivin' this thing?"

"Over a lot of bad roads and through back country," Jim answered.

"More like through Palo Duro Canyon," Jake retorted. "Well, leave me the keys, and I'll get started on her later. You're gonna have to plan on a couple of weeks before you get her back."

"I reckon I've got no choice," Jim said. "What am I getting for a replacement while mine's in the shop?"

"That black Charger over in the corner," Jake answered. "She's got a lot of miles on her, so she'll be goin' up for sale at the next department surplus equipment auction, but she still runs solid. The keys are in the ignition."

"All right, Jake. I'm gonna be doing some work while I'm here, so I'll pick it up when I'm ready to leave," Jim said. "See you later."

Jim headed inside the main office. Laurie Jean Swenson, the administrative assistant at the front desk, greeted him warmly.

"Good morning, Ranger Blawcyzk. What brings you by?"

"Good morning, Laurie Jean. I had to drop off my truck for repairs. While I'm here, I want to go through some of the back case files. I'm hoping to find something, or more likely someone, that will lead me to whoever's behind the outfit which was running the drug distribution out of New Braunfels and Kendalia. I have a gut feelin' it's a pretty large organization. I know the DEA has already taken the information we passed along to them and is working with their counterparts in Mexico, to try'n see where some of the drugs come from down there. I'm hoping I might find somethin' to help me figure out who might be killing those old ladies, too."

"Well, you know where to find the files," Laurie Jean said. "Just call me if you need any assistance."

"I'll do just that," Jim said. "You're a peach. I'm gonna pop in to say howdy to Chief King and let him know I'm here, then get to work."

"After you stop in the cafeteria to get a can of Dr Pepper out of the soda machine," Laurie Jean said, with a smile.

"You know me only too well," Jim said.

Jim had been plowing through records for almost four hours when the phone on the desk rang. He picked it up.

"Ranger Blawcyzk," he answered.

"Ranger, it's Laurie Jean. I have a call from the Comal County Sheriff's Office for you. I'll put it right through."

"All right, thanks."

Jim waited until a voice came on the other end of the line.

"Ranger Blawczyk?"

"You've got him."

"This is Deputy Charles Hunt. We have an apparent homicide near Spring Branch. It's another elderly woman. From what our deputy on scene tells us, it may be related to the two Hays County killings."

"What's the address?"

"1435 State Park Road P31. That's near the junction with Bell Ranch Road. June Taylor is the deputy you'll meet on scene."

"I'm on my way."

Jim slammed down the phone, hurried to the garage, and got into the black Dodge Charger he'd be using until his Tahoe was ready. He started the car, hit the accelerator, and turned on the lights and siren. He had eighty miles to cover before he reached the murder scene. He muttered a curse under his breath when he noticed the gas gauge needle pointing to E. Rather than return to the DPS garage, he turned into a nearby filling station, pulled up to the sole unoccupied pump, jumped out of the car, took his state credit card out of his wallet and inserted it into the pump, then opened the Charger's gas cap and slid the nozzle into the filler neck. Less than two minutes later, the tank full, he sent the big Dodge rocketing toward Spring Branch.

There was only one Comal County Sheriff's Department car parked in front of the taped-off driveway to the apparent crime scene when Jim arrived. Deputy June Taylor flagged him down.

"You made damn good time, Jim," she said, when he rolled down the window. "But what the hell are you doing in that? I was looking for your Tahoe."

Jim had to laugh before answering. Taylor was in her late forties, thrice divorced, with four teenaged daughters at home, and nothing if not blunt spoken.

"Mine's in the shop," he said. "It got a little beat up."

"You mean you pounded the crap out of it,"

Taylor answered. "I'll take down the tape, let you in, then ride back up to the house with you."

"Okay."

Jim waited while Taylor pulled down the tape, then pulled into the drive and waited for her to replace the tape.

"Are you alone?" he asked, puzzled, when Taylor got in his car. There should have been at least one more deputy, to guard the driveway and keep out intruders or reporters.

"Yeah, I damn sure am," Taylor answered. "There's a big wildfire burnin' on the other side of Canyon Lake, and the damn wind's pushin' it along pretty quick. Evacuations have been ordered, so every available person has been sent up there to get the damn rich folks out of their damn vacation houses in one helluva hurry. Of course, most of them damn sons of bitches don't want to leave, so it's gonna be one helluva job forcin' those bastards to get the hell off of their damn fat butts and get the hell out."

Jim had to chuckle. Evidently Taylor had been ordered to tone down her language. This was the first time he'd ever heard her get through more than one sentence without tossing in a few F-bombs.

"Where's the house?" Jim asked. "What've we got here?"

"Just around that bend ahead, behind those pin oaks," Taylor said. "The owner is—*was*—Pearly

Mae Huston. She was eighty-three, but real spry for her age. There's the house now. Pull up behind my cruiser."

"Who's that in the Camry?" Jim asked, upon seeing a dark red Toyota parked in front of the house, with a man sitting behind the wheel, when they rounded the bend.

"That's Bishop Theodore J. Pawley, from the Spring Branch Church of Worship and Praise in Jesus Christ," Taylor said. "Mrs. Huston was a member there all her life. He's the one who discovered her body, which is in pretty bad shape. I'd say she's been dead a while."

When the minister started to get out of his car, Jim parked, then rolled down his driver's window and called to him.

"Bishop, I'm Texas Ranger James Blawcyzk. I'll be the chief investigator into Mrs. Huston's death. If you could just wait a few minutes while I finish speaking with Deputy Taylor, I would appreciate it. We won't be long."

"Of course, Ranger." Pawley sat back down and closed his car door.

"Damn it, June, you know no civilian should be alone at a crime scene," he told Taylor. "Suppose that *hombre* decided to start wandering around, and disturbed evidence. That could wreck any chance we might have of building a case before we even got started. And there should be someone watching the driveway."

206

"Dammit, you think I don't know that, on both counts, Jim?" Taylor said. "But what choice did I have? I've known Bishop Pawley for years. When I told him to stay in his car until I got back, he assured me he'd do just that. If you can't trust a damn preacher man, who can you trust?"

"When I'm workin' on a case, I wouldn't trust my own parish priests, if there was a chance they were somehow involved," Jim answered. "Neither should you trust anyone."

"Point taken. I don't, including damn bastard smart-mouthed Rangers," Taylor retorted. "As far as the driveway, there's a Spring Branch constable on his way. He should arrive within a few minutes. He's already been instructed not to come up to the damn house, but to park his damn butt at the bottom of the driveway and keep curious folks the hell away. Are you satisfied now?"

"Not really, but as you just said, what choice do I have? What's done is done, and can't be taken back. Finish telling me about what you found here."

"All right. As I've already said, we got the call from Reverend Pawley, saying he'd found Mrs. Huston, and she was dead. I haven't had the chance to ask him what he might've touched inside the house. I know he didn't touch the damn phone, because the call came from his cell.

"When I arrived, I went inside and found Mrs.

Huston's body, lying on its back in the kitchen. Even though the corpse is in bad shape, I could see right away she'd been shot in the forehead, so of course, the first damn thing that came to my mind was this could be connected to the other two killings of elderly women who lived alone, out in the damn country. I didn't do a damn thing, except back out of the house, then call the damn Rangers. From the quick look I had, she's probably been dead for more than a day or so. Bishop Pawley comes out to check on her every damn Wednesday, and he said she was just fine when he left her last week."

"Any family?"

"Yeah, but not nearby. She has two daughters who live in Houston, and a son up in Kansas City. A whole helluva passel of grandkids. Her husband died around eight or nine years ago, the best I can recall. His family, and hers both, have been around here for generations, goin' back before the damn War of Northern Aggression. They were slaves, then sharecroppers, but eventually Henry's—that was Pearly Mae's husband—anyway Henry's grandfather saved enough to buy these thirty acres out here in the damn middle of nowhere, back during the Depression in the 1930s when land could be bought for little more'n a damn dime an acre. It's never been much of a place, just a damn sorry hardscrabble farm."

"It doesn't look all that bad," Jim said. "What about friends?"

"Any she had have mostly died off," Taylor answered. "The ones she did have left were mostly from the church. And most of those were too damn frail to drive out this damn far for a visit. Her only regular company, as far as I know, was Bishop Pawley."

"I guess that's enough of the basics for me to get started," Jim said. "I'll just talk to Pawley for a few minutes, so he can go home, then I'll examine the body, and start searching the house. If you wouldn't mind, June, it'd be a real help if you take a look around the outside while I'm talking with him."

"Not at all. That'll give me something to do instead of just sitting on my damn butt," Taylor answered. "I'll watch for the county coroner's van to show up, too."

"Also, is that Hyundai alongside the house Mrs. Huston's?"

"Yeah, I reckon it is."

"Then the car will need to be taken to the lab for a forensics search of it, too. Call for a hook, if you wouldn't mind."

"I'll get right on it."

"Appreciate that, June. *Gracias*."

Bishop Pawley got out of his car when he saw Jim approaching. He was a tall, barrel-chested

African-American, in his late sixties, with a deep baritone voice. His graying hair was cut short, his dark eyes shaded by a pair of sunglasses. When they shook hands, Jim felt as if his had just been crushed in a vise, so powerful was the preacher's grip.

"Bishop, before we begin, I'd like to extend my condolences on the loss of one of your church members," Jim said.

"Thank you, Ranger. I appreciate your kind thoughts," Pawley answered. "I also want you to know I will assist in any way possible to help apprehend the coward who would murder an elderly woman, in cold blood."

"I'm sure you will," Jim said. "Unfortunately, I can't take you inside, or even on the porch, to get out of this heat, since this is a crime scene. I can interview you in your vehicle, or mine, wherever you'll be more comfortable. I should warn you the air conditioning doesn't work very well in the one I have. My regular truck is in for service, so that car's the replacement DPS gave me until mine is ready."

"Then we'll definitely be more at ease in my car," Pawley answered. "Be my guest."

He opened the front passenger door, then walked around the back of the car and settled behind the wheel.

"Do you mind if I smoke, Ranger?" Pawley asked. He pulled a grape cigar from his suit coat's inside pocket. "I regret to admit smoking is the one vice from my misspent youth I haven't been able to give up, even after finding Jesus."

"It's your car, Bishop. Now I'm going to ask you . . . do you mind if I record our conversation?"

"Not at all."

"Fine, then let's get started."

While Pawley lit his cigar, Jim pulled out his digital recorder and turned it on.

"Texas Ranger James Blawcyzk, of Company F, investigating the apparent homicide of Pearly Mae Huston, an eighty-six-year-old black female, of 1535 State Park Road P31 in Comal County. Comal County Deputy Sheriff June Taylor is assisting me. This is an interview with Bishop Theodore J. Pawley, who discovered Mrs. Pawley's body. He is the pastor of the church Mrs. Pawley attended. If you would, sir, for the record, could you please give me your full name and address."

"Of course. My name is Bishop Theodore Jonah Pawley, pastor of the Spring Branch Church of Worship and Praise in Jesus Christ. My residence is located at 845A Old Boerne Road in Spring Branch, Texas, which is also the location of my church."

"Thank you. Bishop Pawley, how long had you known Mrs. Huston?"

"Pearly Mae, Mrs. Huston, had been an

active member of my church for more than twenty-seven years. She was a fine, upstanding, Christian woman, with a deep and abiding faith in the Lord."

"I understand. Now, why were you here at Mrs. Huston's home today?"

"I came out to check on her welfare, as I did every Wednesday. I do that for several of my elderly congregants, since it is difficult for them to drive to church every Sunday. Hopefully, within the near future, we will have enough saved to buy a used church bus to transport people to church on Sunday.

"Sadly, as is happening with so many churches, my congregation is growing older, and smaller. Young people just don't seem to care about religion any longer. They are more concerned with the pleasures of this world. Satan has gained control over so many young minds. Do you mind my asking if you're a Christian, Ranger Blawcyzk?"

"I am, Bishop. Catholic. Now, getting back to the matter at hand. Can you describe exactly what you found when you arrived here today?"

"Of course." Pawley took a puff on his cigar before continuing. "I arrived a bit later than usual, just after eleven-thirty. Normally, Mrs. Huston would be waiting for me on the porch. I wasn't unduly concerned when she wasn't, this time, since the weather is so humid. I *was* rather surprised that she didn't hear my car when I pulled up, and come out to greet me. She always did that if she wasn't outside when I arrived.

"When I knocked on her door and there was no answer, my concern increased even more. I tried the door and found it unlocked, so I opened it partway and called for Mrs. Huston. When she still didn't answer, I went inside and found her, lying on the kitchen floor. I knew immediately that she was dead.

"At first, I thought it had probably been a heart attack or stroke, then I saw the dried blood and bullet wound to her forehead and realized she had been shot. I quickly left the house and called the sheriff's office."

"Did you touch anything in the house? Anything at all?"

"Nothing but the doorknob, and perhaps the door itself, Ranger."

"You didn't touch Mrs. Huston, or perhaps shake her in an attempt to rouse her?"

"No, I did not. As I've already told you, I knew she was dead as soon as I saw her."

"Please forgive me for pressing on this point, but exactly how could you know she was dead?"

"From the condition of Mrs. Huston's body. In addition, I spent three years with the Army as a medic in Viet Nam, so I have had firsthand experience with the dead and dying. I know from my military service when a person is beyond saving. In this case, Mrs. Huston had obviously been deceased for some time."

"I understand, Bishop. I only have a few more questions. Do you know of anyone who would want to hurt Mrs. Huston? A relative or acquaintance who might hold a grudge, or was angry with her for some reason, perhaps an argument?"

"No one at all. Mrs. Huston was loved by everyone she knew. All three of her children urged her to move closer to them, but she was an independent, some might even say stubborn, woman, who was determined to live out her days here at the family homestead."

"She didn't happen to mention to you anyone who might have threatened her, or anyone coming around here that she was worried about?"

"No. No one."

"What was her mood like when you visited last week?"

"The same as always. Cheerful and full of joy for life and the Lord. A few minor complaints about the infirmities of old age, but nothing out of the ordinary."

"And you didn't see anything unusual, anything out of place?"

"Not a thing. Our visit was the same as we've had for the last several years. Mrs. Huston always baked a cake or cookies, and we sat and talked over sweets and coffee. There was not one thing different."

"Just one more question, Bishop, then you can leave, and go about your business," Jim said. "Please consider your answer carefully before you give it."

"Of course, Ranger."

"Deputy Taylor told me this place, the Huston homestead, has always been a rather poor farm, implying that it didn't provide much of a living, or financial stability, for the family. Yet, to me, it appears to be, while certainly not luxurious, at least fairly prosperous. The house, at least from the outside, seems well-maintained, perhaps even remodeled in the not-too-distant past.

"The vehicle Deputy Taylor told me belonged to Mrs. Huston is no more than a year old. At first glance, it doesn't appear Mrs. Huston had any financial worries. Can you provide me any information on that?"

"I'll do my best. Up until two or three years ago, Deputy Taylor's statement would have been one hundred percent accurate. Mrs. Huston was barely getting by. In fact, myself or my wife would often bring her food. Several times, we paid her electric bill so her lights wouldn't be shut off. Then, gradually, things seemed to get better for her. She had repairs made to the house, bought the car you mentioned, and no longer had problems paying her bills or buying groceries.

"The county had been threatening to take her land for back taxes, and she even paid those off, in full. I wondered about her new source of income, but of course, I couldn't ask her about it. I do know her tithe to the church increased considerably."

"And she never divulged to you the source of her apparent newfound revenue?"

"Only to say that the Lord, in His mysterious ways, had answered her prayers, and she would be able to keep her home. I know that her children weren't able to help her—at least, not very much. All three are doing fairly well, but they have growing families, so they have their own needs to worry about.

"I just assumed Mrs. Huston had perhaps received a small inheritance from a distant relative. The money could not have come from gambling, because she never took a trip to the casinos in Louisiana or Mississippi. She also never bought a lottery ticket, not even a scratch-off. She felt gambling was a sin."

"So, you have no idea?"

"Not really."

"Thank you for your cooperation, Bishop Pawley. This concludes our interview."

Jim switched off his recorder and fished a business card out of his shirt pocket. He handed that to Pawley.

"Here's my card. If you happen to think of anything, no matter how trivial, that you believe might help my investigation, please get in touch with me at once. If you can't reach me, call Company F and leave a message, or contact the county sheriff's office, and have them get in touch with me."

"I will, Ranger." Pawley took a card of his own out of his jacket pocket and handed it to Jim. "Here's how to reach me. If you need any other questions answered, I'll make myself available. Now, I suppose I'll need to break this tragic news to my wife. She and Mrs. Huston were dear friends. Am I free to leave?"

"You are, sir," Jim said. "I only ask you don't say anything, to anyone, about how Mrs. Huston died. Wait for a statement to be released by DPS or the Comal County Sheriff."

"Not even my wife?"

"If at all possible. Just tell her the death was untimely, without specifics. I'm sure your wife is a fine person, and wouldn't divulge what has happened here purposely, but you know how things can sometimes get out, despite our best efforts."

"I do indeed, Ranger. I won't lie to Lydia, but I'll be evasive."

"I appreciate that, Bishop. I'll be in contact if I need more information, or if I have any for you."

"And I'll be praying for your success, Ranger. If you don't mind."

"Not at all, Bishop. In my line of work, I'll

take all the prayers I can get, anytime. Thank you again."

They shook hands, then Jim got out of the car. Deputy Taylor, who had been leaning against the front fender of her Explorer and checking her text messages while waiting, gestured for him to come join her.

"Have you got something?" Jim asked, once he reached her.

"I damn sure have. I think so, anyway," Taylor answered. "Take a look over here, next to the driveway, opposite Mrs. Huston's car."

She led Jim to the spot she meant, then pointed at the softer soil alongside the hard-packed dirt and crushed stone drive.

"Right there. I checked, and that tread mark for certain doesn't belong to the damn Hyundai sittin' there. It doesn't match any of the tires from our cars, neither, although none of use drove up here."

"How about Bishop Pawley's Camry?"

"No, his car was in the same damn place you saw it when you drove up. Besides, that tire track looks too damn big to have come from his Toyota, doesn't it? And the footprint next to it damn sure didn't come from Pawley's patent leather loafers."

"It sure didn't," Jim agreed. "Besides, there was no dirt on his shiny black shoes, only some dust."

"You looked at his damn feet?" Taylor said, looking at Jim doubtfully.

"Part of bein' a Ranger. You learn quick to look at everything. I even looked at *your* feet," Jim said, with a soft laugh. "Maybe we've finally caught a break. Soon as we're done in the house, I'll go get my evidence kit and make a cast of these."

He stopped short at a distant rumble of thunder.

"Damn! It hasn't rained for weeks, so it's gotta rain *today*. I'd better make those casts first, then process the house."

He began to turn for his car, then stopped short once again.

"Damn!"

"Now what's wrong?" Taylor asked.

"When this call came in, I left so fast I forgot to get the evidence collection kit out of my car. June, you wouldn't happen to have any dental stone in your vehicle, would you?"

"No, I damn sure wouldn't," Taylor said. "I don't carry any in my purse, either, just in case you're wondering." She laughed.

"I don't imagine you do. It's a bit heavy to lug around," Jim said. "Guess I'm gonna have to make do. The Cost-mart down on 281 should have most of what I need. I've got to come up with something in place of fingerprint powder, though. June, do you happen to know where the nearest tack shop or farm supply store's at?"

"Sure. There's a Tractor Supply right across 46 from the Cost-mart. It's fairly new, so it might not have been there your last time up this way."

"They'll have what I need." Jim gave a glance at the sky when thunder rumbled again, nearer this time. Storm clouds were building to the northwest. "That's if I can beat this son of a bitch storm. It's liable to wash out these prints before I can get the casts. June, do me a big favor. Take pictures of these, from all angles. Then see if you can find something to divert any water that comes down the slope. Once you do that, see if you can find a tarp or something to cover them, then move your car over them, without driving on 'em, of course. That'll at least give us half a chance to keep the rain from washin' them away. With a lot of luck, I'll beat the storm."

"Sure, Jim."

June pulled out her phone and started taking pictures, while Jim headed for his car at a trot. Once he got moving, he sent the Dodge down the driveway as fast as he dared. The Spring Branch constable had arrived, as well as several satellite trucks from the Austin television stations. Jim rolled down his window, shouted to the constable to take down the tape and that he'd be back shortly. Once that was done, Jim hit the pavement and gunned the Dodge, fishtailing slightly when he turned right onto solid blacktop. He hit the lights and siren, then jammed the accelerator pedal to the floor.

Jim parked right in front of the entrance to Costmart, leaving the car running and lights flashing, but, since luckily Jake had given him two sets of keys, making certain to lock the doors. All that had to happen would be someone stealing a Highway Patrol car he'd left unlocked. That would get him most likely fired, and at the least would be downright embarrassing.

He hurried inside, and went straight to the baking and cooking products section, where he grabbed a roll of butcher paper. After that, he went to the front of the store, and took a jar of Vaseline from the shelf, along with a box of nitrile gloves and a package of medicine droppers.

Lastly, he headed for the household supplies, where he got two boxes of plastic bags, one sandwich size, the other gallon. Much as Jim was loath to use his Ranger badge as a means to obtain special service, sometimes it was necessary, and this was one of those circumstances. When he reached the checkouts, he cut to the head of the line of the least busy register, apologizing as he did so.

"I'm sorry, folks, but this is official business. I'm in the middle of an investigation, and need this stuff. I've gotta beat the storm that's brewin'."

A couple of the customers muttered under their breaths, but most Texans respected the long tradition of the Rangers' service to the state. Several even told Jim, "No problem, go right ahead, Ranger."

Jim paid for his purchase, then headed across State 46 to the Tractor Supply store. There, he went to the horse supply section, got two bottles of Wonder Dust and paid for that. Less than ten minutes after reaching the Cost-mart, he was headed back to the crime scene.

When Jim got back to the Huston farm, two or three more news vehicles were parked along the side of the narrow road. The Spring Branch constable saw him coming, lowered the tape and waved Jim into the drive, blocking any reporters from following. When he reached the house, Jim noted with satisfaction that Deputy Taylor had found a large piece of plastic sheeting, covered the tread mark and footprint with that, then held it in place with her car.

"You're not a minute too soon," Taylor said, once he was out of his car. "That damn storm's gonna blow up any minute now, and unless I miss my guess, it's about to rain like hell."

Indeed, the sky was now covered with dark, scudding clouds, the wind gusting fitfully, moaning through the trees. The rumbles of thunder were much louder, and lightning sliced through the clouds.

"This shouldn't take long," Jim said. "We won't have to wait for dental stone to set. You're about to see how we can make an imprint of footprints and tire tracks in a pinch. It looks like you did a fine job of keeping 'em protected. You got the pictures, right?"

"I damn sure did," Taylor said.

"Good. Email them to my office, will you? Now, let's get started. Move your car back."

As soon as Taylor backed her car off the plastic, Jim rolled it up and set it aside, weighing it down with one of the two by fours.

"Real good job saving these prints," he told Taylor. The deputy had dug a small ditch just upslope from the prints, and had also placed a couple of two by fours just above that ditch, in an uphill pointing "v" to divert any water. He picked up the plastic and handed it to her.

"Hold this while I get to work."

He unrolled a length of the butcher paper, held it flat with dirt on each corner, then coated it with Vaseline. He opened one of the bottles of Wonder Dust, and sprinkled most of the contents liberally over the Vaseline.

"Now we just take this paper, turn it over, press down on the prints, and we'll have a nice impression of them. It won't last anywhere near as long as dental stone, of course, but it'll hold together long enough to take more pictures, and also get it to the lab for forensics and comparison."

Jim first took an impression of the tire tread, then repeated the procedure for the footprint. After that, he took a couple pictures of each makeshift cast.

"I'm gonna run these to my car, since I'd rather not roll 'em up," he told Taylor. "I'll meet you at the front door."

The rain started coming down as Jim ran for his car. He had no sooner gotten the casts in the trunk when the skies opened up, in a typical summer Texas cloudburst. By the time he got back to the house, he was drenched, his soaked shirt clinging to his skin, water dripping from the brim of his Stetson and down his back. He yanked off the hat and shook as much water from it as possible.

"Where's your raincoat, Jim?" Taylor asked, her voice sweet and innocent. "I didn't realize see-through shirts were now part of the Ranger dress code."

Jim glared at her.

"My damn slicker's back in my Tahoe, in Austin, along with my spare clothes," he answered. "Not one more damn word. Let's get inside. I've got gloves here, and plastic bags to slide over our boots, since my booties are also in my car. Unfortunately, like all my other stuff, my masks are back in Austin, so unless you've got a spare, I'll have to go without."

"Damn! I thought I'd finally get to see you shake your bootie," Taylor said, laughing. Jim started to frame a retort, then also had to laugh.

"That would probably give you a heart attack," he said. "It sure wouldn't be a pretty sight. Let's get this over with."

Once they were inside, Jim turned his recorder back on, then took out his camera and began taking photographs of the scene.

"Ranger James Blawcyzk, still assisted by Comal County Deputy Sheriff June Taylor, continuing the investigation into the apparent homicide of Pearly Mae Huston in her residence at 1535 State Park Road P31 in Comal County, Texas. Initial observations indicate no sign of a struggle, also that nothing appears to be disturbed, nor any items removed from the home. That will be confirmed after a thorough search of the building. The victim's car is still in the driveway, locked. It will be removed to the DPS lab for a forensics examination."

Jim continued dictating his findings as he walked into the kitchen.

"Mrs. Huston's body is lying in a supine position, on her kitchen floor. An apparent bullet wound to the forehead is present. The body is fully clothed, but is in an advanced state of decomposition, which was most likely accelerated by its location in a closed, un-air conditioned house during ninety plus degree weather, accompanied by high humidity. An accurate estimated time of death will be impossible, until a complete autopsy is performed, but I would place a range of the past forty-eight to one-hundred-and-forty-four hours, two to six days, pending the medical examiner's report."

Jim paused the recorder while he took more photographs, then switched it back on.

"Closer examination of the forehead wound shows it appears to have been made by the same caliber weapon, and the bullet fired from approximately the same distance, as in the homicides of Pamela Sue Dearing and Susan Hollister. That will be confirmed by ballistic tests. The blood spatter pattern would indicate the bullet is still in the victim's brain. I am proceeding to roll the body over to confirm there is no exit wound."

Jim left his recorder on while he started to roll Huston's body onto its side. As he did, the bloated corpse spewed forth a foul mixture of gases and bodily fluids from its mouth and nose, spraying Jim in the face and staining his clothes.

"Dammit!" Jim cursed. "Of all the times to be caught without a BDU. This one had to let loose now."

He pulled the handkerchief from his hip

pocket to wipe the sticky, odiferous mess from his face, as best he could. Taylor, for her part, was alternating between gagging and laughing hysterically. She finally had to leave the room when Jim began wiping as much of the stuff from his clothes as was possible. He could hear her laughing out on the back porch.

"I'm glad you're finding this so funny, June," Jim called. "As soon you can get yourself back under control, I'd like to get back to work so we can finish up here sometime before midnight."

"I . . . I'm sorry, Jim," Taylor stuttered, when she returned. "I know I shouldn't have found it funny, but I did. Damn funny. If we didn't have to keep what we have here under wraps, I'd probably have posted some damn photos to Facebook, or maybe Instagram. Even a video for Youtube. But if I hadn't laughed, I'd have gotten damn sick to my stomach."

"The stench in here is bad enough without you puking and adding to it, so I'll take the laughing," Jim said. He glanced at his recorder, saw that it was still running, cursed when he realized it had recorded his outburst, then finished rolling Huston's body onto its stomach.

"There is no exit wound, so the bullet is apparently still inside the skull," He continued. "There are no other apparent injuries to the back of the torso or extremities. Livor Mortis is still evident. Blood has pooled . . ."

By the time Jim returned home, it was well after dark. He had already called Kim, told her what had happened, and asked her to leave a trash bag outside the back patio, along with a bar of soap and some old towels. He parked the car near the barn. Frostie came bounding off the front porch, his tail waving, but when Jim got out of the car, he caught a whiff of the smell still clinging to him, stopped short, and ran back to the front door, whining and crying.

"I can't blame you there, buddy," Jim said, with a rueful chuckle. He picked up the things Kim had left him, then headed for the hose attached to the barn hydrant. Copper had his head hanging over the fence, expecting his evening treat and petting. Instead, once he caught a whiff of his rider, he snorted, tossed his head, and galloped to the other end of his corral.

"Oh, like you think your dang manure smells so sweet, don't ya?" Jim yelled after him. He unbuckled his gunbelt and draped it over the back of an old bench alongside the barn, then sat down to pull off his boots and socks.

"At least I can salvage my boots," he muttered. "I sure don't want to have to go to the expense of needin' to replace those. Glad that stuff missed my hat, too. The rest of my clothes are goin' straight to the landfill."

He hung his hat on the back of the bench,

unpinned his badge and put in inside his hat, then shucked off all his clothes, shoving them in the trash bag. He turned on the hose, picked up the soap, and spent the next half-hour scrubbing himself vigorously. After he toweled off, he stuffed the towels into the trash bag and tied it shut. The fluids' odor still clung to him like cheap perfume. He shook his head again, picked up his boots, hat, and badge, then headed for the house. Kim met him at the back door.

"Jim, you still smell something awful," she said. "Like one of Josh's dirty diapers."

"I know," Jim said. "I'm gonna soak in the tub for about an hour. I think I'll borrow some of your scented bubble bath. Maybe that will help."

"Do you want me to run down to H-E-B and get you a few cans of tomato juice, like people do for skunked dogs?"

"That's just an old wives' tale," Jim said. "It doesn't work for dogs, and it sure won't work on me."

"It would be interesting to see you as a redhead, though."

"Not to mention a redskin, to be politically incorrect," Jim answered. "I'd laugh, but I'm too doggone worn out. Don't wait up for me. I'm gonna sleep on the patio tonight, so I don't get any of this stink on our sheets and pillows. I'll see you in the morning. Good night, Kim."

He gave her a quick kiss on the cheek.

"What kind of pathetic kiss is that?"

"The kind you get if you don't want to smell like I do."

"In that case, it's perfectly acceptable. Good night, honey."

10

Several days later, Jim was in his office when the telephone rang.

"Ranger Blawcyzk."

"Good morning, Jim. It's Mary Huggins. I'm glad I caught you in."

"Howdy, Mary. You just caught me. I won't be here much longer. I'm on my way to Johnson City in a few minutes, to testify at the Adams trial."

"In that case, I'll get right to the point. Are you making any progress on those murders?"

"Not a heckuva lot."

"Well, I might have some good news for you. I've got the results on those tire tracks and footprints you sent in. Perhaps those will help."

"They sure might, Mary. What have you got?"

"The tire is a Michelin Pilot MXM4, size P235/55R17. They're specified for passenger cars and sedans, recommended for highway driving, so they're most likely pretty popular in Texas, I would think. They come as original equipment on several brands, Nissan, Toyota, and some Volkswagen models, as well as several Ford and General Motors products. And, of course, they're also sold in most tire shops, including Cost-mart.

I'm afraid I haven't narrowed things down for you much."

"At least it's a start. I appreciate your help, especially since it's not really your job. It's just that I'm so backed up."

"There's no need to explain, or apologize, Jim. I like helping you boys out whenever I can. It's a break from the daily routine. As long as I get my regular work done, Major Voitek has no issue with me lending a hand, you know that. I'm glad to help out. Now, about the shoe. The print came from a left athletic shoe, a Nike Air Max 95 Premium, size 12 or 13, men's. Again, just like the tire, it's a fairly common item."

"But a pretty pricey one, too, Mary. Not everybody can afford such a fancy sneaker. The size is even more help. We're looking for someone with big feet."

"That also means he could be tall," Mary said. "Or a clown."

"Could be," Jim answered. "Anything else?"

"There is one more thing. The photos you took of the shoe, as well as the impression, seem to show a piece missing out of the sole, just in front of the instep, about a quarter of an inch or so wide. That might just be a flaw in the photo and impression, but it seems pretty clear."

"So, all I need to do is check the left foot of every man in Texas wearing a big Nike, to see if his shoe is missing a chunk, and I'll have our killer. That's probably only a few hundred thousand *hombres*."

"All of whom would probably object to some stranger asking to see their feet, even if he is wearing a Ranger badge," Mary said. "Not to mention you'd receive some mighty strange looks . . . or perhaps a punch in the mouth."

"You're right," Jim said, laughing. "I reckon I'd better come up with another plan. I'm obliged, Mary. You've been a big help. If it wouldn't get me in trouble with your son, not to mention my wife, I'd take you out for drinks, dinner, and dancing."

"Jimbo doesn't tell me what to do, retired Ranger or not," Mary retorted. "Be careful, or I'll take you up on that offer."

"I probably couldn't keep up with you. You'd wear me out. Thanks again, Mary."

"Anytime, Jim. You take care. Good-bye."

"You too, Mary. Bye."

Jim hung up the phone, then leaned back in his chair and sighed. So far, the few leads he had in both of the major cases he was working on had taken him absolutely nowhere. He'd been following the paper trail of the companies found in the evidence obtained from the New Braunfels Airport for weeks now, with no success. They all led in circles or down blind alleys. The main corporate entity was apparently based in Grand Cayman, where of course no cooperation could be expected from banking or government officials, for shell corporations headquartered in the Caymans was a lucrative source of revenue for the islands. The corporate name was probably a phony, anyway. He'd have to keep digging, and hope he found something.

Tacked to the bulletin board on the wall opposite his desk were photos of Pamela Sue Dearing, Susan Hollister, and Pearly Mae Huston. The files, and his notes, on each case were spread across his desk.

"I sure wish you ladies could tell me something from the grave," he said to the pictures. He continued talking to himself, while tapping a pencil on the desktop.

"Let's see what I've got. Three elderly women, who all lived alone out in the country, murdered, but for what reason? There was no sign of forced entry at any of their places, meaning they most likely knew their killer, and let him or her in. No sign of a struggle, no evidence of rape, and nothing missing, as near as can be figured, from any of the crime scenes. So . . . what's the motive?

"I can eliminate race, since Mrs. Huston was black, the other two women, white. Everyone I've talked to says they were all the salt of the earth, too, with not an enemy in the world. But someone wanted all three of 'em dead, that's for damn sure. Whoever killed 'em is damn smart, too. No fingerprints, no drinking glasses or anything else that I might've gotten a DNA sample from, no nothing, period. Nobody saw him, or her, either.

"The only leads I've got are those tire tracks and footprints, and those are damn slim. Even they might not belong to the killer. I keep comin' back to what Bishop Pawley said about Mrs. Huston suddenly having some extra income. The only problem with that is neither of the other two women seemed to be making any money, other than their Social Security. No money in the bank, no cash found in their houses, except for a few dollars. And that means they sure weren't killed for their cash, that's for certain. But that extra money Pawley mentioned keeps gnawin' at my brain. It's the only motive I can come up with, at least for now."

Jim glanced at the clock on the wall and sighed again.

"I'd better be on my way to Johnson City. At least I'll have some time to think on this while I'm driving. Being behind the wheel or in the saddle, ridin' Copper, always seems to clear my head."

As much as Jim wanted to concentrate on the two major cases that had him stumped, he was fully aware he still had to work on the other cases assigned to him. Still, spending a good part of his day making the hour-long drive to Johnson City, take probably two hours testifying, then driving back, was the last way he needed to spend his time at this point. However, it was all part of being a Texas Ranger, one of the most overworked and underpaid law enforcement agencies in the country, if not the world. Covering four counties that together were bigger than the combined size of Rhode Island and Delaware meant the workload was always heavy.

Besides, this was an important case, and rather unusually, Jim was testifying for the defense, instead of the prosecution.

Clifford Adams was a young black man, in his early twenties, who had been arrested on charges of breaking and entering, larceny, and third degree sexual assault. He worked as a gardener and handyman for Letitia Williams, a wealthy widow, who was a prominent member of the community in Johnson City. It was she who had accused him of the crime.

Even though it was in the middle of the night when the crime took place, so Williams could not swear she was able to positively identify her assailant's face, Adams was arrested and indicted based on her accusation, his fingerprints, and DNA evidence. His attorney was unable to convince the court that, since Adams worked for Williams, it was only natural his prints and traces of his DNA would be in the house.

When the indictment came in, his attorney asked the Rangers for assistance. Jim had done a lot of digging, and was able to show there were no traces of Adams's DNA on the bedclothes where the alleged assault took place, nor any of his fingerprints in that room. Ms. Williams refused to be examined, to determine whether any of Adams's DNA was present in her genitalia.

Jim did find evidence of another person being there, fingerprints that were not in the NCIC database, and a splotch of dried blood on the rug that did not match Adams's type. There were also some minute skin flakes up against the wall behind the bed, scrapings which belonged to a white male.

Despite his findings, the county attorney refused to drop the charges. Jim suspected that would happen, even in light of what Jim had uncovered, since the case involved a young, poverty-stricken black man accused of crimes against one of the most influential white women in Johnson City.

He was also aware the deputy who had arrested Adams, Frank Jarvis, was a known bigot and white supremacist, although that couldn't be given as evidence in court. It would be considered either hearsay, or Jim's opinion, not a fact.

Now, Jim was about to testify for the defense, in hopes of keeping a young man he was convinced innocent from going to prison. Despite years of progress, racism still ran rampant in many parts of Texas.

As he parked his car outside the Blanco County Courthouse, Jim murmured a silent prayer that, with his testimony, something would finally go right, and Cliff Adams would be acquitted.

After testifying for nearly two hours, Jim left the courtroom feeling a bit better. It was always hard to read a jury, of course, especially a small-town jury, but he had a definite feeling this one had believed his statements, and Clifford Adams would soon be a free man. The prosecutor had been unable to shake him into stumbling over any of his testimony, in fact, Jim had torn some of his challenges to shreds.

Since it was just after noon, he walked across the street to Pecan Street Brewing for lunch. He ordered pecan sweet fried chicken, with garlic mashed potatoes, washed down with one of their brewed-on-the-premises craft beers. He finished his meal with a slice of Mexican chocolate cake and a Dr Pepper.

He left the restaurant, intending to go straight to his car, but instead, walked around the corner and up North Nugent Avenue, to Texcetera Art Gallery. He wanted to find something to bring home to Kim, and this interesting little shop would be just the place to find it.

Anne, the manager, and Sandy, one of the sales

associates, were behind the main counter when he walked in.

"Howdy, ladies," Jim said. "Glad to see you're both here."

"Ranger Blawcyzk. Hello. It's been way too long since we've seen you," Anne replied. "How have you been?"

"I've been doin' okay," Jim answered. "I just haven't had the chance to get up this way. I had to testify at Cliff Adams's trial, so I figured as long as I was in town I'd stop in, and pick up something for my wife, and maybe a little something for my mother."

"Well, we're certainly glad to see you again," Sandy said. "You know where to look for what you want, so just call us if you need any assistance."

"I'll do that," Jim said. "I'll want a six pack of Dublin Bottling soda to start. Two root beers, two vanilla creams, a ginger ale, and a lemonade. On second thought, make that two six packs. Double each flavor."

"Of course. I'll start getting that ready for you," Sandy answered.

Jim could have spent hours browsing through the shop, which featured items created by area Texas artisans and artists, but he wanted to get back home in time for supper, a rarity for him. He bought a pair of sapphire blue and emerald green fused glass cabochon earrings for Kim, and a hand blown red and orange candy dish for his mother.

Unfortunately, he had his own weakness for glasswork, and he ended up buying four pieces for his office, two copper and stained-glass wall hangings by Deb Wight, one titled "Red Hot Totem", the other "Tweety Spire" for his den, as well as a stained-glass and copper piece called "Red Bird" by the same artist, for the kitchen. He also purchased two fused glass pieces by Cindy Cherrington, a wall hanging depicting a desert sunset entitled "Painted Sky", and a small pebble filled zinc tub holding two fused glass cacti in full bloom. Those would go into his office in Buda.

"Now you see why I don't stop by here that often," Jim said, as he paid for his purchases. "I can't afford to."

"You *are* one of our best customers," Anne said. "You can just visit without having to purchase anything, you know."

"That's easier said than done," Jim said. "I'll pull my car around and load these things up."

Anne and Sandy had the fragile items carefully bubble-wrapped and boxed by the time Jim got back. They helped him carry his purchases outside and load them into the trunk of the Dodge. After making his good-byes, Jim started the journey back toward home.

Jim had just driven through the small settlement of Cedar Valley, which had been established in

1867 but had never grown to more than a dot on the map, when his phone rang, and Kim's cell number appeared on the Dodge's dashboard display. He pushed the button on the steering wheel to answer the call.

"Hi, Kim," he said. "What's up?"

"Jim, where are you?" Kim answered.

"I'm headed east on 290. Just went through Cedar Valley. My truck's finally ready, so I'm headed to the DPS garage to pick it up. After that, I'm going to the office for a while, then I'll be home for supper, on time for once. Is something wrong? You sound worried."

"I think we're being followed."

"What?"

"I think we're being followed. Your mother's with me, and she thinks so, too. I called you before calling 911, to see if you were close by."

"Where are you, and what makes you think that?"

"We're on East 11th by the Capitol, just coming up on Brazos Street, heading for the highway. We took Josh for his checkup, and when we left Dr. Gonzalez's office, a green Audi pulled out behind us. It stayed behind us until we got to the Travis County Courthouse. I had to stop there to leave some papers with the county clerk. When I turned into the parking lot, the Audi kept going, but when we left the courthouse, it was behind us again. It's still back there."

"Kim, listen carefully, and do exactly what I say. Without using your turn signal, make a right on San Jacinto, another on East 10th, then a left on Congress Avenue. Let me know what that car does."

"All right."

Jim waited tensely until Kim's voice once again came over the Dodge's speakers.

"I just turned onto San Jacinto. The Audi turned too. It's two or three cars behind us."

"Speed up, then make the right on East 10th."

"What if I get pulled over?"

"If you *are* being followed, that's the best thing that could happen."

"All right."

Jim could hear the engine of Kim's Equinox rev as she stepped hard on the accelerator pedal. He flipped on the Dodge's rooftop strobes and increased his own speed.

"It's still behind us, Jim."

"Take the left on Congress."

He heard Kim's SUV accelerate even more, then its tires squeal when she made the turn onto Congress Avenue.

"I just ran a red light, Jim. So did the Audi. It's still two cars behind us."

"I'm going to have the Austin police notified to try and intercept you. Stay on Congress Avenue. Don't try for the highway, because that would make it easier for whoever's in that car to force you off the road, or whatever else they've got in mind, then get away. Keep goin' onto South Congress, and I'll meet you at the CVS at South Congress and West Stassney Lane. I'll be there in about fifteen minutes. Whatever happens, don't stop! If you catch any red lights, check to see the road's clear, then lay on your horn and run 'em."

"Jim, this is your ma. Couldn't you catch up with us at 290 and Congress?"

"You'll probably be past before I reach there. Tell Kim to go as fast as she can without wreckin'. I'm gonna radio for assistance from Austin PD now. Whatever you do, don't hang up. I'll be right back on the phone."

Jim turned on his two-way radio.

"Ranger unit 810 to Dispatch."

"Dispatch. Go ahead, Ranger 810."

"I need you to notify Austin PD and the Highway Patrol to have every available unit near Congress Avenue, in the area between the Capitol and Stassney Lane, to look for two vehicles, first a blue 2016 Chevrolet Equinox, Texas plates Bravo Zebra Mike 1987, second a green Audi, year, model, and plates unknown. Last known location proceeding south on Congress, below East 10th. The first vehicle is driven by my wife, who is apparently being followed by the second vehicle. I need the second vehicle stopped for questioning. Use extreme caution, as my infant son and my mother are also with my wife. I'm en route to South Congress and Stassney and will attempt to make a stop there."

"10-4, Ranger 810. Notifying Austin PD and Highway Patrol now. Stand by."

"10-4."

Jim put down the mic to speak to Kim again. When he heard a flurry of what sounded like gunshots, he hit his siren and jammed the accelerator pedal to the floor.

"Kim, was that gunfire? Where are you now?"

"Yes, Jim, it was. Whoever's in that car is shooting at us!" Kim's voice was frantic. "What should I do?"

"Tell me where you're at."

"Just crossing the bridge over the Colorado River. They're going to kill us."

"No, they're not. Not if you stay calm. Keep driving to where I told you. Austin PD has units on the way, so they should reach you before I get there. Keep swerving as much as you can, so you're a more difficult target to hit. What the hell was that?"

The sound of shattering glass had come over the phone.

"They just shot out the back window!" Kim screamed.

"Are any of you hit?"

"I-I don't think so."

"Kim, you concentrate on driving, and let Ma

handle the phone," Jim said. "Ma, is Josh all right?"

"He is. I don't know where the bullet struck after it went through the window, but it didn't hit any of us."

"Good. Hang on one minute."

Jim picked up the mic again.

"Ranger 810 to dispatch."

"Go ahead, Ranger 810."

"Shots have been fired. At least one bullet struck my wife's car. It blew out the back window. They just crossed the Congress Avenue Bridge over the Colorado. Where the hell are the Austin units?"

"Nearest units are approximately fifteen minutes away. Four have been dispatched, and will be on scene as quickly as possible. Two state troopers are also en route."

"They may be too late, if they can't get there sooner."

"Will notify Austin PD and Highway Patrol shots fired and urgency of situation."

"10-4, Dispatch. Keep me posted on all units' progress."

"10-4, Ranger 810."

"Ma, are you still there?" Jim called back into the phone.

"Yeah, we're just passing Oltorf Street. The men in the Audi were closing in, but got cut off by a garbage truck. I'm sure they'll get around it in a minute, though. In fact, they just passed him. They ran another car off the road to do it."

"Ma, listen carefully. You too, Kim. The nearest Austin units are too far away to help. I'm still going to try and get to Stassney and Congress before you. If I'm not there, you keep driving down South Congress. I'll catch up to you."

"Shouldn't we pull into a store or gas station?" Kim asked. "They wouldn't dare try anything with people around."

"No. If those bastards are tryin' to kill you, people being around won't stop them. Just keep coming toward Stassney. Ma, do either of you have your guns?"

"Of course. I've got my .38 in my purse. Kim has hers, too."

"Good. Start shootin' back at those *hombres*. You probably won't hit anything, but just might make 'em back off a bit. Not you, Kim. Just get to Stassney. Ma, once you're turned around, tell me if you can read the plate on that car, or see how many men are in it. Whoa! You stupid son of a bitch. Sorry, some idiot just came right out in front of me. Good thing I had room to get around. Ma, you heard me?"

"I sure did," Betty answered. "I'm already looking out the back. There's two in the car, one driving, the other one doing the shooting. It looks like he's using a semi-automatic rifle. I can't read the plate, but it's not Texas. White background, dark letters, but not one of the new Texas plates."

Jim heard his mother's pistol fire, followed by a shout of triumph from her.

"I got their windshield! That slowed them down for a minute, anyway. I guess they didn't plan on two ladies shooting back at 'em. They must've forgot this is Texas."

Over his radio, in the background, Jim could hear the locations of several Austin units and state troopers as they reported their positions and ETAs. None were close enough to be of immediate help.

"Ma, try'n hold 'em off. Kim, are you doing okay?"

"Amazingly, yes. I'm not nervous, just mad."

"Good. Location and speed?"

"We're just going over 290. I'm doing about seventy-five."

"Then you're only a few minutes from Stassney. So am I. I'm gonna stay off the phone now to concentrate on getting through the damn traffic. I'm not hanging up. If anything happens, just yell. I'll hear you."

Jim keyed his radio mic.

"Ranger 810 to Dispatch."

"Go ahead, Ranger 810."

"Subject vehicles just crossed over 290, still southbound on South Congress. Will attempt to intercept at South Congress and Stassney. Have all units converge on that intersection."

"10-4, Ranger 810. Advise major MVA at U.S. 290 and Texas 1. All lanes closed, blocked by overturned 18-wheeler. Suggest you use alternate route."

"10-4, Dispatch. I'll take West William Cannon, then cut back. ETA six minutes."

Traffic on 290 was already backed up past West William Cannon when Jim neared the intersection.

"Dammit!" he muttered. "Car, I sure hope your struts are still in decent shape." He swerved to the right, manhandled the Dodge over the curb and onto the grassy shoulder, smashed his head on the roof when he drove over a depressed storm drain, then made a hard right onto a service road that ran behind a strip mall, which contained several small businesses and restaurants.

The road looped around the mall, making a hard left, then a sharp right before exiting onto West William Cannon. Jim wrestled his car around the left, scraping its side on the concrete retaining wall on the right, then roared past the Postal Annex and cut short the right, jumping the curb and knocking over two signposts. He swerved right again onto West William Cannon, then floored the accelerator once more. Over his radio, he could hear the other police units as they radioed each other; over his phone, the sounds of gunfire still came. He took his right hand off the wheel for just a moment to make a quick Sign of the Cross.

Jim intended to take Garrison all the way to South Congress, then head north on that to hopefully intercept the men chasing his family near West Stassney. However, Garrison was being repaved, with all traffic being detoured north on Manchaca Road, then west on Stassney to South 1st.

Jim weaved in and around vehicles as he fought his way through the bottleneck, cursing whenever an obstinate or unaware driver refused to move over. He even shoved one shiny black Mercedes sedan off the road, when the young female behind the wheel not only refused to budge, but kept swerving in front of him, and gave him the finger.

"Good thing I've got a dashcam to record what she did," Jim said, as the Mercedes spun off the road and stopped in a grassy field of Garrison Park. "Let her make a complaint. She'll be the one in trouble."

Each delay only increased Jim's anxiety. His knuckles were white, so tightly was he gripping the wheel, sweat was rolling down his brow and soaking his shirt, which clung to his back like a second skin. His mother hadn't answered his calls, so he was beginning to fear the worst. If he didn't reach South Congress before Kim and her pursuers, he might not catch up with them until it was too late.

Finally, he reached the intersection of Manchaca and West Stassney. Now, it was little more than a mile to South Congress. Jim blew past several cars, then, just as he made the right onto West Stassney, a warning chime sounded, and a red light flashed on the instrument panel.

"Damn!" Jim muttered. The Dodge was over-heating, the needle at the top of the temperature gauge. In the rearview mirror, he could see steam coming from under the vehicle, luckily at this speed being blown back and not blocking his vision. "Don't you quit on me now, you glorified piece of scrap metal. There's only a few blocks to go."

Jim pressed harder on the accelerator, trying to get the last bit of speed out of the struggling Dodge. The engine was now making fearsome knocking noises, threatening to throw a rod at any minute.

Jim drove past Blue Bird Lane. The CVS store came into view. He saw Kim's car flash by, then he was entering the intersection, at the same moment as the Audi. The shooter was leaning out of the front passenger window, still firing. With the lives of his family, as well as others, innocent bystanders who might be hit by a stray bullet, in the balance, Jim didn't hesitate. He broadsided the car at full speed, sending the Audi into a spin, then a tumbling roll.

Jim caught a quick glimpse of the shooter being

knocked half out of the Audi before the hood crumpled and the airbag in the Dodge deployed, knocking his hat from his head and blocking his vision. The Dodge skidded sideways, then came to rest on the low concrete median divider on the other side of Congress Street. Jim wasn't certain but that he might have blacked out for a moment or two from the impact. He shook his head to clear his vision, unbuckled his seat belt, then tried to force open the driver's door. When it refused to budge, he took out his pistol, smashed out the window with the gun's butt, and went through the window frame feet first.

The Audi was lying on its roof, wrapped around the base of a large billboard in front of the Auto Show Place used car dealership. Flames were licking from under the hood.

Gun in hand, Jim raced up to the car. Its roof was crushed, the right-side doors jammed shut, the left inaccessible. What was left of the shooter was lying half out of the car, his body mangled and bloodied. He was obviously beyond help.

Jim took a fast look through the shattered windshield. The driver was hanging upside down, held in place by his seat belt, bloodied and unconscious, quite possibly already dead. Jim shoved his gun back in its holster, ran to the back of the car, then began tugging on the rear passenger's door. Two passersby rushed up to assist him.

"I don't think we can get it open before this thing explodes!" one of them shouted, in Spanish. "We'd better get away from it pronto."

Jim answered in Spanish.

"This isn't Hollywood. Cars don't generally explode like in the movies, they just burn. Keep tryin' to get this door open."

An Austin patrol unit rolled up to the scene. The two officers inside jumped out and hurried to Jim's aid.

"We'll give you a hand, Ranger," one of them said. "We've already called for fire and EMS."

"Don't worry about the one *hombre*, he's already finished. Try'n get the driver out of this thing," Jim said. "If he's still alive, and recovers, he'll be placed under arrest. Let's hope he does, because he's probably the only answer as to who's behind all this. I've got to check on my wife, baby, and mother. These bastards were tryin' to kill 'em. Let me borrow your car."

"Sure thing, Ranger."

Jim jumped into the Austin unit. Once Kim realized she was no longer being chased, she had pulled into the filling station at the corner of South Congress and Ainsworth Street, two blocks south. Another Austin police unit was parked behind her car. The two officers were standing outside Kim's bullet-riddled SUV. They nodded to Jim when he got out of the car after he drove up.

"Your family's fine, Ranger, especially considering what they went through," one of them said. "They're more worried about you. There's an EMS unit on the way to check them over, just to make certain they're not injured."

Kim jumped out of her car and threw herself into Jim's arms. Now that the danger was over, she broke down, sobbing.

"Take it easy, Kim." Jim tried to soothe her. "It's all over. You're safe. All of us are."

"Are you all right, Jim?" she asked.

"It's all in a day's work," Jim answered, with a nonchalance he certainly didn't feel. A peace officer was supposed to keep his emotions in check, but when someone was trying to kill his family, that was impossible. Jim was shaking inside. His mother came around the car, carrying Josh. She placed the baby in Jim's arms.

"He's just fine, Jim. Not even a scratch. In fact, he slept through almost the entire thing."

"Ranger, what happened here?" the other officer asked.

"That's what we're gonna have to find out," Jim answered. "Since me and my family are involved, I'm not gonna be able to take charge of the investigation. I'll need one of you to call Company F, since my cell phone's back in what's left of my car. Give them a quick idea of what happened, and tell them to send one of the Rangers who cover Austin or Travis County down here, and also Lieutenant Stoker. If they want to talk to me, put me on your phone."

"Right away, Ranger," the officer answered. "You might want to sit down until EMS arrives. You're looking a bit shaky."

"I'll do that as soon as I see what happened to the men who were chasing my family," Jim answered. He handed Josh to Kim, and gave her a quick kiss on the cheek.

"Honey, I'll be back in a few minutes," he said. "I just want to see if the driver is able to talk. The shooter's already dead. He won't be trying to kill anyone ever again, at least not this side of Hell. You try and take it easy until then."

"I will, but are you certain you aren't hurt?" she answered. "You look like you've been burned."

"That's just from the air bag going off when I rammed that Audi," Jim said. "It's no worse than a bad sunburn. I'm fine. Let me get goin', so I can get back here quick as I can. Ma, keep an eye on her for me."

"I will," Betty assured him.

"Good. See y'all in a bit."

Jim got back into his borrowed car and returned to the wrecked Audi. By now, it was almost fully engulfed in flames. More police units were converging on the scene. Two engines from the Austin Fire Department had arrived, and were charging their hoses. A few moments later, two streams of water were dousing the flames, the thick black smoke from the burning vehicle turning into clouds of white steam. A random thought crossed Jim's mind.

"It looks like the Church has just elected a new Pope."

He shook his head and chuckled, then, exhausted now that the tension of the chase was over and his family was safe, slumped against the side of his borrowed, wrecked car and sighed. A voice he recognized as that of Division Commander Eliezer Montalvo from the Austin police called to him.

"Jim, what the devil happened here?"

After getting an initial statement from Jim, Montalvo had insisted he be checked over for injuries. When Jim protested in no uncertain terms, Montalvo turned to Jim's wife. While the Austin officer couldn't overrule Jim's objections, Kim certainly could, and did, so Jim was sitting on the back bumper of an ambulance, with his tie removed and shirt open, while an EMT held a stethoscope to his chest, when Ranger Sean Jordan arrived.

"Howdy, Jim," Sean said. "It seems you've caused a little excitement."

"I didn't start it, I just finished it," Jim answered. "I appreciate your getting here so quick, Sean. You're gonna have a lot to unravel."

"So I understand," Sean said. "Where's your family? Are they all right?"

"They're with one of the Austin units," Jim answered. "They're probably doin' better'n I am."

"Then they must be just fine," the EMT said. "I can't find anything wrong with you, Ranger, except for the burn you got from the airbag, and the bump on your head where you hit it on your car's roof. Your blood pressure's just a bit higher than normal for a man your age, and your pulse is a little fast, but that's both to be expected under the circumstances. All you really need is some rest. I *am* sure you'll be feeling a lot of bumps and bruises come morning."

"I told Kim and Eli this would be a waste of time. I was right." Jim stood up and began buttoning his shirt. "C'mon, Sean, let's start seein' if we can get started to the bottom of this. Is Lieutenant Stoker on his way?"

"He is. He should be here in about forty-five minutes to an hour. He was down in Seguin when the call came in. If you don't mind, I'd like to hold my questions until he gets here."

"Not at all," Jim said. He tucked his shirt back in, then picked up his tie and knotted it back around his neck. "I've gotta retrieve my hat. It's in my car. It sure wouldn't do to not be dressed to code when the lieutenant shows up."

"You're right. He *is* a stickler for that," Sean

agreed, with a soft laugh. "Once you've done that, I'll get started processing the bad guys' car, if it's cooled off enough to let me work it."

"There won't be much left to work with. What about the driver?"

"Montalvo told me he's crispy as well-done bacon," Sean answered. "So's the shooter. They were pinned so tight Austin FD couldn't pull either one of them out."

"So they're both toast."

"Burnt toast. It's gonna be one helluva job I.D.'n those *hombres*."

"You mind if I watch? I'd particularly like to know if that car had Michelin tires on it."

"Hell, don't just watch, you can lend a hand. With all these witnesses around, no one'll be able to claim we tampered with the evidence."

"Appreciate that."

Once they reached the twisted, melted remains of the Audi, it was still smoking, and it would be another hour at least before Sean could start processing it, a fire department lieutenant told him. The Austin police had set up a blue tarp around the vehicle, to shield it and the bodies inside from curious spectators.

"Are any of the tires left on it, Sid?" Jim asked the fire lieutenant.

"As a matter of fact, the left rear is still there. It's even still inflated. That and the left rear fender are about the only parts left."

"Sean, I just want to take a quick look, and see what kind of tire that is," Jim said. "Do you mind, Sid?"

"Not at all. Just be careful."

"Obliged. Sean, let's check that tire."

The two Rangers walked behind the tarp.

"Damn, Jim, you weren't kiddin' when you said there wouldn't be much left."

"It's even worse than I thought," Jim said, glancing at the charred skeleton of the shooter, still pinned in the wreckage. "Let's check that tire."

It only took a moment to examine the tire. It proved to be not a Michelin, but a Hankook.

"That eliminates one theory," Jim said. "This isn't the same car that was at the Huston place. I reckon that probably means those *hombres* weren't the same ones who killed her, unless they switched cars."

"You think whoever's killing those women might've come after you, Jim?"

"It's far-fetched, but possible. It's no secret I'm investigating those murders. Whoever's behind 'em might've decided to kill me and derail that. I know one thing. When I do find out whoever it was who tried to kill my family, they'd better hope the Devil gets to 'em before I do. Going after me is one thing, but my family . . ."

"I'd feel the same way," Sean said.

"Sean, since we can't do anything here for a while, do you mind if I ask you a favor?"

"Not at all. What is it?"

"Would you mind interviewing Kim and my mother before Lieutenant Stoker gets here? I'd hate to keep them hanging around for an hour, maybe longer, especially since they've got my boy with them. He's bound to get tired and cranky. Austin PD has already told me they'd give them a ride home. If the lieutenant has any questions, he can ask those later."

"Not at all. I'd be happy to do that."

"I appreciate it."

Jim's family left right after Sean was through interviewing them, about ten minutes before Lieutenant Stoker arrived on scene. The Audi had cooled to the point where Sean could process it, so Stoker found the two Rangers behind the tarp, going through what was left of the vehicle.

"Sorry it took me so long to get here," he apologized, after greeting Jim and Sean. "Traffic was a mess no matter which route I tried. Jim, it seems you're at it again. I hear you've raised quite a ruckus. You want to tell me about it . . . just the short version, for now."

"Sure, Lieutenant. I was on my way back from court in Johnson City when my wife called me. She said she was being followed. Why she called me first, instead of 911, I have no idea.

You'll have to ask her. I told her to do a couple of maneuvers to make certain she was being followed, and sure enough, she was. It turns out it was a good thing she called me first, anyway, because neither Austin PD nor the Highway Patrol had any units close enough to help . . . at least, none closer than I was.

"I started heading this way, and notified DPS dispatch. By the time I got off the radio with them, shots were being fired at my wife's car. At least a couple of them hit it, but luckily, none struck any of my family. Even with my ma shooting back at them, those bastards wouldn't quit."

"Hold on just a minute, Jim. Your *mother* was shooting back at the men chasing her and your wife?"

"Of course, lieutenant. She's a Texas woman, the widow of a Ranger. You didn't think she'd go around unarmed, did you? Kim would have been shooting at those sons of bitches too, but she was too busy driving. They sure weren't not gonna fight back."

Stoker shook his head.

"It's not just the men in your family, but the women, too. Unbelievable. Continue with your story."

"Hold on just a minute, Lieutenant." An Austin policeman came around the tarp. He carried a large paper sack, and a cardboard tray filled with cans of soda. "The Perfect Chick up the road sent a whole mess of fried chicken and all the fixin's for us. They've set up a table by the mobile command unit. Commander Montalvo knew y'all'd be busy, so he had me bring some over to you. Jim, I've brought what I know you needed most."

He handed Jim two ice cold cans of Dr Pepper, and the sack to Sean.

"You're a lifesaver, Bill," Jim said. "I'm more'n a touch parched."

"Tell Commander Montalvo we appreciate it," Stoker said. "Jim, you can finish your story, then we'll eat."

"There's not much left to tell in the short version. I saw Kim's car go by, then I entered the intersection at the same time as the men chasing her. I knew they had to be stopped, and right then, before my family or anyone else got hurt. So I slammed into their car. I blacked out for just a minute, I think. When I came to, I had to break the window to get out of my car, since the doors were jammed shut. The Audi had rolled over, hit that pole, and caught fire. A couple of men tried to help me pull the shooter and driver out of the car, then two Austin police officers, but we couldn't do it. The shooter was already dead anyway, and the driver probably was, too."

Stoker sighed.

"I can see it's gonna be a long rest of the day,"

he said. "Where's your wife and mother now?"

"I sent them home, Lieutenant," Sean answered for Jim. "While I was waiting for this car to cool so I could start processing it, I questioned them both, so there was no need to keep them here. After you read my notes, if you have any further questions for them, you can call them."

"That's fine," Stoker said. "Let's take a couple of minutes to eat, then get back to work. Jim . . ."

"I know. I can't take part in the investigation. I've just been watching Sean work. With your permission, I'd like to continue to do so."

"I don't see where it will do any harm," Stoker said.

"*Gracias*. I'm obliged."

Several hours later, all the evidence gathering at the scene had been done. The remains of the would-be killers had been removed from their wrecked and burned car, and taken to the morgue for autopsies and identification. Lieutenant Stoker had finished questioning Jim. The Audi and Kim's Equinox were being loaded on flatbeds, to be taken to the DPS garage to be examined. Another flatbed driver was hooking up the wrecked Dodge Jim had been driving.

"So far, we've got practically nothing," Sean said. "Those Virginia plates on the Audi came back to Hertz. I'll have to find out where the car was rented, and by who."

"Whom." Jim said.

"All right, *whom*. It probably won't matter anyway. I'll guarantee it was rented under a false name and address. That means more digging."

"It's time to wrap things up for tonight, and start fresh in the morning. Jim, I'll give you a lift home," Stoker said.

"You don't have to, Lieutenant," Jim answered. "My truck's ready. I was on my way to pick it up when all hell broke loose. All I need's a ride back to the DPS garage."

"You've got it," Stoker said. He shook his head. "I can just imagine what Jake will say when he sees what you did to that car."

Jim looked at the two men loading up the wrecked Dodge.

"Hey, hold on just a minute!" he yelled. "Sean, Lieutenant, be right back. I've gotta get some things out of the trunk."

Jim hurried over to the Dodge. The keys to the car were jammed in the broken ignition, so he had no way to open the trunk.

"One of you boys got a prybar or tire iron?" he asked.

"We sure do, Ranger," the flatbed driver answered. "You need that trunk popped?"

"That's exactly what I need."

"Not a problem. It'll only take a minute."

The driver got a prybar out of his toolbox, jammed one end under the lip of the Dodge's trunk, then pushed down on the other end. The trunk easily popped open.

"Thanks," Jim said. He reached into the trunk and took out the cartons containing his purchases from Johnson City.

"You did good today, ol' gal," he told the Dodge, patting its left rear fender. "At least you went out with a bang."

"That's all you wanted?" the driver said.

"Sure is. Seems like the stuff inside might have somehow survived this wreck. Thanks, men."

"Not a problem, Ranger."

"What's in those boxes that's so all-fired important, Jim?" Stoker asked.

"A few things I picked up in Johnson City for Kim and my mother," Jim answered. "A couple for me, too. I sure hope they're still okay."

Commander Montalvo walked over to join them.

"Jameson," he said to Stoker, "we can take care of what's left here, if you boys want to head for home. About all that's still got to be done is finishing loading Jim's car, and sweeping up the debris. You don't need to hang around for that."

"We appreciate that, Eli. If you need anything, don't hesitate to call. Sean or myself will probably talk to you tomorrow. Good night."

"Good night, men."

As they walked to their cars, Stoker spoke to Jim.

"I'm about to say something you don't want to hear," he said. "Don't say anything until you hear me out. I want you, no, I'm ordering you to take the rest of the week off. I'll clear it with Major Voitek. I'm certain he'll agree. Hold on just one damn minute, and let me finish," he said, when Jim started to protest. "I'm not suspending you, or putting you on administrative leave. You had to stop those bastards, any way you could, and you did. But you've been through a lot today. You've got a ton of personal and sick time accumulated, and I want you to take some of it to spend time with your family, not to mention get some much-needed rest for yourself and recharge your batteries. You can come back to work on Monday."

"I can't take the time, Lieutenant," Jim answered. "Someone out there is tryin' to kill me, and they damn near killed my wife and baby today, not to mention my mother. I can't just sit around and let whoever's behind this take another run at me again. I've got a hunch it's whoever's running the drug operation out of New Braunfels and Kendalia I busted up, and if it is, they sure ain't gonna give up. I might've put a dent in their operation, but they sure aren't out of business, not by a long shot."

"It could be someone completely different, someone you put in jail in the past, or someone who just wants to take out a Ranger, Jim," Sean pointed out. "They just happened to pick you."

"I doubt that, and you don't believe it either. You remember I said those sons of bitches on the motorcycles were tryin' to kill me, but the Austin PD disagreed. Well, after today, I'm more certain than ever that's exactly what happened. Besides, I've got the two big cases I'm working on, plus all my others that are backlogged. I can't just walk away from 'em."

"I'm not asking you to walk away from them," Stoker said. "But you need to step back for a spell. Sometimes a few days' rest will bring a new perspective. You might come up with something you've overlooked. You've been pushing hard, real hard."

"No harder than any other Ranger."

"I'm not going to argue with you, Jim. You're worn out, you're probably hurt worse than you realize, and no matter how tough your wife and mother are, right now they need you more than the Rangers do. Take the time, and if I need anything from you, or if anything develops on any of your cases, I'll call you. Another thing. I'm going to have a state trooper guard your house until we get to the bottom of this."

"Now you've gone too far, Lieutenant," Jim said.

"I don't believe I have. Once you fully realize what happened today, you won't, either."

"All right, I reckon you're leaving me no

choice. Just don't assign a handsome young fella. In fact, assign a woman."

"You mean you think your wife might fall for another man?"

"Not my wife. My ma."

"Now I *know* you need the time off." Stoker laughed. "Let's go get your truck so you can make it home before you fall asleep behind the wheel. Sean, have a good night."

"As long as my wife understands. It's hard to explain to your woman why you get home late five days out of six."

"Mykeisha will be fine. Don't forget, she's a peace officer too."

"Yeah, a county deputy in a small town. Maybe we should trade places."

"There's not a chance of that. Mykeisha's too intelligent," Jim answered, laughing, then yawning. "I guess you're right, Lieutenant. I'm plumb exhausted."

"Now you're making sense, Jim. Let's go home."

11

Logan Daniels stared at his television in disbelief. He was watching the KXAN ten o'clock news. With every word of the reporter, he muttered another curse. Reporter Heather Ramirez was standing at the intersection of South Congress and Stassney.

"Good evening," Ramirez said. "Earlier today, chaos erupted along a stretch of South Congress Avenue, culminating here at its intersection with Stassney Lane. Details are still coming in, but we do know that two men, who were allegedly chasing and shooting at another vehicle, are dead. This is the scene from earlier today. I must warn our viewers that some of the video is graphic, and may be disturbing."

The image changed to Ramirez, at almost the same location, earlier that day. Behind her was the ambulance with Jim sitting on its back bumper while the EMT examined him.

"A dangerous chase took place today on some of the busiest streets in Austin. The situation is still unfolding, but we can tell you that apparently, a vehicle containing two men was involved in a chase and shooting with another vehicle, which held two women and an infant. The chase ended when a Texas Ranger, who you see behind me being checked for injuries by Austin EMS, stopped the chase by deliberately crashing into the men's car just north of here, at the intersection of South Congress Avenue and Stassney Lane. KXAN is about to show you exclusively some amateur video of the conclusion of the chase. Warning: the images are extremely graphic, and may be upsetting to some viewers."

The image changed again, to a shaky video taken from a cell phone. The reporter narrated the video as it played.

"You can see the blue SUV, with its back window shot out, the men were allegedly chasing speed by, then the green vehicle pursuing it, with the apparent gunman leaning out of the passenger window. Then, a black vehicle, which we have learned was driven by the Texas Ranger you just saw, deliberately broadsides the car, which then rolls over and catches fire. The two men are trapped in the vehicle. You can see the apparent gunman lying half out of the vehicle. In a moment, you'll see the Ranger and another man attempt to free him. The video then stops, as the witness also went to assist the Ranger. His name is Matthew Birnbaum, and this is what he had to say . . ."

"I heard gunshots, then more than one vehicle moving very fast, then a siren. I saw the first two vehicles coming south on Congress at a high rate of speed, so I took out my phone and started recording, then I saw the black police car crash into the green car. As soon as the officer in the black car freed himself, me and another man went to help him, but there wasn't anything we could do."

"We have some more images from the scene," Ramirez continued. The screen showed the fire department extinguishing the burning Audi, the arrival of several Austin police units, and Kim's shot-up Equinox. The station had blurred Jim's family's faces. "As you can see, there was an extremely heavy police response. The entire area around South Congress and Stassney has been placed on lockdown, with both roads, as well as the side roads in the vicinity, closed. Traffic is snarled for miles. Austin Police advises us they have no idea when the scene will be cleared and the roads reopened, but that the investigation will take at least several hours."

The image once again returned to a live shot of the reporter.

"We have received some additional information from the Texas Rangers, which they emphasized is very preliminary, as they are still early in their investigation, along with the Austin Police Department. According to their spokesperson, who did not wish to be named at this time, the bodies of the two men who died in the crash have been taken to the medical examiner's office for autopsies and identification. According to the Rangers, the men were burned beyond recognition, so determining who they were will be a time-consuming process.

"They have also told us about an unusual twist to this entire event. The two women allegedly being chased were Kimberly Tavares Blawcyzk and Elizabeth Barrett Blawcyzk. They are the wife and mother, respectively, of Texas Ranger James C. Blawcyzk of Company F. With them was the Blawcyzks' six-month-old infant son.

"From what has been determined so far, Mrs. Blawcyzk realized she was being followed, and called her husband, who then notified Austin PD and Texas DPS. Evidently, Ranger Blawcyzk happened to be the police officer nearest the location where all this took place, and it was he who ended the chase by deliberately crashing into the alleged assailants' car. Needless to say, there will be many further developments in this case. KXAN will be following the situation closely, and will bring you updates as soon as they become available. Back to you, Beth and Josh."

"Thank you, Heather," Beth Jennings said. "In other news . . ."

Daniels switched off the television, picked up his cell phone, and called Tarquin Sarkanian.

"Hello, Logan."

"Tarquin, you son of a bitch, did you see tonight's news?"

"You mean the bit of excitement they had over by Garrison Park and South Austin today?

271

I've been following that since this afternoon."

"That was more than just a *bit of excitement*. You said Blawcyzk would be dead by now. Instead, he's still alive, and unless I'm a total idiot, he's mad as hell. I assume what happened today was your doing?"

"Indirectly, yes," Sarkanian admitted.

"That's twice you've screwed up, Tarquin. First the motorcycles, and now this. What do I tell my bosses?"

"Tell them to be patient, Logan. I've never failed you yet, have I?"

"No, but it looks like you're comin' awful damn close with this damn Ranger. What happened today? How could you go after his damn wife and kid? You'd better have a good explanation."

"Let's go back to the motorcycles for a moment, Logan. How the hell was I supposed to know that any damn horse, even a police horse, would stand and hold its ground, rather than spooking and throwing its rider, with half-a-dozen crazed bikers coming after it? No one could have foreseen that. And I've already told you, if they happen to be caught, which I doubt, none of the men I hired will talk. Even if they do, they have no way to figure out who I am, let alone you or your employers.

"Now, as far as what happened today, the only explanation I have is the men I used for this attempt got the wrong car. I gave them the information on Blawcyzk's car, a dark blue Chevy Tahoe SUV. His wife's car, from what I could determine by looking at the pictures on the news, is also a blue Chevy SUV. They followed the wrong one, that's all."

"You're trying to tell me those damn fools couldn't tell one car from another? And Blawcyzk wasn't even in an SUV, but a black sedan. Even worse, they didn't realize they were following two women? What were they, two damn queers, who didn't know the difference between boobs and—"

"Let's not speak ill of the dead, Logan," Sarkanian broke in. "Yes, today was a mistake, a big one. I won't deny that. Let's make it right. We start by looking at the positive. First of all, if Blawcyzk is, as you say, mad as hell, he's liable to get careless. That'll make it easier to get to him."

"He's liable to be more damn cautious, knowing someone is trying to kill him, is what he's liable to be. Not to mention every other damn Ranger in the state will be watching his back."

"Yes, but when the new bait is dangled in front of him, especially if he thinks his family is still in danger, that's when he'll get careless. Let me finish, Logan.

"Second, there is absolutely, positively no way those men can be traced. The car was a rental, and they had false identification and used a counterfeit credit card. From what I gathered, the

Rangers will have a hard time identifying them, even with dental records. Even a DNA match will be almost impossible. We have no worries on that account."

"Except Blawcyzk's still alive, and if you don't take care of him soon, I won't be, Tarquin. That means you'll never see the rest of your money. And before I die, I'll make certain my employers know it was you responsible for Blawcyzk not being in Hell."

"Take it easy, Logan. Your threats are meaningless. As you're well aware, attempting to kill me would be a damn big mistake.

"Second, have you forgotten I always guarantee my work, or my client gets a full refund? Let's turn our attention to the two immediate problems. First, Blawcyzk. Yes, I'll admit, taking him out is going to be a bit more difficult than I envisioned. However, the job will get done. Next, how to mollify your employers. We start by assuring them I won't quit until the job is complete. I'm not going to charge you the expenses for the bikers, or today."

"You'd have a damn lot of nerve if you did, Tarquin."

"Since I'm not, that isn't an issue, is it? As far as the delay, think of all this as foreplay. The longer it lasts, the sweeter and more satisfying is the climax."

"You're a damn smooth talker, Tarquin. If I

hadn't worked with you before, I'd tell you to go to Hell right now."

"I know you won't be that hasty, considering what I know about you, and could take to the authorities, Logan. Merely assure your employers that I am going to handle Blawcyzk personally this time. If that isn't enough to satisfy them, then I'll keep my advance, and instead of the Ranger I'll kill *you,* Logan. But before you die—slowly, and in great pain—you'll tell me who your employers are, and then I'll kill them, too. Is that clear, Logan?"

"Perfectly, you bastard. I guess I've got no choice."

"I knew you'd listen to reason. As far as my legitimacy, you're more correct than you realize. I never did know who my father was. Good night, Logan."

Daniels' phone went dead. He cursed Sarkanian one more time, then got up and took a bottle of Scotch from the cupboard. He uncorked the bottle and took a long pull.

After he hung up, Sarkanian slumped back in his chair. Blawcyzk, no matter what he had told Daniels, was going to be far more of a problem than he'd imagined. He had to put together a foolproof plan, and soon. He needed to choose his resources more carefully to complete this assignment.

12

"Jim, are you sleeping?" Kim asked, later that night.

"Just about," Jim answered. "Why?"

"I don't know how you can sleep after what happened today. We have to talk."

"If I couldn't sleep every time I was involved in something like that, especially when I was still a state trooper, since chases happened more often back then, I'd never get any sleep. Hard as it might seem to believe, especially right now, it's actually far safer to be a Ranger than a trooper. We aren't on the front lines every day like troopers are."

"You're missing my point. I never imagined someone coming after me, or Josh," Kim said. "Does being a Ranger mean so much to you that you don't care about your family's safety?"

"That's not fair, Kim. You knew I was a Texas Ranger when you married me, the latest in a long family line of Rangers. We went over everything that means, including the dangers—even, yes, that there could be a slight possibility someone would try to get to me through you. Unfortunately, it happened. I'm not downplaying what took place today. You don't know how scared I was during the whole thing, until I stopped those men, and knew you, Josh, and my ma were all safe.

"I was honest with you before I gave you the ring, and told you I'd never want to be anything but a Ranger. You said you understood, and all that mattered was our love for each other. I hope you're not asking me to choose between you and the Rangers right now."

"I don't know what I'm asking you to do," Kim answered. "All I know is I'm scared for all of us, and that if you weren't a damn Ranger, none of this would have happened."

"But something just as bad might have. None of us can hide from life, honey. Besides, we're probably the safest family in the state right now. We've got a state trooper guarding us, if you need to go anywhere that trooper will accompany you, plus both you and Ma have guns, and know exactly how to use them. Don't forget, Frostie will warn us if anyone's coming onto our land. And whoever's behind this will be caught. You can count on it. The Rangers won't rest until they are. Just because I'm home until Monday doesn't mean I won't be working on this case, too. I've got my computer and my phone. That's all I need to keep digging."

"I know all that, Jim, but I'm still worried. In fact, let's not talk about this anymore, at least for tonight. I'm so upset I might become angry and say something I don't mean. I've also got a full day tomorrow, and on top of that, now I have to call the insurance company, then arrange for a rental car."

"You wouldn't be human if you weren't worried," Jim assured her. "I'll be home the next four days, so if you still want, we can talk about this some more after we get some sleep. C'mere."

Jim took Kim in his arms. She snuggled close to him.

"This is all we need right now. Each other, and sleep."

They kissed each other good night, then fell asleep in each other's arms.

Despite his objections the previous day, Jim was grateful Lieutenant Stoker had insisted on posting a state trooper at the entrance to his ranch. He wasn't overly worried about whoever had tried to kill his family making another attempt, at least not this soon, but the trooper was able to prevent the many media reporters wanting to talk to Jim or his family from accessing the Blawcyzk property, saving Jim that chore. He made several phone calls before reaching the person he needed to speak with most.

"Howdy, Jerry. It's Jim," he said, when the party on the other end answered. "You busy today?"

"Hello, Jim. I had a feeling I'd hear from you today. I've got a meeting scheduled this morning, but nothing this afternoon that can't be pushed off."

"That's great. How about we go to the gym for some racquetball, then a swim and the sauna or steam room? It's been too long since we both worked up a good sweat."

"That sounds like a fine idea," Jerry Golden agreed. "Say around two o'clock? I'll call and reserve a court."

"I'll see you then."

Jim started for Kim's office to let her know he would be gone for most of the afternoon, but she was in the kitchen, getting a cup of coffee when he came in from the deck.

"Who was that on the phone?" she asked.

"Jerry Golden. I'm going to meet him at the gym. Maybe a good game of racquetball will help clear my head. That is, if you don't mind."

"Not at all. Things seem far less scarier in the daytime than they do at night. I have to wait here anyway, since the rental car company can't deliver my car until this afternoon. In fact, some strenuous exercise will probably do you some good. Whether you want to admit it or not, you're still tense from yesterday. I can sense it. So, go ahead, have a good time. I'll be just fine."

"You're a Texas woman, all right, through and through," Jim told her, then kissed her on the cheek. "If your rental hasn't come before I leave, I'll tell the trooper out front to make certain to check both drivers' credentials real carefully, before she lets them in."

"All right. I hear your mother calling me. She must have my conference call ready. Do you mind making supper tonight?"

"Not at all. Something simple. Burgers and dogs on the grill?"

"That's fine with me. I'll see you later, cowboy."

At quarter-to-two, Jim pulled his battered ten-year-old Chevy Silverado pickup into the front lot of the Austin Men's Fitness Club. The facility was an upscale establishment, and included, in addition to the usual treadmills, cardio, and weight equipment, several racquetball and handball courts, an Olympic sized pool, as well as steam rooms and saunas.

Whenever he went to the gym, Jim almost always took his old pickup, which looked completely out of place amongst the variety of luxury cars which dominated the lot. He loved watching the rich young professionals, who were the majority of the club's members, look askance at his faded, once-blue-but-now-gray, dented old truck.

Today, some of them gave him an especially disdainful look as he parked the truck, since he'd stopped at the feed store on the way, and the pickup was loaded with hay. He noted with satisfaction that Jerry's dark silver Cadillac

Escalade was already parked in the second row. He got out of his truck, took the duffel bag containing his gym clothes from the pickup's passenger seat, then headed inside.

"Good afternoon, Ranger Blawcyzk," the clerk behind the desk greeted him.

"Afternoon, Bert. I saw Mr. Golden's car outside."

"Yes, sir, he said to tell you he'd be waiting for you in the locker room."

"All right. Thanks, Bert."

Jim headed down the hallway and into the locker room. Quite a number of other members were there, changing from street clothes as they prepared to work out, or toweling off from showering after finishing their exercise.

Jerome Golden was sitting at the end of a bench in front of his locker, pulling on his gym shorts and a University of Texas T-shirt. Jerry was about two years older than Jim. He stood five-foot-eleven, almost half a foot shorter than Jim's six-foot-four, and blockier, weighing close to one hundred ninety pounds, but was by no means fat. He had wavy, dark brown hair and eyes a lighter shade of the same hue. He and his wife, Esther, owned a medium-sized pharmaceuticals distribution company.

Three years previously, the Goldens had been arrested and convicted for illegally distributing prescription drugs, as well as over the counter medications used to manufacture illegal substances such as methamphetamines. In a plea deal, they had received no prison time except that already served, just a heavy fine and probation, and were allowed to keep their business. What the public didn't know was the plea deal included Jerry becoming an informant for the lawman who had arrested them. That lawman was Jim Blawcyzk.

Both Jerry and his wife had stayed true to the terms of their probation. Jerry had provided valuable information that allowed Jim or the Austin police to make several major drug busts. Over the past two years, what started as Jim and Jerry's partnership of necessity had turned into friendship.

"Jim, there you are," Jerry said, when he saw him walking down the row between lockers. "I arrived here a few minutes early."

"So did I," Jim answered. "Is the court free, or are we gonna have to wait a while?"

"No, it's waiting for us," Jerry answered. "Soon as you've changed, we can get started."

Jim unlocked his locker, then took off his Texas A & M baseball cap and peeled out of his Cowboys Unlimited Live Free or Die T-shirt. Jerry finished tying his sneakers and stood up. He gave Jim a backhanded slap to the belly.

"Are you ready to get beaten badly again, buddy?" he asked.

"Not a chance, pal," Jim said. "You're gonna lose so bad you'll think you got caught up in a Texas tornado."

"I don't suppose you'd care to make a bet on that?"

"Why not? Loser buys the drinks."

"You're on."

Jim and Jerry played three games of racquetball, with Jim winning two out of three.

"Looks like you're buyin' the drinks today, Jerry," Jim said, as he wiped the sweat off his forehead.

"Seems so. I'd make it double or nothing racing in the pool, but I know I'm nowhere near as fast as you in the water," Jerry said. "Let's go cool off."

After swimming laps for an hour, the two men went back to the locker room, removed their swim trunks, and wrapped towels around their waists.

"Which do you prefer today, Jim, the sauna or the steam room?" Jerry asked.

"The steam room, if it's not too crowded," Jim answered. "The eucalyptus oil does wonders for my sinuses."

"That's fine with me."

They headed down the corridor which led to the saunas and steam rooms. The saunas had six men each already lounging in them, one steam room was also full, but the other held only one man, who was just leaving.

"Hey, Russ. How hot's it in there today?" Jerry asked him.

"It's plenty damn hot," Russ Tambor answered, holding the door open for them. "Almost as hot as Houston. You'd better not spend too much time in there."

"Appreciate the advice," Jim answered. He and Jerry stepped into the steam-filled room, which was heavy with the pleasant scent of eucalyptus. They spread their towels out on the lower bench, sat down and leaned back. Sweat began oozing from their every pore.

"Okay, Jim, you didn't ask me to come here just for some exercise," Jerry said. "Now, since no one can hear our conversation, what are you after? I think I've already got a good idea."

"If you saw the news yesterday, then you know exactly what I'm after. I want the damn son of a bitch who's responsible for trying to kill my whole family. Have you heard anything?"

"I hear lots of things," Jerry said, with a shrug. "Nothing really specific, though. Have you got any inkling of who you think it is?"

"I've got plenty of ideas, but right now I'm thinking it has to be whoever's behind the operation that was running out of New Braunfels."

"Ah, yes. I did hear the persons who control that enterprise were quite upset when you intercepted their shipment, to put it mildly. In fact, damn mad as hell would be a more accurate description."

"But you don't know who those persons might be."

"I can't exactly come right out and ask now, can I? Russ was right. It *is* hotter than usual in here today. Even the steam's so damn thick I can barely see you from over here, and I'm only two feet away. It's a bit hard to breathe, too."

Jerry got up and turned on the cold water shower. He stood under it to let the water run down his overheated skin.

"I have heard that it's a local operation, based right here in the Austin area. But that's all. Have you come up with anything?"

"Not so far. I've done a lot of digging through a lot of paperwork, but it's just been leading me in circles. Shell company after shell company. As near as I can tell, the operation has set up a main office in the Caymans. You know that's probably nothing more than a post office box and a bank account. Stop hoggin' that shower so I can cool off a bit, too."

"All right."

Jerry moved aside so Jim could drench himself with the cold water. Once he was sufficiently cooled, Jim sat back down.

"Telling me it's a local operation doesn't help much, Jerry. You haven't heard more?"

"Not at all. Just enough to confirm your suspicions could be right."

"Okay, I'll take your word. You'll let me know if you hear anything else, won't you?"

"Of course, Jim. I'll make some more discreet enquiries, to see what I can come up with. Listen, I've got to get out of this damn room, and I mean now. Something's not right."

"I'll say it isn't. It's way too hot in here, and the smell sure isn't eucalyptus oil, not anymore," Jim agreed. He also was having trouble breathing, and when he stood up became extremely lightheaded. He staggered into Jerry and nearly fell. Both of them stumbled through the door, then collapsed on two of the chairs in the hallway, pulling in great draughts of fresh air.

Leon, one of the attendants, saw them and hurried over.

"Oh, my goodness. Mr. Golden. Ranger Blawcyzk. What happened?"

"I . . . I dunno," Jim gasped. "The steam room's way too hot. Something's wrong with the air, too."

"Oh, my Lord. Let me get you both some cold towels, then I'll call maintenance. Do either of you need an ambulance?"

"No. No, we'll be . . . just fine, Leon, now that we're out of there," Jerry answered.

"Very good, Mr. Golden."

Leon picked up four iced towels from a stand in the alcove nearest the steam room. He placed one on each man's head, then spread out the others and draped those over their bodies.

"I'll fetch someone from maintenance right now."

"You don't have to. I'm already here, Leon," Pat Foley, one of the maintenance men, said from behind him. "Russ Tambor told me he suspected there was a malfunction with the steam room, so I came to post it closed while I checked. It appears he was right."

"He sure was," Jim said. "It got way too hot, real fast, and there's something wrong with the air, to boot. It's almost as if it was filled with carbon monoxide, that's how hard it was to breath. Smells like sulfur in there, too. Don't go inside until you're certain the air is safe."

"I won't, Ranger Blawcyzk. Are you and Mr. Golden all right?"

"We are now," Jim said. "We just need to catch our breath a bit more, and cool off. We'll take a cold shower. That should take care of things."

"As long as you're certain. I'll let you both know what malfunctioned as soon as I figure it out."

"We appreciate that, Patrick."

Once they had their strength back, Jim and Jerry showered, dried, and redressed. As they crossed the parking lot, Jerry asked, in little more than a whisper, "Jim, you don't think someone deliberately tampered with the system for that room, to try and kill us both?"

"That had crossed my mind," Jim answered. "However, I don't think so. The only one who knew I was coming here was my wife. Did you tell anyone where you were headed?"

"Only my secretary, and my wife."

"Then no one but them knew when we'd be here, so it would be hard for someone to have time enough to fiddle with the system. Also, Russ Tambor said the room seemed to be running hot when he came out of it. Unless Pat turns up something suspicious, I'd say whatever happened was probably just an accident. Coincidence, but an accident."

"But you can't be certain."

"No, I can't be, which means you need to be careful too, Jerry. Now, where are we going for those drinks?"

"Right across the street, to the South Side Sports Bar," Jerry said. "I would have chosen the Goose and Gander, but that's a little too snobbish for the way you're dressed. Besides, they'll be showing a rerun of a Cowboys game at the South Side. They know us both there, too. And for a sports bar their selection of liquor is quite extensive."

"That's fine with me," Jim said.

A few minutes later, they were standing at the bar.

"What're you boys having today?" Josie, the raven-haired, full-figured young bartender, asked them.

"Chivas Regal, on the rocks," Jerry requested.

"Of course. A long neck Lone Star for you as usual, Jim?"

"Not today." Jim shook his head. "Jerry's buying. I'll have a Zubrowka Bison Grass Vodka please, Josie. Make it a double."

"That stuff's awfully potent," Josie warned him. "It's imported all the way from Poland. They make it really strong."

"My ancestors were imported from Poland, too," Jim answered, smiling. "I can handle it."

"All right."

Once they had their drinks, Jerry lifted his glass.

"To your health, Jim," he said.

"Yours too, Jerry," Jim answered, as they clinked glasses. "Right now, I can't think of a more appropriate toast."

13

Late Friday morning, Jim was on the back deck, lying on the glider. Frostie had his head resting on Jim's stomach, while Jim scratched the dog's ears. Both were just lazing away on this warm, humid summer morning. Kim came out to join them. She was carrying a tray of ham and Swiss cheese sandwiches, along with a bag of potato chips, cans of Dr Pepper, and white chocolate chunk macadamia nut cookies, which she placed on the wicker dining table.

"Jim, are you going to just waste the whole day sleeping, or would you at least like to have some lunch?"

"I'm just following Lieutenant Stoker's orders," Jim answered, as he sat up. "Although I suppose I could force myself to eat something. Where's Josh?"

"He was sleepy, so I fed him and put him down for his nap early. This way we can have a nice lunch, just the two of us."

"And Frostie," Jim said, as the dog sniffed at the table, then looked at Jim with pleading eyes. "Don't worry, I'll give you a taste, buddy."

Frostie waved his tail and licked his chops.

Jim sat at the table, then reached for a sandwich, handful of chips, and a soda.

"This will really hit the spot," he said. "I'm glad you took a break from working. I'd love to help you, but I'd be lost. I have no idea how you do what you do."

"It doesn't matter," Kim said. "I love my job as much as you love yours."

"Although it's a lot less stressful."

"I'm not certain. There are times when it can be *really* stressful. Of course, my work doesn't usually involve dead bodies, and bullets coming at me."

"Touché Kim, listen. I've got a great idea for the weekend. Mike Blakely messaged me earlier. He's playing at the dance hall in Luckenbach tomorrow night. Annie's going to be performing with him. We should go. We can spend the weekend in Fredericksburg. We'll take Josh and my mother, and I can watch Josh while you two go shopping. We'll stay at the Hoffman Haus, maybe even get massages. I know I could use a deep tissue massage to get the knots out of my muscles."

"That does sound wonderful, Jim, but I'm so busy. I'm not certain I can take the time."

"Now you sound like me. Let's just forget everything, and do it. We both need to get away."

"All right, you've convinced me," Kim said. "Go ahead, make the reservations. Let Mike and Annie know we'll see them in Luckenbach."

"I already have," Jim said, grinning. "Made our reservations, too. I even talked the B & B into letting us bring Frostie. You'll wear your new earrings, of course."

"Of course I will. I'm still amazed all that glassware survived the crash."

"Anne and Sandy told me they'd pack everything really well. I guess they did."

"Jim, you don't think anyone will try to chase us again, while we're in Fredericksburg, do you?"

"I doubt it. I think, since their last attempt failed, whoever it was wouldn't attempt anything this soon. They probably wouldn't come after anyone but me next time, either. The more I think on it, the more I believe they made a mistake. They thought they were chasing me, but somehow ending up chasing you instead. Once they started, they probably realized their mistake, but were too stupid or too stubborn to stop. Besides, we'll be using your rental car, and they won't know it. We can be certain no one is watching the house, not with the state troopers out front, and extra patrols from the Travis County Sheriff. We'll just forget everything but having a good time. I'll tell Ma as soon as we finish lunch."

At that moment, Jim's cell phone rang. He glanced at its display.

"It's the Austin police, Kim. Maybe they've got something for me."

He picked up the phone.

"Ranger Blawcyzk."

"Jim, hello. It's Commander Cody. I've got some good news for you."

"It's about time someone had some. What have you got, Jack?"

"We might have caught a break. Willie Wiley from Willie's Wild World of Wheels over on San Jacinto had a yellow Suzuki dirt bike with a busted out headlight brought in this morning. The owner wanted it fixed *pronto*. Wiley told him he'd have the bike ready in a couple of hours. As soon as the owner left, he called us. We sent a man down to check the bike, and it has a bullet in the headlight housing, just like you said it would. We've had a John Doe warrant prepared since the day you had the problem. When the owner came back for his bike, we were waiting for him. He's at Headquarters right now, along with his machine. Can you come down and identify the bike? Ask some questions if you want? I've already called Sean Jordan, but he's tied up on another investigation. He said you could stand in for him."

"I'm on my way," Jim said. He hung up the phone.

"Sorry, Kim, Austin PD has a biker who could be one of those who attacked me and Copper. His dirt bike's got a bullet hole in its headlight. I need to go downtown to try and identify it. Be back quick as I can. Can you tell Ma about the trip for me?"

"Certainly. She can use some time away too."

"I knew I married the best gal in all of Texas," Jim said. He gave Kim a quick kiss, started into the house to change clothes, then turned back and grabbed several cookies and another can of Dr Pepper.

"For the road."

Kim just shook her head.

Shift Commander Jonathan "Jack" Cody was waiting for Jim when he walked into Austin Police Headquarters.

"Hello, Jim. It didn't take you long to get here."

"Howdy, Jack. I wasn't doing anything much when you called, just planning a weekend in Fredericksburg with my family."

"That's a real fine idea. How are they?"

"Still a little worried, of course, but they're doing fine, otherwise. Soon as I catch the son of a bitch behind all this, they'll be more at ease."

"Well, perhaps recovering this bike will give you a lead. It's down in the impound lot. I'll take you to look at it before you talk with the owner. He's waiting for his lawyer to show up before he'll let us question him anyway. The lawyer's on his way, so it shouldn't be long."

"Sure. Let's go."

Cody led Jim to the impound lot, where a yellow Suzuki dirt bike was sitting in the front corner, behind a locked gate. Cody unlocked the gate, opened it, and both men went to the motorcycle.

"That's it, Jim. What do you think?"

"It looks like the one I shot at," Jim said. He squatted on his heels to get a better look at the broken headlight and its housing.

"That's definitely where I hit it, too. I purposely aimed not to hit the operator. I can see the bullet's still in there. I'd say this is the bike. A ballistics test will show whether or not that bullet's from my gun. The only question is, will it be too degraded to get an accurate test?"

"I've got my doubts about that, too," Cody said. "Maybe we should try and run a bluff, and see how our suspect reacts."

"That's not a bad idea. Let's try it."

"What's the guy's name?" Jim asked, as they headed back inside.

"One Bobby Lee Martin. He's nineteen, and lives with his family on Tortuga Trail. His address comes back to the biggest waterfront house on the street. Sits right on the river."

Jim whistled.

"Boy howdy! That's some high priced real estate. So the first question is—"

"What's a kid from that neighborhood doing running with a gang of renegade bikers, if he is one of those we're after." Cody finished for him. "I reckon we'll find out. Jorge Ortega's the arresting officer. You know he'll do a thorough job. In here."

Cody opened the door to one of the interrogation rooms. Four men were inside, one, Detective Sergeant Jorge Ortega, the second, a teenager with close-cropped black hair, tattoos covering both his arms, and a surly expression, was clearly Bobby Lee Martin. The man sitting next to him Jim didn't recognize, but assumed it was Martin's father. The fourth man he certainly did recognize, Stanley Vogel, a partner with Hughes, Vogel, and Barnard, one of the most high powered, and expensive, law firms in Austin, which specialized in criminal defense. He and Jim had sparred many times in court. The fact only one of his clients was found not guilty after Jim's testimony had led to a deep-seated antipathy toward the Ranger on Vogel's part.

"Jim, you know Detective Ortega, of course. The young man is our suspect, Bobby Lee Martin. I believe you're acquainted with Stanley Vogel."

"We've met," Vogel said, with a curt nod in Jim's direction.

"I'm Bobby Lee's father, Darrell Martin," the fourth man stated, before being asked. "You've no doubt heard of me. Martin Oil Exploration. And I have to say I don't appreciate my son being arrested. Let's get this farce over with so I can take him home."

"I can't say as I have," Jim answered.

"You can take your boy home all in good time, Mr. Martin," Cody said. "This is Texas Ranger James Blawcyzk. Your son was arrested because several weeks ago, a group of dirt bikers allegedly attempted to run him down, while he was riding his horse in Searight Park. Ranger Blawcyzk was forced to defend himself by firing at the lead rider, who was on a yellow Suzuki. The bullet shattered the bike's headlight. Your son's bike matches the description of that one. That's why we're here. Sergeant, I'll leave you to your questioning now."

"Thanks, Commander. Ranger, pull up a chair. Now that you're here, we can get started. Mr. Vogel, before we continue, I do want to state for the record your client has been read all his rights. He requested to have his legal counsel present, so you were called. He has also agreed to have this session audio and video recorded."

"That's fine, Detective."

"Jim, to bring you up to speed, the younger Mr. Martin has already been advised of the date the alleged incident took place, and the possible charges he is facing. Mr. Martin, do you still say you were not present in Searight Park at the time Ranger Blawcyzk states he was set upon by six bikers?"

"That's right. I've never been in Searight Park in my life. It's against the law to ride bikes or quads in there, you know."

"I'm well aware of that, Mr. Martin. Since you say you weren't at Searight Park that day, can you tell us where you were?"

"I was, I dunno, wait, I took out my boat, and went swimming that afternoon."

"Was anyone with you?"

"No. I wanted to get away by myself for awhile. I planned on meeting friends later."

"Did you see anyone on the river who you recognized, and who might be able to back up your story?"

"No. Like I said, I wanted to be alone."

"So you don't really have an alibi for the time in question?"

"No, I guess I don't."

"Bobby Lee, you don't have to answer any of these questions if you don't want to," Vogel broke in.

"I want to answer them. I'll prove this Ranger is a damn liar."

"I'll grant you permission for now, but if I tell you no further answers, I'll expect you to listen," Vogel answered. "Proceed with your interrogation, Sergeant."

"Thank you, Mr. Vogel. Mr. Martin, I'm going to assume for the moment that you are telling the truth, and were not at Searight Park on the day in question. How, therefore, do you explain the broken headlight on your motorcycle? Can you tell us where and when that happened?"

"It happened just the other day, I guess. Me and some friends were out riding on some dirt roads. A rock must've busted out my headlight. I didn't even realize it was broken until I looked at my bike the next morning."

"But it wasn't a rock, it was a bullet," Ortega pointed out. "You didn't hear a gunshot, nor see anyone with a gun?"

"Nope. A bunch of bikes bein' pushed hard makes a lot of noise. I didn't hear anything, or see anyone."

"Are you trying to tell all of us in this room you didn't feel the impact of the bullet hitting your machine, that you didn't see any flying glass or pieces of plastic?"

"No, I didn't."

"If you'll pardon my saying so, Mr. Martin, that's rather hard to believe. Neither you, nor any of your friends, realized someone had shot at you? And not one of you noticed the broken light on your way home?"

"I already said no one saw it."

"Detective, if my son says he didn't realize his bike had been damaged, then he didn't," the elder Martin interrupted. "This is enough of this inquisition. You have no right to be hassling my boy."

"Begging your pardon, Mr. Martin, but we have every right," Ortega said. "We are trying to solve a very serious alleged crime. Hopefully, we will be able to prove your son was not involved."

"Let the detective ask his questions, Darrell . . . for now," Vogel said.

"Thank you, Mr. Vogel."

"Mr. Martin," Ortega resumed, "Can you tell us where you were riding that day, and what day it was? Also, the time of day?"

"We ride all over the place. I can't recall where exactly we were that day."

"Do you recall the exact day? How about who you were riding with?"

"I ride with a lot of different guys, all the time. I can't say for certain who was with me that day, or what day it was. I just don't remember."

"Mr. Vogel, if you or either of your clients has no objection, I would like to ask Ranger Blawcyzk to make a statement as to his version of what happened."

Both Martins looked at Vogel.

"I have none," the attorney said. "Ranger Blawcyzk may speak his piece."

"Thank you. Ranger Blawcyzk, if you would."

"Of course, Detective. I was riding my horse that Sunday, as I do almost every Sunday. We had just started back home, when I heard a group of dirt bikes on the trails. Motorized vehicles aren't permitted on the trails in Searight, so the riders were already violating the law, just by being there. The bikes kept coming nearer. When they came into view, they immediately sped up, and came directly at me and my horse, coming at us from two directions.

"When it became apparent they were trying to hit us, I fired a warning shot, then another. They came as close as possible to my horse without actually hitting him, then regrouped and came at us again. It was then that I fired at the nearest rider's machine, not the rider himself, but his bike, a yellow Suzuki. I wanted to hit his front tire to disable the Suzuki, but my bullet hit the headlight.

"Once they realized I was no longer firing just to warn them off, the bikers, there were six of them, split up and took to the woods. I realized I could chase them, and quite possibly catch up to at least one, but the odds were my horse would most likely have been injured, or possibly other users of the park if they were caught up in a chase.

"Instead, I notified the Parks Division of the Austin Police and reported what had happened. They searched for the bikers, but with no luck."

"Ranger Blawcyzk, you had a brief look at Mr. Martin's motorcycle when you arrived here today. Would you say it is the same machine you shot the headlight out of?"

"It is."

"You have no way to prove that, Ranger!" the younger Martin exploded. "There's lots of yellow Suzukis out there. You can't prove it was me in the park that day."

"I thought you said you had never been in Searight Park in your life, Mr. Martin," Ortega said. "Why did you just say 'that day'?"

"I . . . I meant I wasn't there, that's all."

"Of course, that's what you meant. Ranger Blawcyzk, do you have anything to add?"

"Just that I, or I should say the Austin Police Department, can in fact prove it was Mr. Martin's Suzuki carrying my bullet. Once the slug is retrieved from the headlight housing, a simple ballistics test will prove it came from my personal sidearm, the Colt .45 Peacemaker that has been in my family for generations. Since I was off-duty, I was wearing my Colt, rather than my service weapon."

"And if the bullet shouldn't match?"

"Then I will apologize to Mr. Martin and his family for the inconvenience. However, I am confident the test will show I fired the bullet. Mr. Martin's bike matches the one I shot at that day, and my bullet struck the headlight, which is where the bullet is lodged in Mr. Martin's Suzuki."

"It wasn't me!" Martin screamed. "Dad, make them stop!"

His glower had been replaced by a look of panic. Sweat was beading on his forehead.

"Detective, this session is over," Vogel stated.

"If that's what you wish, counselor. However, let me advise you again of the charges your client is facing. Once you hear those for a second time, you may decide it's in his best interest to consider cooperating with us."

"Mr. Martin?" Vogel said.

"You're my attorney, Stan," the elder Martin said. "You'll know how best to handle this."

"All right. Detective, go ahead and explain the charges. Mind you, this is not an admission of any involvement or wrongdoing by Bobby Lee Martin. This is merely to ascertain what is being considered by the authorities."

"Of course. As of now, if the physical evidence from Mr. Martin's motorcycle corroborates Ranger Blawcyzk's statement, Mr. Martin will possibly be facing attempted murder charges, since the attack on Ranger Blawcyzk appears to be a deliberate attempt to cause injury or death. It is also possible that charge could be upgraded to attempted murder of a police officer, and also conspiracy to attempt murder of a police officer. At a minimum, your client will be charged with felony reckless endangerment. Other charges could also include destruction of public property, unauthorized use of a motorized vehicle on a prohibited trail, and cruelty to animals. Austin PD also reserves the right to add other charges, once our investigation is completed."

"You're really reaching, Detective. I told you that before. You don't have any proof my client was even present at the time of the alleged assault."

"I don't believe I am, counselor. Once the ballistics test is completed, we can place your client at the location. If he tries to claim someone else was using his motorcycle, he'll have to provide us the name of that person. There's more, hear me out," Ortega said, when Vogel tried to interrupt.

"You're no doubt aware that a recent attempt was made on the life of Ranger Blawcyzk's family. While the investigation into that incident is far from complete, all indications are the attempt was really aimed at Ranger Blawcyzk himself. Now, if, as Ranger Blawcyzk has stated, and will testify to in front of the grand jury, it is determined that not only was your client present at the Searight Park attack on Ranger Blawcyzk, but that attack was, in fact, an attempted murder for hire, you are well aware if your client is convicted on those charges he could easily end up spending the rest of his life in Huntsville."

"You're reaching again, Detective."

"Again, I don't believe so. Looking at your client, he seems quite worried. Are you, Bobby Lee?"

"Of course he is!" his father answered. "What kid wouldn't be?"

"Not as worried as your son appears. I know a guilty man when I see one, and I'm looking at one right now."

"Objection!"

"This isn't a trial, counselor, just a preliminary interrogation. Now, since the Austin Police Department is investigating the incident at Searight Park, and the attack on Ranger Blawcyzk's family jointly with the Texas Rangers, I am authorized to tell your client that, if he cooperates with us, we are prepared to offer a plea bargain which would result in no jail time, merely a fine, restitution, and community service. This is a one-time offer, right now. Otherwise, we'll prosecute your client to the fullest extent of the law. Ranger Blawcyzk . . ."

"Mr. Vogel, Mr. Martin, Bobby Lee, I spoke with Major Voitek, the Commanding Officer of Company F, and Commander Cody of the Austin Police, who is present here, on a conference call while I was en route here. We agreed to what Bobby Lee would be charged with, and the penalty, if, and I emphasize *if,* he provides us every bit of information he has. Do you want to hear the details of the plea bargain?"

"Darrell?" Vogel said.

"Bobby Lee?" his father said.

"Dad, I . . . I don't know what I should do."

"Then perhaps you should listen to the offer, son," Cody suggested. "If you aren't guilty, or if you don't like the deal, you can always turn it down."

"Go ahead and listen, Bobby Lee," Vogel said.

"That's good advice, Mr. Vogel," Jim said. "What we are offering is a reduction in the charges to misdemeanor breach of peace. Bobby Lee would have to pay a fine, and restitution for damage to the trails in Searight Park. His community service, one hundred hours, would be performed in the Austin city parks, doing repair work. If he successfully meets all the conditions of the plea, and commits no further crimes, all charges will be removed from his record after twelve months."

"That's all?" Vogel asked.

"That's all. You understand, we are only offering this deal if your client tells us, truthfully, if this incident was indeed a planned murder attempt, and whatever information he can provide us about the person or persons behind it. It's an extremely generous offer, because of the need to stop the people who hired him. Since this is Bobby Lee's first offense, other than some speeding violations, we can arrange this deal. Any questions?"

"What about my friends?" Bobby Lee blurted out.

"Bobby Lee, don't say another word," Vogel warned.

"That's up to you, son," Jim said. "We're not

asking you to turn in your friends. However, if they also have information we can use, and provide it to us, they'll get the same deal you've received. They are still wanted, so it might behoove them to surrender voluntarily. Of course, if you'd rather, you can take your chances in court. Mr. Vogel can tell you how successful he has been defending his clients when I've been the arresting officer, and testified against them."

Vogel didn't say a word, merely glared at Jim.

"The deal's on the table," Ortega said. "It won't be for long."

"I'll need some time to discuss this with my client," Vogel said.

"Of course. You have fifteen minutes. We'll wait outside."

The three lawmen went into the hallway and down to the water cooler while Vogel conferred with the Martins.

"What do you think, Jorge?" Jim asked. "Will they go for it?"

"I'm not certain. Vogel isn't stupid. He has to realize we're not positive we can match the bullet to your gun. He might want to wait until after the ballistics test."

"Yeah, but that boy is awfully nervous," Cody said. "He's guilty, he knows he is, and he's scared to death at the thought of being taken from his nice, comfortable home and spending time behind bars. We didn't even have to mention whoever hired him and his friends might kill them to keep them quiet."

"I don't think his daddy wants to see him in jail, either," Jim added. "It wouldn't do to have the family name spread all over the news for a son that's been arrested on possible attempted murder charges. I know one thing. We can't sweeten the deal any more. It's take it or leave it, as it stands."

"I love the way you shoved the knife in that lawyer's back and gave it a twist when you reminded him how many times he's lost a case where you've been involved, Jim," Cody said. "Nice touch."

"Yeah, I probably shouldn't have said what I did, but I couldn't resist. Hey, the door's opening. Vogel's waving us back. Whatever decision they made, it was quick."

They headed back into the room, and took their seats.

"Well, counselor?" Ortega said.

"If my client takes the deal, there will be no prison time, correct?"

"No. As we said, a fine, restitution, and community service, with the record expunged after twelve months."

"Can you keep his name out of the papers, and off the television?"

"We can't promise that, because of course he will have to appear in court, and the proceedings and results will be public record. However, lots of kids Bobby Lee's age get into minor scrapes with the law. I doubt anyone will pay attention to his pleading guilty to a misdemeanor breach of peace."

Bobby Lee broke in.

"Mr. Vogel, I want to take the deal. That's my decision."

"But I'm your attorney. This should be my decision, and perhaps your father's."

"No. It's time I stood up for myself. Ranger, I was there that day, as you said. I was the leader of the pack. It was my bike you shot. When the bullet hit it, that damn near scared the crap out of me. I'll take the plea bargain."

"Not quite so fast, son," Ortega said. "Remember, you have to be able to help us find the persons we're looking for."

"I don't know how much I can help, but I'll tell you everything I know."

"Detective Ortega, my client has taken the decision out of my hands," Vogel said, clearly displeased. "As soon as the paperwork is ready we'll sign it."

"It was being prepared while we did our questioning," Cody said. "I'll have it brought right down."

He picked up the phone on the table, dialed an extension, and told the person who answered to bring down the forms.

"They'll be right down," he said, "Jim . . ."

"The leader of the pack, now he's gone gone gone gone," Jim had been singing softly. He stopped when Cody glared at him, and gave him an innocent "Who, me?" look.

"What?"

"You know damn well what."

Cody turned his attention back to the Martins.

"Mr. Martin, your son made the right decision just now," he said. "If he's involved with whoever is trying to kill Ranger Blawcyzk, that decision might have just saved his life. Whoever it is, they're ruthless, and would have no compunction about eliminating any possible witnesses, including Bobby Lee."

"Will you offer him protection?" the elder Martin asked.

"We'll see if that's necessary once we hear what he has to say."

Once the papers were signed, Ortega turned the questioning over to Jim.

"All right, Bobby Lee. Just to remind you, this conversation is still being recorded," Jim said. "Take your time, and in your own words, tell me why you and your buddies attempted to kill me. You can stop whenever you like, as long as you give me all the information you have. I'll break in if I have any questions, as will Detective Ortega or Commander Cody. Are you ready?"

"Yes, sir, Ranger." Martin took a swallow of water, then began.

"First, I want to start by saying none of my friends are aware of who made the arrangements with me. Dad, you won't want to hear this, but for the past year and a half I've been dealing drugs, mostly meth and crack. Using them, too. I always knew I'd get caught someday. Anyway, I've been buying them from a dealer named Sharky. That's the only name I have, Sharky. I'm sure it's not his real name, but I don't know if it's a nickname or his last name. I don't know if you've ever heard of him."

"I have," Ortega said. "His real name is Ernesto Maldonado, and he's one *muy malo hombre*. He's been busted several times, for drugs, assaults, and robbery. He got turned loose just about two years ago. We haven't been able to pin anything on him since, but we're aware he's put himself right back in the game. His territory's in the Central East district."

"That's right, Detective," Martin agreed. "We usually meet either in the Oakwood Cemetery or behind the liquor store on Chicon Street."

"Go on," Jim said.

"Sure. About a week before we came after you, Sharky told me he had a friend who needed a favor. He wanted another dealer taken out, but needed it to look like an accident. He told me where to find the person, when, that he'd be on

311

a horse, and if me and my friends could catch him on a back trail and spook the horse, he'd get thrown and break his neck, or get busted up so bad he'd end up crippled for life, and be an easy target to finish off later. I swear, he never told me we'd be going after a Texas Ranger. Sharky told me it was another dealer."

"How much was he paying you?" Jim asked.

"He was paying me in drugs. Twenty thousand dollars' worth of crack and meth. He also told me not to tell my friends what we were up to. He said make it look like we were just chasing the guy, like has been happening in other parks. I could do what I wanted with the drugs, share them with my friends, use them myself, or sell them."

"That brings up another question," Ortega said. "Did you or any of your friends ever harass other people using the park trails?"

"No, never. That's the truth. We always found dirt roads or abandoned parking lots. Once in a while, we'd do stunts on the streets, but that was it. We wanted to have fun, but not hurt people."

"Jim, that's an awful lot of drugs," Cody said. "Whoever wants you dead has enough money to make it happen."

"Which points more and more toward the New Braunfels – Kendalia operation. Bobby Lee, did Sharky give you any clue as to his friend might be?"

"No, sir, Ranger. Only that, if we did this job right, there would be more for us."

"Son, why did you do this?" his father asked, tears running down his cheeks. "Your mother and I gave you everything you ever wanted. You didn't need any money. You're our only child, and we wanted the best for you."

"Except being there when I needed you, Dad. You were always too busy with work to play with me, and Mom was always out socializing at her fancy parties. I was lonesome, and my friends were the only ones I could talk to. I got into drugs, then discovered I could sell them to the other kids in the neighborhood and make myself some real cash. I never intended to get in so deep. Ranger Blawcyzk, you probably won't believe me, but I'm sorry for what happened."

"I do believe you, son. I hope I'm right, that you'll turn yourself around, and make something of your life. Do you have anything else you can tell us?"

"No. I'm sorry. I wish I did."

"There's no need to apologize. You did the right thing, and gave us a place to start. Once Sharky is picked up, we should be able to get more from him. Mr. Martin, I'd suggest you check Bobby Lee into a drug rehabilitation program. Getting off drugs is something he can't do alone. In fact, unless you or Mr. Vogel have an objection, that should be a condition of his plea bargain."

"I have none," Bobby Lee's father said. "I'll arrange that as soon as we're done here."

"If my clients don't have any objection, neither do I," Vogel said.

"Excellent. I'd suggest a secure facility, for Bobby Lee's protection until we track down the persons we're after," Jim said. "Detective Ortega will process the arrest. Bobby Lee, you'll be released on your own recognizance. Here's my card. If you think of anything else, anything at all, or if you think someone is after you, call me immediately. Mr. Martin, please let me know where your son will be at during rehab. I'd like to keep track of his progress. Unless there is anything else, I believe we're done here."

"There is one other thing, Jim," Ortega said. "Two days ago, Maldonado, Sharky, was killed in a drive-by shooting. No one saw a thing, of course. We won't be getting any information from him. I didn't want to reveal that until Bobby Lee agreed to take a plea bargain."

"Does that mean our deal is invalid?" Bobby Lee asked. "I didn't know Sharky was dead, honest. We were supposed to meet later today. He said he couldn't pay me the twenty thousand in drugs, since the Ranger wasn't dead, but he'd pay me another twenty-five hundred's worth, just for trying. He'd already given me twenty-five hundred as an advance."

"No, you held up your end of the bargain," Jim

said. "Jorge, unless you still need me, I'd like to get back home. It's not often I get a day off. Email me the transcript, will you?"

"Sure thing. I'll be doing some checking with the late Sharky's associates, too."

"I knew you would. I'll have Sean Jordan get in touch with you, since the Rangers will need to be involved too. *Adios*, Jorge."

"*Vaya con Dios*, Jim."

"I'll walk you out, Jim," Cody said.

"Okay."

"Damn, I hate to see that kid get off so easy," Cody said, as they were walking toward Jim's car.

"Same here, but it was the only way we'd ever have gotten him to talk. It's just too bad about Sharky. We could have put some pressure on him to see if he'd give up whoever asked him to arrange my killin'."

"If he even knew who made the arrangements."

"True," Jim said. "But we did make a little progress. Here's my car. You take it easy, Jack."

"And you be careful, Jim. Real careful. Enjoy your trip."

14

"Here we are in Fredericksburg," Jim said, late the next morning. "We'll be at the hotel in a few minutes."

"I'm so glad you decided to make this trip," Betty said. "It's been far too long since the two of you had some time to yourselves."

"You needed some time to relax too, Ma," Jim said. "That's why I insisted you come with us. I know you and Kim will have fun shopping while I take care of Josh."

"I still say we should have taken my rental car, not your Ranger vehicle," Kim said.

"I told you why we're using the Tahoe. I had to bend like a damn pretzel to get into that compact car your insurance company allowed. There's no chance I could have ridden in that oversized skateboard all the way here and back. The processing of your car should be done in a couple more days. Once it is, then it goes straight to the body shop. You'll have it back in a couple of weeks, at the most. There's the turn for our hotel."

A few minutes later, they were pulling up to the Hoffman Haus, an historic bed and breakfast in the heart of downtown Fredericksburg. The accommodations ranged from rooms in the main house to various historic buildings that had been moved to the site, then renovated and modernized to accommodate guests.

"Jim, you didn't tell me the Hoffman Haus was this fancy," Kim exclaimed. "We could have just stayed at a less exclusive place."

"Not this trip. We're doing it up right," Jim said. "It's not quite as expensive as it looks. Let's check in."

They got out of the car and entered the exquisitely decorated lobby. The woman behind the desk smiled, and greeted them warmly.

"Howdy. You must be the Blawcyzk family. Welcome. I'm Leslie. And this must be Frostie. May I give him a treat?"

"I'm sure he'd love one," Jim said.

Leslie came out from behind the desk with a doggie biscuit, which Frostie gently took.

"He's so sweet," she exclaimed. "And your baby is so darling. What's his name?"

"Joshua, but we all call him Josh," Jim said. "This is my wife, Kim, and my mother, Betty."

"I'm so pleased to meet y'all. The Basse House is all ready for you. Just sign in and I'll get the keys."

Jim filled out the registration form while Leslie ran his credit card.

"Here's your keys," Leslie said. "If you need anything, anything at all, just call the front desk. We always strive to make your stay with us as relaxing as possible. I'm certain you need that, Ranger Blawcyzk. Yes, I know who you are from the news reports. No one will even know you're here, I promise you that. I have arranged a deep tissue massage for you, and hot stone massages for the ladies, as you requested. Breakfast will be delivered to your room tomorrow morning at nine, sharp. Enjoy your stay."

"Thank you. I'm certain we will," Jim said.

Once they reached the Basse House, Kim and Batty gasped in surprise.

"Jim, this is magnificent," Kim said.

The Basse House was a stone dogtrot cabin, built by a German settler in 1871. The two sides of the building held the bedrooms, while the dogtrot joining them had been enclosed, and now served as the living room. There was also a kitchen, which was original to the building, but had been modernized with a stove, refrigerator, and oven. A welcoming front porch held rocking chairs, and overlooked the Texas Garden.

"If you think this is something, just wait until you see the inside. If it's anywhere near as nice as the pictures on the website, we may never want to leave."

Jim unlocked the doors and they stepped inside.

"The Basse Suite is ours, Kim. The Burrier Suite is yours, Ma. Soon as I bring the luggage inside, we'll rest a spell, then you two can head for downtown. I'll take a nap with Josh. When he wakes up, I'll do some exploring with him."

"Jim, this is too beautiful for words," Kim exclaimed. Both bedrooms, or suites as the B & B called them, were furnished with antiques, luxurious bedding, and chandeliers.

"It sure is," Betty agreed. "You're right, Jim. I never want to leave this place."

"Neither one of you can fool me," Jim said. "You can hardly wait to hit the shops."

Fredericksburg still maintained much of its charm from the town's early days as a German settlement. East and West Main Streets were still also called the Hauptstrasse. Quaint shops, restaurants, and plain old tourist traps lined the downtown streets.

"You're right," Kim conceded. "We'll just freshen up a bit and be on our way. What time are our massages?"

"I took the last appointments of the day, so you have plenty of time," Jim said. "Go on, do what you have to do and get going. Josh and I want to rest. You too, Frostie, right?"

Frostie waved his tail, hopped on one of the sofas, and curled up.

At three that afternoon, Kim and Betty returned from their shopping expedition, laden with boxes and bags.

"I see you had a successful day," Jim said.

"We did," Betty answered. "There were so many

cute things, and the prices weren't all that bad, especially for a tourist town. How was your rest?"

"We only napped for a little while, then I took Josh out to do some exploring of our own. We went down to that new Texas Ranger Heritage Center, which is nice. After that, we stopped by the Old German Bakery and Restaurant for some sauerbraten, pastries and kuchen. They make the best lebkuchen in the state."

"We should have known, Betty," Kim said.

"That's not all. After we—well, *I* ate, I took Josh to Dooley's Five and Dime. I bought him a bag of plastic cowboys and Indians for when he's a little older, a stuffed horse, and also his first cap gun and cowboy hat. Since he's already a Junior Texas Ranger, he can't go without a pistol and cowboy hat. I got him his first toy police car, too."

"You didn't," Kim said.

"I did. They're in the sack right on the table. Here's a picture of him wearing them."

Jim turned on his phone to show Kim and Betty a photo of Josh with a small child's size cowboy hat perched on his head, and a way-too-large gunbelt, holster, and cap gun wrapped around his waist. Alongside him were the bag of cowboys and Indians, the stuffed horse, and the police car.

"And so it begins," Betty said. "The next thing

you know, Josh will have a pony. Jim's father was just like that with him."

"Jim, really. Don't you think Josh is just a little too young?" Kim said.

"It's never too young to start a boy, or a girl for that matter, to learn about our Texas heritage," Jim answered. "Not to mention how to ride a horse."

"Don't even bother, Kim," Betty advised, when Jim's wife started to frame a retort. "You'll just be talking to a brick wall."

"A brick wall who's on his way to his massage," Jim said. "See you in ninety minutes. After you ladies have your spa treatments, we'll head over to Auslander for supper, then on to Luckenbach."

Jim had tried to convince his mother to come along to Luckenbach, with Josh, but she insisted that side trip should be for just Jim and Kim, that she would be perfectly content staying at the hotel with Josh and Frostie. So, after supper, Jim and his wife made the short drive to Luckenbach, the town made famous by Willie Nelson and Waylon Jennings.

Only about seven people lived there now, but its old dance hall and combination bar/general store were still popular attractions. Even when there wasn't a concert indoors, there was an impromptu music circle on the small outdoor stage just about every night.

Jim got drinks at the bar, a long neck Lone Star for him, a glass of white wine for Kim. They went inside the dance hall, and found seats on a bench near the middle of the room. Several local musicians were playing, and continued for about half-an-hour. When they stopped, one of them introduced well-known Texas singer-songwriter-author Mike Blakely, and his wife, Annie. Mike opened with a song from *Keepsake*, his recently released CD, *My Same Old New Mexican Dream*, followed by *Charlie Siringo*, then *Rancho Quien Sabe*. After that, he stopped singing to welcome the audience, and introduce himself and Annie.

"We have two special guests with us tonight," he continued. "Our good friends Jim Blawcyzk, and his lovely wife, Kim. Stand up, both of you."

Reluctantly, Jim and Kim came to their feet, Jim tipping his Stetson to the crowd, Kim giving a slight wave.

"Even though he hasn't asked me to, I'm going to play some of Jim's favorite songs tonight," Mike said. "First will be *The Last Comanche Moon*. I don't know if his wife's aware of this, but Jim's the only person who's ever told me I should have saved the horse in this song, not the girl. Kim, how do you feel about that?"

Kim blushed, then laughed and punched Jim on his arm.

"That's about how I thought you'd feel," Mike said, laughing along with the rest of the crowd.

"Then, we'll do a favorite sing-along of all my friends, *Here's to Horses*. As you probably guessed from what I just told you, Jim's a real horse lover. Later on, Annie and I will sing *Pacing Horses*, and *The Old Bar 7*. Some of these I haven't performed live in quite some time, so I apologize if I'm a bit rusty. The last song for Jim will have special meaning for him. Since he's a Texas Ranger, I'm going to dedicate *Go Easy* especially to him. So, here goes."

Mike began the opening narration to *The Last Comanche Moon*.

Mike and Annie's show ran over an hour-and-a-half, with a thirty-minute intermission. It was just after one in the morning when Jim and Kim arrived back at the Hoffmann Haus. The night was still hot and sultry.

"Boy howdy, a swim in that above ground pond is mighty tempting," Jim said. "I'd imagine we'd get in a bit of trouble if we took one, though."

"I have a better idea," Kim said. "There's the Jacuzzi in the bathroom, along with the rock-walled shower. It's also the only bathroom I've ever seen with its own fireplace. I bought a bottle of Riesling today, which is chilling in the refrigerator. We can light the candles on the mantel, pour two glasses of wine, get into the Jacuzzi, and see where things go from there. Unless you'd rather not."

"Rather not? I don't think so. As long as you don't take your new earrings off."

"I'll remove everything but, as long as you remove your cowboy hat."

"I think I can manage that."

"Then let's get busy, cowboy."

The next morning, following breakfast, the Blawcyzk family attended the 11:15 Mass at St. Mary's Church. After a quick lunch at Burger Burger, they made the drive back home.

"Well, that was fun," Jim said, as he pulled into the yard. "Too bad it's over so soon. Tomorrow, it's back to work."

"For all of us," Betty said.

15

There was one thing about his job that Jim absolutely despised, and today he was doing it. He, along with Sean Jordan and Jorge Ortega, had stood outside the funeral home where the services for Ernesto "Sharky" Maldonado had taken place, watching the attendees arrive to see if any were associates in Maldonado's illegal drug distribution enterprise. Now, they were in Oakwood Cemetery, ironically the same cemetery where Maldonado had completed most of his drug deals. They were standing a short distance from Maldonado's grave while waiting for the committal service to conclude.

"I feel like a ghoul being here," Jim complained. "I always do. I don't care how bad an *hombre* was, I hate ruining the family's privacy at a time like this."

"True, but this is one time it was worth it," Ortega said. "It looks like the minister's done. Folks are starting to leave. Let's go talk to our pigeon, before he flies the coop."

The three men walked over to where the cars from the funeral procession were lined up. A man was just opening the door of a black BMW 440i. Ortega walked up behind him, slammed the door shut, and spun him around.

"Leaving so soon, Georgie Boy?" he said. "You've barely spent enough time to pay your respects to the family. I couldn't think of letting you do that."

"Ortega, you no good son of a bitch. What the hell are you doin' here? Can't you leave the dead rest in peace?"

Several of the mourners started toward Ortega. They stopped when Jim and Sean shook their heads.

"Ranger business, people," Sean said. "Just keep going to wherever you're headed."

"I was about to ask you the same thing, Georgie Boy. What the hell are *you* doing here? The last I knew, you and Maldonado were in the middle of a turf war, and you had each sworn to kill the other. I suppose you're going to claim you had nothing to do with his shooting."

"That's right, I didn't. Me'n Sharky had come to a truce. I've got no damn idea who killed him."

"Now, why don't I believe you? I'd like you to meet a couple of friends of mine, Georgie Boy. These are Texas Rangers Sean Jordan and Jim Blawcyzk. Rangers, meet George "Georgie Boy" Washington. A testament to our first president he's not. In fact, Georgie Boy is pretty much scum. He'll sell crack to his own mama. Isn't that right?"

"My mama's dead, fool. Why are you hasslin' me? Ain't you got nothin' better to do, Ortega?"

"Not today, I don't. But I'm not the one who

wants to talk to you, Georgie Boy. The Rangers, here, do."

"Why would the damn Texas Rangers want to talk with me?"

"I'll let them answer that. Sean . . ."

"You see, it's like this, Georgie Boy," Sean said. "The Rangers are always looking to bring in drug pushers, and you certainly qualify on that count."

"You ain't got nothin' on me, Ranger. You think I'm some kind of dummy?"

"I'm sure it wouldn't take us long to dig up something on you . . . one way or the other," Sean answered. "But that's not why we're here. You see, someone's got a contract out on Ranger Blawcyzk. He's got some questions for you. Since this is my territory, I allowed him the courtesy of coming in to talk to you. Kind of like when the gangs have a meeting, and one comes into the other's territory. Let me tell you what he wants to know. He wants to know who wants him dead. I'm sure even someone dumb as a brick like you can understand that. So, you'll answer his questions like a good Georgie Boy, you hear me?"

"I don't know nothin' about a hit on no Ranger. Anyone who'd get involved with tryin' to take out a damn Ranger is a damn fool."

"We'll let Ranger Blawcyzk decide that. Jim, go ahead."

"Thanks, Sean. Mr. Washington, I have no interest in you, the gang you might belong to, or what kind of criminal activities you're involved in. As Ranger Jordan said, someone's been trying to kill me. Information has been obtained, information possibly linking the late Mr. Maldonado to the person or persons responsible for the attempts on my life, one of which also involved my family. Detective Ortega believes you might know something about that."

"I don't know nothin' about nothin'," Washington said.

"C'mon, Georgie Boy," Ortega said. "You can do better than that. Not a deal goes down in Central East that you don't know about it. If Maldonado was involved with whoever put the contract out on Ranger Blawcyzk, you had at least an inkling about it. You've got two choices. You can answer the Rangers' questions here, or down at Headquarters. Of course, if you don't tell us what we want to know, we might just have to search your car."

"You'll need a warrant for that."

Ortega walked to the back of the BMW, grabbed the bottom edge of the license plate, and bent it in half.

"Golly gee, will you take a look at that, Georgie Boy? Improper display of a license plate. Probable cause, my friend. Shall we start the search? I'll bet we find something real interesting."

"You ain't no damn friend of mine, Ortega, you bastard," Washington said. "All right, you win . . . this time. I'll tell you everything I know. Hell, it doesn't involve me anyway, so why shouldn't I? Besides, Sharky's dead and in the ground, so he ain't gonna give a damn."

"Now you're being smart, Georgie Boy. Go ahead and tell the Rangers what they want to know."

"It won't take long. About a year ago, Sharky seemed to come across a lot more cash, out of nowhere. He bought a flashy new Escalade, pimped it up big time, and moved into a fancy apartment in a downtown high rise. I don't know the address, 'cause we weren't exactly friends, as Ortega says. I'm sure you've already got the address, anyway. But he bragged about the place all the time, showed everybody he came across pictures of it. He took a lot of women up there, and rumor has it some young boys, too, kids in their teens."

"But you don't know where he got the money?" Sean asked.

"No, I sure don't, Ranger. I wish I did, so I could get in on some of the action, too."

"That wouldn't be too smart, if it involves killing lawmen," Jim said.

"I guess you're right, at that," Washington conceded. "Anyway, I heard talk he was workin' for some guy out of West Lake Hills, doin' what he called odd jobs and handyman work. Well, there ain't no handyman I ever knew made the kind of money Sharky was throwin' around. He never said who he was workin' for, but one time his phone rang. He told the guy on the other end he'd have to call him back, and I overheard the guy's name. All I can tell you is he had a funny soundin' name, kind of foreign like."

"Any clue as to what nationality? Muslim? Indian? Russian? Middle Eastern? French? Anything?"

"I don't know, Ranger. It kind of sounded like the real name of the guy who made the Chipmunks records."

"You mean David Seville?"

"Yeah, but that wasn't his real name. It was Ross Bagdasarian. I know you'll think I'm supposed to be too young to have heard of the Chipmunks, and that I probably listen mostly to gangsta rap or hip-hop. You'd be right, but my mama loved the Chipmunks Christmas album, and listened to it from Thanksgiving to New Years. I liked it too. Still do. Anyway, that's all I know."

"But you'll get in touch with me or Ranger Jordan immediately, if you do learn anything else. Right, Georgie Boy?" Ortega said.

"Right, Detective."

"Good. Now get outta here. Oh, if I were you, I'd get that license plate fixed before you go too far. I wouldn't want you to get pulled over."

"Go to hell, Ortega."

Washington got in his car, fired it up, and roared out of the cemetery.

"You know, I damn near ended up just like

330

him," Sean said. "I grew up in the Dallas hood. My father disappeared when I was just three years old, and my mother took to working the streets. I started running with a gang when I was nine years old. Then, my grandmother took me in after my mother got sent to jail. She was a tough old bird, my grandma. Didn't take any guff from anybody. She got me started in the right direction, then, when I was in high school, a cop came to career day, name of Tyrone Jubilee. I'm not kiddin', that was his name. Anyway, for some reason, he took a liking to me. When I graduated, he got me into the law enforcement program at the community college, and I never looked back. So here I am, an honest-to-gosh Texas Ranger."

"Well, honest-to-gosh Texas Ranger, I'd say you've got some work cut out for you," Ortega said.

"I sure do. Jim. What Washington gave us isn't much, but it's a place to start. I'll get digging, and with any luck make a couple of connections. I'll follow the dots and see where they lead."

"I've got to get back to my office, and finish the paperwork on a bunch of closed cases," Jim said. "But first, I'm starved. Either one of you want to grab some lunch?"

"That sounds like a good idea," Sean answered. "You have any place in mind?"

"Yeah, someplace quick and cheap," Jim said. "I've had a hankerin' for Pancake Heaven for a couple of weeks now. How about we head for the one on 290?"

"That's fine with me," Sean said. "How about you, Jorge?"

"Cheap, greasy, but good food. Sounds like eating my wife's cooking. Sure, why not?"

"Then let's go."

The Pancake Heaven was busy as usual, so they had to wait about fifteen minutes for a booth. Jim ordered his usual, a double order of pecan waffles and bacon, accompanied by a large glass of cold milk. Sean had steak and eggs with hash browns, and coffee, while Jorge had a grilled bacon chicken deluxe and a Diet Coke.

"A Diet Coke with *that?*" Jim said, laughing.

"Hey, every little bit helps."

They were just finishing their meals when Jim's phone rang. He glanced down at its display.

"214? That's Dallas. Who the devil would be calling me from Dallas?"

He picked up the phone.

"Ranger Blawcyzk."

"Ranger Blawcyzk? This is Bruce Sherman, out of Company B. I'm the new Ranger assigned to McKinney."

"Howdy, Bruce. What can I do for you?"

"I'd like you to take a run up here, if you wouldn't mind. We have another murder of an elderly woman—actually, two elderly sisters.

From what I've seen so far, this could be connected to the murders down your way. I've also uncovered something that's mighty interesting. I think you should take a look. I know it's a bit of a drive, and I apologize, but I really believe it will be worth your while."

"There's no need to apologize. I'll be there in about three hours. What's the location?"

"5970 Telephone Road in Melissa. That's also Texas 277. It's a gravel road that parallels U.S. 75, so sometimes GPS doesn't pick it up."

"I'm on my way."

Jim clicked off the phone, pulled some bills from his pocket and tossed them on the table.

"Sorry, fellas, I've gotta run," he said. "That was Bruce Sherman, the Ranger out of McKinney. Two more elderly women have been murdered, this time up north of Dallas. He thinks it's connected to the murders down here, and wants to see what I think. Talk to you later."

A block from the Pancake Heaven was a convenience store and filling station. Even though the Tahoe's tank was more than half full, Jim stopped there to top it off and grab a cold six-pack of Dr Pepper. Once he was done, he hit the strobes on his truck, then in less than three minutes, was on I-35 North, heading for Melissa.

16

A bit less than three hours later, Jim pulled into the driveway of 5970 Telephone Road in Melissa. A Collin County deputy was guarding the taped-off driveway. He lifted the tape so Jim could enter. Near the house, a dark blue 2017 Ford F150 crew cab pickup was parked behind a vintage, 1956 black and red Mercury Monterey four-door hardtop, which appeared as if it had just come off the showroom floor. When Jim pulled up, a young Ranger got out of the Ford.

"Howdy, Ranger Blawcyzk," he said, as they shook hands. Bruce Sherman had a good, firm grip. "I really appreciate your coming all the way up here to help me."

Bruce Sherman was a few inches shorter and a few pounds lighter than Jim. He was dressed in tan khaki pants, a crisp white shirt, and a light blue and white striped tie. A white Stetson covered his sandy hair, and shaded his blue eyes. He had a polite, "Aw shucks, yes ma'am, yes sir" cowboy-style personality. Even at this first meeting, Jim was sure that politeness covered a rock-hard determination to keep on the trail of a lawbreaker until he or she was brought to justice. It could probably fool many an outlaw into thinking they were dealing with someone soft, until they figured out too late Bruce had snared them.

"As I told you on the phone, it's no trouble, especially if this is connected to the other murders. And the name's Jim. I've got the same rank as you, Texas Ranger. What have you got here, Bruce?"

"Two elderly sisters, Elsie Borden, age seventy-four, and Alice Borden, age seventy-three. Both shot in the forehead, at close range. Neither ever married. No known living relatives. Their closest neighbor says they pretty much stayed to themselves. He said they were nice enough, but kind of eccentric. Do you want to take a look inside, Jim?"

"Sure."

After donning nitrile gloves and booties, Bruce and Jim went into the house.

"This place looks like something out of the nineteen fifties," Jim said. "It's neat as a pin, though."

"It sure does," Bruce agreed. "The television's an old black and white—with rabbit ears, no less. Even the stove and refrigerator are at least fifty years old. So's the plumbing fixtures." He shook his head. "It's a real shame we'll have to make a mess of that nice old car out there when we check it for evidence. The bodies are right down the hallway, in the bedroom."

Bruce led Jim into the main bedroom. The

335

bodies of the Borden sisters were lying side by side on the bed, dressed in flannel robes. They looked as if they were sleeping . . . except for the bullet holes in each of their foreheads.

"As you can see, they were shot at close range," Bruce said. "My best guess is with a nine-millimeter, but that will have to be confirmed once the bullets are retrieved. Until then, I'm just speculating. It appears as if the killer forced them to lie down, then shot them. They've been dead for at least a couple of days, probably no more than four or five."

"Now let *me* speculate," Jim said. "There are no signs of a struggle anywhere in the house, and not one shred of evidence as to who the killer was, or why he killed these women."

"In the house, no," Bruce agreed. "However, there's something outside I want to show you."

Bruce led Jim out the back door, and off the back porch.

"Boy howdy, for a place that's not much more'n forty miles from Dallas, and less than ten from McKinney, not to mention with a real busy highway less than a few hundred yards away, this property might as well be in west Texas," Jim said, as they crossed the yard. "It sure is isolated."

"It sure is," Bruce agreed. "What I want to show you is right over here, on the other side of the barbed wire fence, in that ditch."

After they worked their way through the fence, Bruce stopped at the edge of a long unused irrigation ditch. Jim could see where the dirt had been disturbed.

"Don't pay any attention to the scuffed-up dirt, Jim," he said. "I did that pokin' around. But take a look under here."

Bruce lifted a piece of plywood that appeared as if it had been lying in the ditch for years.

"What do you think?"

Jim gave a low whistle. Under the plywood was a hole, filled with half burned, but many still legible, empty prescription strength Sudafed boxes, along with a Cost-mart store-brand equivalent, as well as various other store or generic brands. Mixed in with them were melted and blackened pieces of tubing, funnels, plastic bottles, and other drug-making paraphernalia.

"These sweet little old ladies were running a crystal meth factory!"

"So it would seem," Bruce said. "The laboratory tests on this stuff will tell us for certain."

"Bruce, how in the world did you find this cache? I have to admit, I'd never have guessed it was back here."

"It was more luck than anything else. I happened to notice a couple of places where the grass was pressed down and dried, like there'd been some weight on it. That made me curious, as it would any lawman. I noticed the barbed wire was a little loose between two posts, which made me even more curious. When I got to the ditch, at first I couldn't see anything out of place. I finally spotted just a corner of that plywood sticking out from under the dirt. I lifted it up, and voila! Evidence of a meth operation."

"Are you sure you're a brand-new Ranger, Bruce? Even a lot of veterans would have overlooked what you found."

"I only got appointed four months ago. And I'm pretty certain any other Ranger would have found it, too."

"Well, you're off to a real good start," Jim said. "It looks like whoever's behind this operation finally got a little careless. I'd bet my hat he, assuming it's one person—a *he*—dug this hole, dumped the stuff in it, and set it on fire. He didn't wait until it completely burned before he covered it up. Probably got a little nervous someone might come by and spot him. Congratulations, Bruce. You just might have come up with what we need to solve these murders."

"I wouldn't say that," Bruce said. "I just found some possible evidence."

"Which is more than anyone else, including me, has been able to do, at least up to this point."

"The big question now, Jim, is why all of a sudden the killings?"

"Offhand, I'd say our suspect has decided the women he's been exploiting have outlived their usefulness to him, so he wants to eliminate any possible witnesses. Let's step back and take a look. All the victims have been elderly women, who had little or no social lives, and few if any close relatives. They lived out in the boondocks, where it's unlikely anyone would notice anything strange, or anyone coming or going. That means it would be easy for our suspect to go undiscovered.

"The victims were all poor, or at least just scraping by, so the money would be mighty tempting. That would explain why one of them, down in Blanco County, suddenly had enough cash to fix up her old house, and buy a brand-new car. It also explains why the first victim was able to fix up her house and replace all her old furniture. She hadn't hit the jackpot at a Mississippi casino, which is what she told everyone. She got that money by manufacturing meth.

"I've no doubt the *hombre* they were working for threatened them with going to jail, or what has happened, killing them, if they said anything to anyone. All we have to do is track him down and prove it."

"Which also means there's probably more women out there who are targets," Bruce said.

"Right. Listen, Bruce, I've got an idea. I'll help you finish up here. After that, I'll head back home. If Major Voitek agrees, I'm going to have a statement ready in time for the morning news programs."

"Sure, but we'll be here a while. I'm hungry. You want some Perfect Chick? I've got a sack of sandwiches in my truck."

"Bruce, I knew I was gonna like you right from the start," Jim said. "I've got a six-pack of Dr Pepper in *my* truck. Soon as I get that, we'll eat."

The next morning, Jim was at Company F Headquarters in Waco, on the grounds of the Ranger Museum complex. All of the Waco, Austin, and Dallas television stations had reporters and satellite trucks there. Reporters and photographers from all the region's newspapers were also present. Jim stepped up to the podium set up in front of Company F's building.

"Good morning," he began. "For those of you who may not know me, my name is Ranger James C. Blawcyzk, attached to Company F, and stationed in Buda. I am the lead investigator in the killings of several elderly women in rural areas outside of Austin.

"Yesterday, the bodies of two more women, apparent victims of the same individual or individuals who murdered the other three victims, were found in their home in Melissa, Collin County, north of McKinney. The investigation into their deaths is still ongoing, so I cannot positively confirm they were indeed killed by the same person responsible for the other deaths, nor can I release their names at this time.

"However, I am able to tell you that, while we are not ready to make an arrest in these cases, we have developed evidence which will help in our hunt. I can say, with confidence, that, based on the evidence we have, the general public, particularly elderly women who live alone, are not in any danger, although everyone, of course, should take the usual precautions to assure their safety. That said, I can also say with a good degree of certainty the killer knew his victims, and will strike again.

"Therefore, I am urging anyone who believes they may be, or have been, involved with the suspect call their local police, local sheriff's department, or Texas Ranger Company F or B as soon as possible. Doing so may just save your life. I would like to thank all the members of the media for helping get this message out. I also thank you for being here this morning. That is the end of my statement. I will not be taking any questions at this time."

17

Late in the morning two days later, Jim was in his office, reading the report Bruce Sherman had sent him on the Borden sisters' murders, along with the autopsy findings and the results of the ballistic tests. The ballistics confirmed the bullets which killed the two women matched the ones from the same nine-millimeter pistol which had killed the three other women. Bruce said he was also hoping to obtain some partial fingerprints or DNA samples from the contents of the burn pit, but realized that was a long shot. Jim had just gotten up to get a cup of coffee when his phone rang. He grabbed the receiver.

"Ranger Blawcyzk."

"Good morning, Jim. This is Mary Huggins. I have a caller on the line. She insists on speaking only with you. She sounds really scared."

"Thanks, Mary. Put her through,"

A moment later, the shaking voice of an elderly woman came on the line.

"Is this Ranger Blawcyzk?"

"Yes, this is Ranger James Blawcyzk. How may I help you, ma'am?"

"I saw you on the news the other day. I'm afraid I'm going to be killed soon. You see, I've been working for the man who killed those other women."

"Can you give me his name, ma'am? Also, yours?"

"I'm too frightened to do that over the phone. Would you come out here to my place? Please, Ranger?"

"Of course. I'll notify the county sheriff to stay with you until I arrive. What's your name and address?"

"No! Not the sheriff!" the woman exclaimed. "I'll only speak to you."

"Okay, I promise I won't call the sheriff. I still need your name and address, though."

"My name is Deidre. Deidre Moore. My address is 1239 Ranch Road 1320 in Blanco County. That's west of Johnson City, and just south of the Pedernales River."

"I'll be there in an hour. If anyone does show up before I get there, don't open your door, and call the sheriff."

"I'll do that, Ranger. And thank you. I'll be so relieved to have this over. It's been a nightmare."

Jim waited until he got in his truck before he called Company F back. Mary Huggins answered the phone.

"Mary, it's Jim. I'm on my way to 1239 Ranch Road 1320 in Blanco County. That woman you had on the phone said she was afraid for her life, that she believes she's involved with the man who killed the other women. Don't have the Blanco County authorities notified, or we'll scare her off. She says she'll talk to me, and me only. I'll call in in soon as I'm on scene."

"All right, Jim."

An hour later, Jim was approaching 1239 Ranch Road 1320. Just as he reached the driveway, a bronze Nissan Maxima holding a man and a terrified looking woman roared out of it, fishtailing as it turned right onto Ranch Road 1320. Jim immediately gave chase, turning on his lights and siren and hitting the accelerator.

The Nissan picked up speed, then swerved off the left side of the road, took down a stretch of barbed wire fence, and continued onto a rutted one-lane dirt track which ran alongside 1320. Jim put his Tahoe right behind the fleeing Nissan, gaining rapidly on the car despite the blinding dust it threw up.

The Nissan skidded on a curve and swerved off the trail, then back on it. The driver pulled over and stopped, apparently realizing his car could not handle the beating it was taking, and he'd never be able to outrun Jim's SUV.

Jim radioed in to dispatch he had made the stop, then got out of his truck and pulled his pistol from its holster. He heard another vehicle, siren blaring, coming from behind. He took a quick glance to see a Blanco County Sheriff's

Department Ford Explorer pulling up behind his Tahoe. Deputy Harvey Kelley, gun in hand, got out.

"Don't worry, Jim. I happened to come along just as you went after that car. I've got your back."

"I appreciate that, Harve."

Jim was halfway to the Nissan when a gunshot sounded, and a bullet slammed into his lower right back. He grunted from the impact, arched with the pain, then another bullet hit him higher, this one on the left side of his back. He staggered forward for two steps, reflexively firing his gun, sending a bullet into the dirt, then pitched to his face.

"Go on, get outta here!" the deputy yelled to the people in the Nissan. The driver put the car in gear and hit the gas.

"I told you I had your back, Jim," Kelley muttered to the downed Ranger, who was lying prone, with his face in the dirt. He picked up the expelled cartridge casings from his gun, broke a branch off a juniper and brushed out the tire tracks and his foot prints as best he could, then drove off.

Jim regained semi-consciousness for just a moment, bleeding heavily and in extreme pain. He dragged himself along on his belly for several feet, trying to crawl back to the road, but passed out well short of his goal.

The sun beat down on him, and buzzards, which always seemed to appear out of nowhere whenever they sensed death, and a meal, began circling overhead. The rancher who owned the land where Jim had been shot was out checking his fences, and the ugly flying scavengers attracted his attention.

"We'd better see what those buzzards are after, Joey," he said to his bay quarter horse gelding. "There might be a calf bogged down in a slough." He cut through the brush, keeping his eyes on the buzzards, which were slowly descending. He came out of the scrub just above where Jim's Tahoe was parked, its engine still running and lights still flashing.

"Oh, my Lord!" he exclaimed, when he saw Jim lying alongside the dirt track. He galloped his horse up to Jim and dismounted.

"Oh, my Lord!" he exclaimed again. "This Ranger's been shot." He could hear Jim was still breathing, but raggedly. "He needs help, and fast."

He took out his cell phone and dialed 911.

"Hang on, mister. Help's gonna be on the way."

18

It took an ambulance from the North Blanco County EMS Service less than ten minutes to arrive after the call came in. Right behind it were two Johnson City Police units.

"Right over here," the rancher called when they rolled to a stop. The EMTs grabbed their medical kits from the ambulance and hurried over to where Jim lay.

"He's been shot," the rancher said.

"Please, sir, stand back and let us get to work."

One of the EMTs took out a pair of scissors and cut off Jim's shirt.

"Joe, this man's bleeding real bad," she said. "He's lost a lot of blood already. Get an IV of Ringer's lactate going and a plasma drip set up, stat. An antibiotic line also. Oxygen too. We've got to get him stabilized. He's liable to go into shock any minute. I'm surprised he hasn't already."

"Right, Jolene." Her partner went to get the needed equipment out of the ambulance.

"Barry, call Travis County STARFlight," Jolene ordered one of the Johnson City officers. "Tell them we need a medical chopper at this location, and they need to get it off the ground now!"

"Sure thing, Jolene," Barry answered.

"Barry, do you know who this is?" the second police officer said. "It's Ranger Blawcyzk. You'd better notify DPS we'll need some state troopers and a Ranger out here, soon as you're done with STARFlight. Notify the county sheriff's office we'll need help blocking off this area, and keeping curious folks away. This is past the city limits and out of our jurisdiction, so the sheriff's office needs to take over anyway."

"I'll get right on it, Chad."

"C'mon, Ranger, keep fighting," Jolene urged as she worked to stop the bleeding from Jim's wounds, while her partner set up the IVs, searching Jim's left arm for a vein still functional enough to take a needle. "Don't you dare give up on me. I've never lost a damn gunshot victim yet, and you sure ain't goin' to be my first. There's a chopper on the way from Austin. You'll be at the hospital before you know it."

While the EMTs worked on Jim, the Johnson City policer officers questioned Emmett Pierson, the rancher who'd found him.

"Em, how'd you happen to come across the Ranger?" Barry Black asked him.

"I was out ridin' fence, when I saw some buzzards circlin'," Pierson said. "I wanted to see what they were after. I thought mebbe one of my calves had got caught in the scrub, or wandered into a bog. Instead, I found this man lyin' right where he's at." He pointed to the drag marks Jim had left. "Looks to me as if he was shot over there, and tried to drag himself back to his truck or over to the road."

"You didn't see anyone, or hear any gunshots?" Chad Brewster questioned.

"No, on both."

"How about any vehicles?"

"Didn't see or hear any of them, neither. I did hear a siren, but I didn't pay any attention to it. I hear those goin' up and down 75 all the time. Sure wish I could be more help."

"You've been plenty of help just by finding this poor bastard before he bled out," Black said. "I hate to do this to you, Em, but you'll have to stay here until a Ranger or state trooper arrives to talk with you. I hope that's all right."

"I reckon it will keep me from finishin' my work for the day, but I guess that can't be helped. I'll just tie Joey where he can graze while we're waitin'."

"Appreciate that, Em."

A short time later, the distinctive "whup, whup, whup" of an approaching helicopter could be heard. The sound rapidly grew nearer. Once the chopper appeared, the pilot circled briefly to determine the best landing spot, then settled the machine to the road, about two hundred feet from the ambulance. Two paramedics jumped out.

"What have we got?" one asked, once they reached where Jim was being treated.

"White male, late twenties to early thirties. Two gunshot wounds in the back," Jolene answered. "Severe loss of blood. I can't tell you what internal organs have been damaged. We've started him on Ringer's lactate, plasma, IV antibiotics, and oxygen. I've managed to slow the bleeding, but haven't been able to stop it completely. Right now, I'd say he's in extremely critical condition."

"Let's get him loaded up. We'll be taking him to St. David's South Austin. That's the nearest hospital from here by air."

"All right," Jolene answered.

Jim was transferred to the helicopter's gurney, then rolled to the waiting machine. Ten minutes after it had landed, the chopper was back in the air, flying at top speed toward St. David's South.

"STARFlight N310KC to St. David's South Austin Emergency."

"St. David's South Emergency. Go ahead, STARFlight N310KC."

"En route to your location from Johnson City with gunshot victim, male, late twenties-early thirties. Shot twice in back. Severe loss of blood. ETA 20 minutes. Need full emergency surgical and vascular team standing by. Transmitting vitals now. Victim is a Texas Ranger. Repeat, victim is a Texas Ranger."

"10-4, N310KC. Will have team standing by."

"How's he doing?" the pilot asked the paramedics, who were working feverishly to keep Jim alive.

One of them shook his head.

"Not good. His blood pressure's dropping, down to eighty-five over fifty, his pulse is erratic, and he's still losing blood. Can't you get any more out of this bird?"

"I've got her red-lined now. I don't dare push her any faster, or the engine's liable to blow."

The paramedics continued working on Jim, while the pilot kept the helicopter at its limit. Fifteen minutes later, the helipad at St. David's Austin South Medical Center came into view.

"STARFlight N310KC to St. David's South Emergency."

"Go ahead, STARFlight N310KC."

"Starting landing approach now. Will be on ground in five minutes."

"10-4, N310KC. Team is standing by."

"10-4, St. David's South."

Once the helicopter was on the ground, even before its rotors stopped turning, Jim was taken out and rushed to the trauma unit's surgical center. The chief surgeon took one look at his wounds and shook his head.

"It's a miracle he got this far. It'll be a bigger miracle if we can save him. People, let's get to work."

• • •

Kim and Betty were in their office, Kim on the phone with a client when the doorbell rang.

"I've got it, Kim," Betty said.

"Thank you, Betty."

Kim returned to her conversation, while Betty went to the front door. She opened it, gasped, and put her hand to her mouth, when she saw Lieutenant Stoker standing on the front porch, along with a female state trooper.

"Mrs. Blawcyzk, good afternoon. This is Trooper Rachel Hutchings," Stoker said. "May we come in?"

"Of course." Betty opened the door wider. Stoker and Hutchings stepped inside.

"Is Jim's wife home?" Stoker asked. "What I have to say, I'd rather tell you both at the same time."

"Yes . . . yes, she is. I'll call her."

Betty went to the hallway.

"Kim. Kim. I need you right now."

"I can't come this minute. I have to finish this call," Kim answered.

"Kim, you need to come here, *right now!* Tell Ms. Escobar you'll have to call her back. This can't wait."

Betty could hear Kim murmur something to her client, then hang up the phone.

"What is it that's so important?" Kim asked, as she walked up the hall.

352

"We have company," Betty answered.

Kim's eyes grew wide with shock and fear when she saw Stoker and Hutchings standing in her living room, holding their hats in their hands. The looks on their faces, as well as Betty's, told her something was drastically wrong.

"Lieutenant Stoker! Something's happened to Jim, hasn't it?"

"I'm afraid so," Stoker said. "He's been shot. No, he isn't dead," Stoker continued, anticipating Kim's next question. "However, he is in very bad shape, from what I understand. The shooting happened outside Johnson City. Jim was medevaced to St. David's South in Austin. He's undergoing surgery right now. This is State Trooper Hutchings with me. We're going to take you and Jim's mother to St. David's. Hurry and gather whatever you need. There's not a minute to lose."

"I'll have to take Josh," Kim said, numbly. "There's no one else to watch him."

"Of course," Stoker said. "Trooper, will you help Mrs. Blawcyzk get her things together?"

"Certainly," Hutchings agreed. "I know this will be hard, Mrs. Blawcyzk, but try not to worry. Your husband is in the best of hands. I've met him several times. He's a fighter."

"Thank you," Kim said. "Josh's room is just down the hall. He's sleeping. I can carry him if you'll help with his diaper bag."

"I'll do whatever you need."

"Thank you."

Kim led Hutchings to Josh's room.

"Lieutenant Stoker, how bad is it, really?" Betty asked.

"I don't have any details, I'm sorry to say, except that Jim's heart stopped at least once while he was in the STARFlight chopper en route to St. David's, but the paramedics did manage to revive him," Stoker answered. "I just know that, apparently, he was ambushed. Fortunately, a rancher found him before he bled to death, and immediately called 911. The investigators from the Blanco County Sheriff's Department are still gathering evidence, along with Ranger LaTonya Quarles. She covers Gillespie, the next county to the west of Blanco, so she'll be in charge of the investigation into Jim's shooting. Can I help you get anything you might need? You'll probably be at the hospital for quite some time."

"No. No, thank you, Lieutenant. I just want to get to the hospital. I can send for things later, if need be. I'm not worried about anything but my son. I lost my husband to the Rangers already. I don't believe I can face losing my son, so soon after that loss."

"I understand. We're all pulling for Jim, and praying for him, too. As soon as Kim has the baby ready, we'll be on our way."

Once they reached the hospital, Jim's family and their escorts were whisked straight to the family waiting room in the trauma unit. The nurse on duty came from behind her station to greet them.

"Mrs. Blawcyzk?" she said. "I'm Head Nurse Charlotte Dean."

"Yes," Kim and Betty answered simultaneously.

"I'm sorry. I didn't realize both of you were Mrs. Blawcyzk."

"Nurse, this is Ranger Blawcyzk's wife, Kimberly, and his mother, Elizabeth," Lieutenant Stoker explained. "Is there any further word on Jim?"

"He's still in surgery, that's all I can tell you. Why don't you take the ladies back to the private waiting room? I'll try to find out something more. Major Voitek is waiting for you there."

"Thank you, nurse."

Stoker took everyone to a small room off the main family lounge. Major Voitek was pacing the floor. He stopped when he saw Jim's wife and mother, then gave them both a hug.

"I'm so glad you're both here," he said. "Jameson, I haven't had any more information from the doctors since you left. Damn, I hate this waiting. Kim, how are you holding up?"

"I think I'm still in shock," Kim answered. "I don't believe my mind has admitted to itself Jim's been shot."

"I'm still a bit numb, too," Betty added. "Major, can you tell us anything about what happened?"

"At this point, not a whole lot. Jim had called in to say he was on his way to meet a woman, who'd called asking for him, saying she believed she was working for whoever's been killing all those elderly women. Apparently, when he arrived at the location, someone, probably the suspect, was fleeing the scene. Jim radioed in to say he'd stopped them, and that was the last we heard from him. A rancher found him lying close to his truck, and called for help. It's fortunate he did, or Jim would most likely have bled to death."

"How bad is it, Major?" Kim asked.

"I honestly can't tell you," Voitek answered.

"Do you have any idea who shot him?" Betty asked.

"As of the moment, no. The obvious assumption is that it's the same person committing the murders, but it's too soon to say for certain. I'm sure Lieutenant Stoker has told you Ranger Quarles and several officers from the Blanco County Sheriff's Department are checking the scene for evidence right now. We've also put out a statewide APB for the vehicle Jim described when he called in the stop."

The door opened, and Nurse Dean entered.

"Any more word?" Voitek asked.

"I promised the ladies I would try to find out anything more, if I could, and I do have a little information I can share. The surgery is going well; however, it will be at least another hour, possibly two, before the surgeon can speak with you."

"Is my husband going to live?" Kim asked.

"I'll have to leave that for his surgeon to tell you, Mrs. Blawcyzk," Dean said. "I honestly don't know what he'll have to say. I know this is going to sound silly, but until the surgery is over, all you can do is rest, try not to worry, as best you can, hope and pray. I did take the liberty of sending down to the cafeteria to have some hot coffee and a pitcher of sweet tea sent up for y'all. I'd offer to send the chaplain up, but he's out sick, and we couldn't find a substitute. And, of course, if I hear anything else at all, I'll let you know immediately."

"Thank you," Voitek said.

Josh began to fuss.

"He's hungry," Kim said. "I'll have to feed him."

"Just like his father," Stoker said. "Always hungry."

Everyone laughed, the tension broken, for just a moment. Kim turned a chair in the corner toward the wall so she could nurse her son with a bit of privacy. The others also found seats, to settle in for what would seem an interminable wait.

It was a bit more than ninety minutes later when Jim's surgeon came into the room, still dressed in his bloodied scrubs, with a surgical mask hanging around his neck. Rachel Hutchings was playing with Josh, as Kim, despite herself, had dozed off, completely exhausted. However, she came instantly awake when she heard the door open.

"Doctor? Is my husband—"

"Yes, I am Doctor Mark Preston. To answer everyone's first question, Ranger Blawcyzk is still alive. He is still in extremely grave condition, and the next forty-eight hours will be crucial. However, he tolerated the procedure well, so unless there are any unexpected complications, his prognosis is quite good."

"Thank You, Lord," Kim exclaimed. A sigh of relief came from the others.

"Doctor, would you mind telling us more about the operation?" Voitek asked.

"Are you a member of the family?"

"No, but I am Jim's commanding officer. So is Lieutenant Stoker."

"Doctor, as Jim's wife, and as I'm sure you'll agree as Jim's mother, Betty, you have our permission to answer any questions Major Voitek or Lieutenant Stoker have," Kim said.

"Excellent, Mrs. Blawcyzk. Thank you. Major, I removed two bullets from Ranger Blawcyzk's back. The first one struck him in the lower back, on the right side. Luckily, it went below the kidney, missing the bottom of that organ by a few centimeters. It also missed the ureters, the tubes that lead from the kidneys to the bladder. If one or both of those had been hit, that would have been a major complication. A wound such as that would have made Ranger Blawcyzk's survival much less likely. Even more fortunate, the bullet didn't hit a bone, break apart, and perforate the small or large intestines.

"The second bullet struck Ranger Blawcyzk on the left side of his back, up higher. Removing that bullet did not present as much of a problem as the first one. It came to a stop in the Latisimus Dorsi muscle. That is a very large, thick muscle on each side of the body, which turns the torso. In a person who was not in the excellent physical condition that Ranger Blawcyzk is in, the bullet would probably have penetrated more deeply, perhaps deflecting into a lung, the heart, or stomach, inflicting a mortal wound. Fortunately, that did not happen.

"With the bullets removed and the wounds closed, we have two major concerns. The first, obviously, is the large volume of blood Ranger Blawcyzk has lost. That leaves the possibility of heart attack, stroke, the loss of limbs if circulation to the extremities collapses, or even brain damage. As of this moment, Ranger Blawcyzk's pulse is steady, and his heartbeat is as strong as can be expected under the circumstances. That lessens the chance of any of those things occurring, so I am not particularly concerned about any of them, unless something drastically changes.

"The second main concern is infection. We will keep Ranger Blawcyzk on massive doses of IV antibiotics as long as necessary, until the possibility of a life-threatening infection is minimized. For the next forty-eight hours, all we can really do is monitor his condition, and take immediate action to interdict any complications."

"What do you think his chances are, Doctor?" Betty asked.

"Unless there are any complications, which I really don't expect, my estimate is seventy percent, or better."

"Will you be in charge of his care?" Stoker asked.

"I will be the lead physician on the team, yes. If there aren't any more questions, I'd like to clean up, then check on my patient."

"Where are Jim's badge and gun?" Voitek asked. "I'll need those, along with the bullets you removed."

"They were bagged and put in a locker for patients' possessions," Preston answered. "You can explain to the nurse on duty you'll need them released to you. As far as the bullets, they were set aside. I'll bring them to you before I shower."

"May we see him, Doctor?" Kim asked.

Preston rubbed his jaw before replying.

"For a moment or two, that's all. He's heavily

sedated, of course, so he won't realize you are with him. However, please speak to him. I have observed patients, even those in a deep coma, can often sense when someone who loves them is present. I also need to caution all of you, if you have never seen a patient who has just come out of surgery, particularly surgery for traumatic injuries, the sight can be quite disturbing. Follow me."

Preston led the group into the recovery room where Jim lay. The gravely wounded Ranger was extremely pale, his skin a deathly white. Wires connected to electrodes glued to his chest, neck, and legs ran to the constantly beeping and flashing machines monitoring Jim's vital signs. IV lines were attached to his arms, while an oxygen tube ran to his nose. A catheter tube ran from under the sheet to a collection bottle hanging on the bed rail.

Kim's eyes welled with tears.

"Doctor, may I hold my husband's hand, for just a moment?"

"Of course," Preston answered. "Just please, use some Purell first."

Kim and Betty sanitized their hands, then each took one of Jim's in theirs.

"Jim, I was afraid this day would happen, just not so soon," Kim said. "I love you so much. Hurry and get better for me and Josh. The doctor says we can't stay long, so I'll kiss you good night."

She kissed him on the cheek.

"Jim, damn you, and damn this whole every-Blawcyzk-male-has-got-to-be-a-damn-Texas-Ranger macho tradition," Betty said. "You've got to get better, so I can kick your butt from here to Waco, you damn son of your father. You're just like him . . . and I love you in spite of that, just like I did him."

She also kissed Jim on the cheek.

"Doctor, do you have any idea when Jim might come to?" Voitek asked.

"He could become somewhat awake sometime tomorrow," Preston asked. "He'll still be pretty drugged up, so anything he says probably won't make any sense. He might not recognize any of you, or understand whatever you say to him."

"When will he be able to answer questions? He may be the only hope we have of finding whoever did this to him."

"With luck, in forty-eight to seventy-two hours. He will become feverish for a while. If the fever gets too high, whatever he says will probably be gibberish. He may even hallucinate. However, on the dose of antibiotics he's receiving, I don't expect that to happen. I hate to ask you to leave so quickly, but it's best for Ranger Blawcyzk if he's allowed to just rest, and let his body start to heal. If there are any changes, I'll be certain you know immediately. He does have several things in his favor. He's young, in excellent

362

physical condition, and he has family and friends to support him. I have a feeling he's a stubborn cuss, too."

"Doctor, you don't know the half of it," Stoker said, grinning. He shook his head.

"Then that's half the battle, right there. I'll order some blankets and pillows brought down so you all can try and get some rest. Mrs. Blawcyzk, do you need anything for the little one? Diapers, a blanket?"

"Thank you, Doctor Preston. We threw some things in a diaper bag before we left the house. We should be fine."

"All right, but if you need anything, just let someone on the floor know."

"Of course, and thank you."

"One more thing, Doctor," Voitek said. "I'm going to order a guard be posted outside Jim's door. No one, and I mean no one, except a hospital staff member, both Mrs. Blawcyzks, or a police officer with proper identification is to be allowed in his room. I don't want whoever shot Jim to try and finish the job, once they find out he's still alive."

"Certainly. That's merely prudent. I'll stop in to update you on Ranger Blawcyzk's condition before I leave."

Jim's family and fellow law officers went back to the private family waiting room, to begin their long vigil.

19

Jim's recovery progressed at just about the pace Doctor Preston had expected. Three days after being airlifted to the ER, he was awake and hungry, grousing that he was only being allowed a bland, liquid diet. His mother and wife were taking shifts staying at the hospital, while the other remained home with Josh, so Kim was with him this morning. Despite his pleading, she refused to sneak a pizza or hamburger, fries, and Dr Pepper in to him. Lieutenant Stoker and Ranger LaTonya Quarles heard his complaints when they walked into the room.

"Good mornin', Jim," Stoker said. "Doctor Preston said you were alert enough to answer questions. It sure sounds like it."

"If that damn Doc Preston doesn't let me have some real food, I'll be too weak to even breathe," Jim answered. "LaTonya, my wife, here, won't bring me a hamburger. How about you come back with some of your famous fried catfish?"

"There's not a chance of that," LaTonya said. "Aren't you aware you came damn near close to singin' with the angels . . . or more likely, howlin' with Satan's demons? Don't worry, Kim. I won't give him anything he shouldn't have. How are you doin'?"

"Much better, now that Jim's back with us."

"Jim, do you feel up to answering questions this morning?" Stoker asked.

"If I don't die of starvation first, yeah, Lieutenant."

"I don't need to be here for that," Kim said. "While you're talking with Jim, I'll go down to the cafeteria for lunch. I think I'll have, let's see, a nice salad, then a steak with a baked potato, and a slice of coconut cake."

"Darling, what was the number of that divorce lawyer again?" Jim said. "I've got grounds of mental cruelty."

"You won't divorce me. We're too much in love," Kim said. She gave Jim a quick kiss. "I'll be back soon. Don't drive the lieutenant or LaTonya crazy."

"It's already too late. He's done it," LaTonya said. "Have a good lunch, Kim."

Once Kim was gone, Stoker and LaTonya pulled chairs up alongside Jim's bed. LaTonya turned on her digital recorder.

"Jim, I'm going to start," she said. "Texas Ranger LaTonya Quarles of Company F, along with Lieutenant Jameson Stoker of Company F, interviewing Ranger James C. Blawcyzk of Company F, in the matter of his recent shooting. Are you ready to begin, Ranger Blawcyzk?"

"I sure am," Jim answered. Just then, a nurse came into the room.

"Ranger Blawcyzk, I didn't realize you had

company," she said. "I hate to interrupt, but it's time for your shot."

"Don't let us stop you," Stoker said.

"You don't understand. It has to go in his buttocks."

"Can't it wait until later, Doris?" Jim asked.

"Not this one. I'd pull the curtain around your bed, but it broke last night, remember?"

"Go ahead and give him the shot, nurse," LaTonya said, as she put her recorder on pause. "It won't bother us. It's not like Jim's got something we haven't seen before."

"Ranger Blawcyzk?"

"Go ahead and get it over with, Doris. LaTonya, don't you dare look. You either, Lieutenant."

"Of course I won't, Jim," LaTonya said.

The nurse rolled Jim onto his side to give him the shot.

"Oh, Lordy, my eyes," LaTonya shouted. "Nice butt, Jim, but I should have worn my sunglasses. It's so pale I'm going blind."

"You said you wouldn't look!"

"I lied."

"Well, at least you were so worried about everyone seeing your behind you didn't even feel the needle go in, Ranger," the nurse said. "I'm all done."

"If you're done looking at Jim's keister, LaTonya, let's get back to the business at hand. He can turn the other cheek."

"Thanks a lot, Lieutenant," Jim grumbled.

LaTonya took her recorder off pause.

"Let's start over, Ranger Blawcyzk."

"I'm ready."

"All right. First, to help you recall the events of that day, I have collected some evidence from the scene. These include tire tracks, a piece of a car bumper which matches the description of the vehicle you stopped, as well as some paint chips from the same vehicle, and a nine-millimeter bullet, which apparently came from your gun. We also found an Illinois license plate stuck in the broken fence. There were also signs the apparent shooter attempted to remove or cover up evidence. No shell casings from the shooter's weapon were found, and tire tracks and foot prints were brushed away. We do know the bullets which were taken out of you, Jim, don't match the ones which killed the five women. They didn't come from the same gun. So far, the limited amount of evidence we've gathered has given us no lead as to the shooter's identity."

"Hell, you don't need any of that," Jim said. "I know damn well who shot me."

"You can identify the shooter? Who was it?"

"Blanco County Sheriff's Deputy Harvey Kelley."

"Harvey Kelley? Are you sure about that, Jim?"

"As sure as I'm looking at you, LaTonya. As sure as I'm lyin' in this damn hospital bed with two bullet holes in my back. The only thing I can't figure is why the sheriff's office didn't know where he was. He must have given them his last location, told them he'd be there for a while, maybe taking his lunch break, then turned off his radio and dash cam and disabled his GPS."

"Of all the damn bad luck," Stoker said.

"What do you mean, Lieutenant?" Jim asked.

"Kelley's body was found in Canyon Lake yesterday. He'd gone out fishing for the day, and apparently fell out of his bass boat. The autopsy report hasn't come in yet, but it looks like an accidental drowning."

"If Harve Kelley fell out of his boat and drowned, I'd bet my hat he had help," Jim answered. "We're friends, or I guess I should say we used to be friends. I've been out on his boat before, fishing and swimming with him. The man could swim like a trout. His death was no accident."

"You're saying someone paid him to kill you, but decided to kill him instead of handing over the money?" Stoker asked.

"It sure looks that way, doesn't it? It would eliminate a witness, particularly if whoever paid Harve is aware I'm still alive—which they no doubt are. Killing him was probably payback for his bungling the job."

"Lieutenant, if you wouldn't mind, can I resume my questioning?" LaTonya said. "Jim, start from the beginning, and tell me everything that happened that day, as best you can recall."

"Sure, Tonya. I was in my office when I got a call from a woman, who sounded really scared. She said she believed she was working for the man who was our suspect, and was afraid she'd be his next victim. She wouldn't talk to anyone but me, she insisted. I got her address, told Mary Huggins, who took the call in, where I was going and why, then headed for the address."

"That was 1239 Ranch Road 1320 in Blanco County, correct?"

"That's correct."

"And the caller gave her name as Deidre Moore?"

"Also correct."

"Go on."

"Okay. Just as I arrived at the address, a bronze Nissan Maxima came shooting out of the driveway, with two people in it, a man and a frightened looking woman . . . I figured the driver had to be our suspect, so I gave chase.

"They went off the road, through a barbed wire fence, and onto a one-lane dirt road, which wasn't much more than a deer track. When they swerved off the road, then back onto it, I reckoned their car must have given out, because they stopped. I radioed the information on the vehicle to dispatch, and let them know I'd made the stop.

"Just as I got out of my truck, Harve pulled

up behind me. He said he'd cover me. Since I'd known him as a good officer for several years, I had no reason to doubt him. The next thing I know is I get a bullet in my back, then another one. I don't remember anything that happened after that until I woke up here."

"Jim, I have to ask you one more time. You're absolutely positive the address you were given was 1239 Ranch Road 1320?"

"I am. You can pull up the recording of the call if you want to check that. Why?"

"Because there's nothing at that address but an old farm house, that's tumbled in on itself."

"What?"

"Nothing but scrub, mesquite, and that collapsed house."

"So I was set up."

"So it seems. My guess is whoever shot you had nothing at all to do with the women's murders."

"What it appears, Jim," Stoker continued, "is that whoever wants you dead saw your plea for anyone who thought they might be a target of the women's killer to call the Rangers. They set up a phony call, and were waiting for you when you showed up. They did a damn good job of baiting their trap."

"And I fell for it, hook, line, and sinker, like a damn fool."

"You had no way of knowing it was a trap. None of us would have," LaTonya said.

"Have you managed to collect any leads at all?" Jim asked.

"Not many. The car was a rental, picked up at Austin Bergstrom. We've obtained the renter's information from them, including a copy of his driver's license, but it's no doubt a fake. The car hasn't been returned. The call you got came from a Houston area cell phone number, registered to a post office box, and was placed from Blanco. The phone's probably still in the car. As far as the P.O. box, it appears to belong to a shell company, probably another of the ones you've been trying to track down. We're attempting to find the woman who made the call, but right now, we're not even certain she exists. It might have been a man imitating a woman's voice. Of course, it could also have been the woman you saw in the car. In that case, either she's in on this, or she's dead."

"You might want to check Canyon Lake," Jim suggested.

"We hadn't made that connection, until you just told us who ambushed you," Stoker said. "As soon as we're done here, I'll get a dive team right on it."

"Who owns 1239 Ranch Road 1320?" Jim asked.

"The county," LaTonya answered. "They took it over for unpaid taxes, way back in 2009. The last of the family who owned it, Helmut Muhler, died and seemingly left no heirs. Obviously, we're going through the records to look for anyone who might have some connection to him."

"Someone sure knew something about the place, at least enough to use it to set me up. Have you got anything else?"

"Not a damn thing," LaTonya admitted. "However, we've still got to go through Harvey Kelley's bass boat and trailer, and are waiting for the autopsy results. Now that you've told us he was the shooter, we'll process his house and car, examine his phone records, all the usual stuff. Perhaps we'll come up with something. Jim, we promised your doctor we wouldn't overtax you. Unless there's anything else you can think of, we'll stop here."

"There's not."

"All right. This concludes the interview with Texas Ranger James C. Blawcyzk."

LaTonya turned off her recorder.

"Say good-bye to Kim for us," she said.

"I'll do that. But Lieutenant, could I ask a favor of you before you go?"

"Depends on what it is."

"Could you bring in my laptop, or give it to Kim or my mother to bring in. There's no point in me lying in this bed, doing nothing but going stir crazy. If I have my computer, I can keep working on both these cases."

"I'll ask your doctor. If he agrees, then you can

have your computer. For now, you take it easy. We'll see you soon."

"Thanks, Lieutenant. Just remember LaTonya, the next time I see you, catfish. And Dr Pepper. Even better, a couple of long neck Lone Stars. If you don't bring those, I'll show you another full moon."

"Anything but that! Good-bye, Jim."

Once Latonya and Stoker left, Jim started to try and piece together anything else he could recall about that day he'd taken two bullets in his back. However, his body's need for more rest betrayed him. Five minutes later, he was sound asleep.

Tarquin Sarkanian's phone rang. He hesitated, knowing who would be on the other end, then picked it up.

"Hello, Logan."

"Don't 'hello Logan' me, you son of a bitch. You screwed up again, Tarquin. Blawcyzk's still alive. What are you going to do about it?"

Sarkanian sighed.

"I'm working on a plan right now. That damn Ranger has more lives than a cat. Who could have guessed that he'd take two nine-millimeter bullets in the back at close range and survive? I was personally driving the car he chased, and saw the deputy gun him down."

"But the damn deputy didn't make certain he was dead, did he? Did he? For that matter, neither did you. I just turned off the news. The damn Blanco County sheriff has just pulled the car you used from Canyon Lake. You'd better hope there's nothing in it that connects it to you. I'll guarantee they also figure out Kelley's death wasn't an accident."

"There won't be anything in that car but a few bass. As far as the deputy, no, he didn't, but he paid the price. And even though an autopsy might show he didn't drown, it can't prove he didn't accidentally hit his head when he slipped, then went over the side of his boat. So you see, it'll be hard to prove his death wasn't an accident. And as you said, neither did I make sure of Blawcyzk," Sarkanian admitted. "I had to get out of there before someone came along. I apologize, but the good news is there's still no way to connect you or your employers to me, and Blawcyzk's out of circulation for a while. I'll have him dead before he's back in action again. I'm going to handle him personally again. And this time, there won't be any slip-ups."

"Tarquin, besides being a damn screw up, you're a lousy liar. You know damn well my receptionist's body is in the trunk of that car. If the Rangers ever make the connection . . ."

"They won't. You've already doctored her employment file to show she left two months ago, that she was taking a job in Florida. Besides, you yourself said you had to get rid of her, that

374

you'd found her rummaging through papers about your real business after jimmying open the file cabinet, and she threatened to blackmail you. Your employers agreed she had to be eliminated. So, she's gone, and the Rangers won't be able to connect her to anything, as long as you don't lose it."

"I won't, but my employers want Blawcyzk dead. So do I, and we mean *now*. You have three days, Tarquin. Three days."

The phone went dead.

The next day, LaTonya stopped by to give Jim an update on what she'd discovered, at least so far.

"Mornin', Jim. I couldn't sneak any catfish past the nurses, but I do have a big chunk of homemade coconut cake in this box. I don't suppose you'd want any."

"The odds of me not wanting any of your cake are the same as you turning as pale as me, LaTonya . . . none. Hand it over."

"Sure. I've got a carton of cold milk, too. You can work on those while I bring you up to speed."

She gave Jim the cake and milk, along with a plastic fork.

"You're a lifesaver, LaTonya," he said.

"I wouldn't go that far, but I can give you some news you can use," she answered. "First, Harvey Kelley didn't drown. He was dead before he went into the lake. The cause of death is blunt trauma to the head and a fractured skull. Unfortunately, it will be hard to prove he didn't slip, hit his head on something in the boat, and knock himself out before he fell into the lake, but we haven't found any signs, like pieces of skin, hanks of hair, or blood that would indicate that happened. He was most likely killed elsewhere, then his body dumped in the lake and the boat set adrift."

"That would make sense," Jim said. "What about the car?"

"It's the one you were chasing," LaTonya answered. "What we found when we pulled it out of the lake was really interesting. There was a woman's body in the trunk. She was in her mid-fifties, a bit on the chunky side. No identification of course, but odds are she was the woman who called in to you, Deidre Moore. We're working on that now."

"Or someone using the real Moore's name," Jim said.

"That's a possibility too. Here's the real kicker. Helmut Muhler, the man who owned the property where you were lured, had a great niece. Would you care to guess her name?"

"Deidre Moore."

"That's right."

"Which means someone connected to the person who wants me dead knew that."

"Right again. Listen, Jim, I've got to get out of here and back to work on this case. Enjoy the rest of your cake, and I'll talk to you once I have anything more that's relevant. See you later."

"See you later. And thanks again for the cake."

While recovering in the hospital, Jim made steady progress over the next several days. Kim and his mother visited every day, of course. He teased them that he could get used to this life, just lying around and basically doing nothing, having his food delivered to him in bed and nurses to give him sponge baths and change his clothes.

Doctor Preston had told him he could work on his laptop, so he spent every moment he didn't have a visitor or was in rehab digging through the records on his cases. Gradually, he was making connections which he hoped would lead him to the person who wanted him dead.

LaTonya Quarles was also working hard, chasing down every lead, no matter how far-fetched. This particular day, Kim and his mother had an important meeting, so they wouldn't be arriving for their visit until that evening. Jim had just finished lunch when Todd Irving, the Austin police officer who was guarding his room that day, poked his head in the door.

"Ranger Blawcyzk, I have a man outside who insists he has to see you. I told him you weren't allowed any visitors, but he said you'd want to see him."

"What's his name?"

"Jerome Golden."

"Jerry? He's damn right I'll see him. Send him on in." When the officer hesitated, Jim told him, "Don't worry, I'll take the responsibility if he kills me, but he won't."

"Somehow, that doesn't put me at ease," Irving said. He opened the door wider. "All right, Mr. Golden, you can go on in."

Jerry came in. He was carrying a sack from the hospital's gift shop.

"Shut the door, Todd," Jim said.

"Are you certain?"

"Yes."

"All right." Irving let the door close.

"Howdy, Jerry. I'm sure glad to see you," Jim said. "I hope this isn't just a social visit."

"No, it's not," Jerry answered. "But first, how are you doing?"

"Good enough I'll be going home the day after tomorrow. I can even get straight back to work in two weeks."

"That's great news. How soon can we get together for some racquetball again?"

"Probably a couple of weeks. I'll have to ask my doctor. Since I'll still be healing, you might actually have a chance to beat me this time."

"Jim, I'd better tell you what I have for you, before one of your doctors or nurses decides to come in. Here."

He handed Jim the gift sack. Inside were a get-well card and a stuffed dog.

Jim looked at Jerry quizzically.

"The puppy is for your baby. The card is for you. Open it. I think you'll find the message is quite interesting."

"All right." Jim tore open the envelope, then opened the card to read its contents.

"Are you sure?"

"I'm positive. The man's been a schemer for years. You probably recall his history."

"I sure do. I was finally getting close to connecting the paper trail, but this cinches it. Listen, Jerry, do me a favor. I want to keep this under wraps until I get out of here. This is not just a Ranger matter. It's personal. Our man's not going anywhere anyway. He's got too good a business going. I want to handle this myself."

"I knew you would, Jim. The only person who knows this, besides me, is my source. Unless something happens to you, this goes no further than this room. Maybe you should destroy the card."

"I should, but I'm gonna hold onto it. That way, if something happens to *both* of us, the evidence will still be available. Jerry, if this works out, maybe I can get your and Esther's probation shortened, or even dropped."

"That would be appreciated. Listen, I'd better run. I've got a meeting in an hour that, with any luck, will land me a big distribution contract. I'll see you later."

"Good luck, Jerry. And I'm much obliged."

Late that afternoon, Jim had another unexpected visitor, Ranger Bruce Sherman. A woman about his age was with him.

"Howdy, Bruce. What the heck are you doin' all the way down here? It's a bit out of B's territory. How'd you get the day off?"

"Howdy, Jim. I didn't. I'm working, but I have a good reason for coming to see you. However, first, I'd like you to meet my wife, Kelly."

"Howdy, Kelly. It's nice to meet you. You're as pretty as Bruce said you were."

"Hello, Ranger Blawcyzk."

"Jim."

"Jim. I'm pleased to meet you, too."

"Okay, Bruce, you have me curious. What brings you by? I don't suppose you snuck any Perfect Chick in for me by any chance?"

Bruce shook his head.

"No, I sure didn't. I wanted to tell you this before you found out from the news, or someone else. There's been another murder of an elderly woman, this time in Weston."

"You didn't drive all the way down here to tell me just that," Jim said.

"No, I didn't. The good news, if it can be called that, is we finally caught the guy."

"You got him? That's the best news I've had in a long time. How'd you do it?"

"A neighbor happened to be stopping by for a visit. She saw a car leaving, but didn't really think anything of it until she went inside the house and saw her friend dead. Luckily, she remembered the make and color of the car, a burgundy Chrysler 300, and that the driver was a long-haired, bearded white male. She also said he'd headed east on Cowan Road. What she didn't have was the license plate number, unfortunately. A description of the car was broadcast, but of course there's an awful lot of red Chryslers on the road. I figured if he was going east, he was heading for 75.

"The only question then was would he head north toward Sherman or south toward Dallas. I decided he'd probably head for Dallas, since there'd be a bigger market for his product there. I also thought, since he was having the stuff made down your way, he was probably working the I-35 corridor between Austin and Dallas.

"I was heading north on 75, planning to sit on the side of it just south of the Collin County Outer Loop to watch for the car, when I saw a red Chrysler going south. By the time I could get turned around, I was afraid I'd lost him. But, he got tied up by construction, where 75 is down to one lane in McKinney. Traffic stopped suddenly, and the woman behind him rear-ended his car, hard enough to pop the trunk open. When that happened, the drugs stashed there were in plain sight. More importantly, the impact gave him such a bad whiplash he couldn't move.

"He tried to run, but as soon as he got out of the car he fell flat on his face. It was probably the easiest capture I've ever made. He had a nine-millimeter Glock in his glove compartment. As soon as a ballistics test is done, I'm certain it will prove to be the same weapon used to kill those women."

"Great work, Bruce. That's one major case that's cleared up. What's the suspect's name?"

"Roland Tanner. His address is 2528 Fruitland Avenue in Farmers Branch. We're just waiting on a warrant to search the house."

"One more piece of dirt off the street," Jim said. "Only a few thousand more to go."

"I just hope you're not upset that I made the arrest," Bruce said. "After all, this was your case to start with."

"Are you serious? It doesn't matter whose case it was, as long as it ends in an arrest. I've got no problem at all with you bringing the Tanner character in. You also just might have saved some more lives, too. Stop being so doggone polite, will you?"

"I can't help it, I guess. I was raised that way," Bruce said. "I hate to leave so quick, but I've got to head back to my office and get the paperwork on this arrest completed. We can get together once you're up and around again. Any idea when that will be?"

"I'm outta here the day after tomorrow, and that's not a minute too soon. I'm about to go stir crazy in here."

"That's good news. Are we any closer to finding out who's trying to kill you?"

"We've got some leads, but nothing solid yet."

"I wouldn't worry too much. Every law officer in the state is looking for him."

"That's easy for you to say, Bruce," Jim said, laughing. "You're not the one who took two bullets in the back."

"I can't argue with you there. I'd better get going. You take care."

"I will. You do the same. Once all this is over, like you said, we'll have to get together. I'd like you both to meet my wife, Kim. I think you'd like her a lot, Kelly."

"I'll bet I would, Jim. She and I can talk about how crazy we both were for marrying a Ranger. It's a date."

"Good. We'll set it up once things are back to normal. Have a safe drive back."

20

Early the next morning, well before dawn, Jim was still asleep. When the door to his room opened, he stirred slightly, opened his eyes for a moment, then closed them again, aware someone had come into the room, but the fact not quite registering. When he felt the person pull down his sheet and lift his arm, he became fully awake.

"Who the hell are you?" he asked the man standing over him, who was dressed in a doctor's white coat, and held a hypodermic needle. He strained to read the person's identification tag in the dimly lit room.

"I'm Doctor Bollinger. I just started my internship here last week," the man answered. "I'm here to give you the shot Doctor Preston ordered, to help you sleep."

"The hell you are," Jim said. "Doctor Preston didn't order any sleep medicine. I've had no problem sleeping at all."

"That's not what your chart says. The orders are to give you a shot to help you sleep. Trust me, this medicine will do exactly that, for a good, long time."

Jim pulled his arm away, and shot an elbow to the man's groin. He dropped the needle and doubled over in pain, then collapsed to his knees. Jim pushed the call button for the nurse, and began yelling for help. At the same time, his door opened, and Paul Curry, the Austin officer guarding him came into the room, gun drawn.

"Don't move, mister," he told the supposed intern, who was now curled up on the floor. "You didn't really think I believed you were a doctor, did you? Ranger Blawcyzk hasn't had a doctor come by to check him at this time of the morning since he left the ICU. Also, a nurse would be giving any routine shot, not a doctor. Are you all right, Jim?"

"Yeah, but you cut it pretty close, Paul."

"I'm sorry, but I had to let him in to make certain he was up to no good. His credentials all appeared legitimate, so I had no real reason to stop him. It looks like you handled him pretty well, though."

"He was just the right height for me to get him where it hurts the most," Jim said.

Curry had Jim's assailant lie on his belly, then cuffed his hands behind his back.

Jim's door opened again, and the nurse on duty came in.

"Ranger Blawcyzk, you needed . . ." Her voice trailed off.

"I don't need anything," Jim said. "However, would you call Ranger Company F? Tell them to send Sean Jordan down here, right away."

"Certainly. Officer Curry, do you need me to call your department?"

"I've already done that, nurse, but thank you. Until another officer arrives, could you have one of your security people stay outside this room? Also, put this floor on lockdown."

"Of course, Officer."

Curry lifted his prisoner and shoved him into a chair.

"Be careful you don't stick yourself with that needle on the floor, Paul," Jim cautioned. "I'm certain it's filled with enough barbiturate to kill my horse. Once help arrives, we'll have to bag it properly for evidence."

"All right, Jim. Meanwhile, let's see who this character really is. I don't suppose you'd care to tell us your name, mister."

"My name's on my identification, Doctor Piotr Bollinger."

"And I'm Tom Mix," Curry answered. "I guess we'll just let you sit there and think about things. In the meantime, you have the right to remain silent . . ."

Sean Jordan arrived within twenty minutes. Several more Austin police officers were already on scene.

"Jim. What the hell's going on?" he asked. "All the nurse told me on the phone was that you needed me here, *pronto*."

"Because that *hombre* in the chair tried to fill me full of a medicine that would help me sleep, permanently," Jim said. "He hasn't said a word, except to give us a name, which I'm certain isn't his."

"Hmmm. Let me take a look at him."

Sean studied Bollinger's face closely, then opened his laptop, turned it on, and brought up a series of driver's license photographs.

"Ah, here we go," he said, then turned the computer so both Jim and his would-be killer could see it. "You'll recall the information we obtained, saying the late and unlamented Sharky was working for a man out of West Lake Hills, a man with a foreign sounding last name. So, I went to the DMV files, got the names and addresses of any licensed driver in that area of town, then narrowed those down by picking out any foreign sounding names, except Hispanic, since Hispanic names sure aren't foreign to Texas. Then, I narrowed the list even more by searching for names similar to Bagdasarian, which our informant said was similar to the name of the man Sharky was working for. Gentlemen, there you see him. Tarquin Sarkanian. That is you, isn't it, Mr. Sarkanian?"

"I'm not saying one damn word until I talk to my attorney," Sarkanian said.

"That's your right, sir," Sean answered. "You can call him as soon as we get you booked. You might want to think about cooperating, however. It seems you are wanted not only in New York, California, and Illinois, but also Canada and several other countries. Keep in mind that Texas is a death penalty state. Let's go."

21

"Jim, I still don't like the idea of letting you go back to work so soon," Lieutenant Stoker said. He and Sean Jordan were sitting in Jim's Tahoe, outside the building which held the offices of XMD Logistics and Distribution. Parked next to Jim was LaTonya Quarles, in her silver Chevy Impala.

"I promise, it's only for this one day," Jim answered. "After that, I'll take the two more weeks Doc Preston wanted me to have to finish recuperating. But I'll be damned if anyone else is going to make these arrests for me. These bastards nearly had my family and me killed, so I believe I have the right to take them down. Are you both ready?"

"We are," Sean said.

"Then let's go."

Jim signaled to LaTonya. The four Rangers got out of their vehicles, went inside, and took the stairs to the third floor. They drew their guns, then Jim turned the knob and slammed open the door. The new receptionist, a young blonde, screamed.

"Texas Rangers!" Jim said. "Just stay where you are, Miss. Don't touch that telephone. Sean, stay with her." Jim went behind her desk, with

Stoker and LaTonya following, and slammed open the door to David Prescott's office. Logan Daniels was with him. Daniels started to reach inside his jacket for a shoulder gun. LaTonya shot him in the side, dropping him where he stood.

"What's, what's the meaning of this?" Prescott said.

"Oh, are you surprised to see me, Mr. Prescott? I'll just bet you are," Jim said. He pulled two folded papers out of his shirt pocket. "This is a warrant; actually, *two* warrants. You and your cohort, there, are under arrest. A partial list of the charges includes manufacturing and distribution of illegal drugs, conspiracy, assault, attempted murder, and conspiracy to commit murder. LaTonya, Lieutenant, they're all yours. Me an' Sean have an appointment downtown."

Half an hour later, Jim and Sean were taking the elevator to the twenty-fourth floor penthouse of a high rise condominium building overlooking the Colorado River in downtown Austin, after obtaining the keys from the building's security manager.

"Let's hope this son of a bitch gives up without a fight, Jim," Sean said, just before the elevator reached the penthouse.

"Here's hoping so, too, Sean, although I'd like nothing better than to hang the bastard by his ankles from his balcony," Jim said.

"I can't blame you for that," Sean answered.

The elevator stopped. Its door opened directly into the penthouse, whose occupant was pouring himself a martini. He dropped the glass in shock when he saw the two Rangers standing there, with their guns aimed straight at him.

"Texas Rangers, Willard Kenney," Jim said. He tossed the warrant he held on a glass coffee table. "This is a warrant for your arrest. You have the right—"

"You have no reason to arrest me," Kenney broke in.

"Oh, but we do, and plenty of evidence to support your arrest," Jim answered. "Your partners Daniels and Prescott are already in custody."

"This is obviously some conspiracy against me, but I'm not going to fight you here," Kenney said. "Go ahead, take me into custody. I'll not resist. I'll call my attorney from the police station."

He held his hands out to be cuffed. When Jim went to place the shackles around his wrists, Kenney slid a syringe and needle from under his shirtsleeve, and jabbed it into a vein in Jim's wrist. Jim immediately became dizzy, but still had the presence of mind and enough strength to press his pistol against Kenney's belly and pull the trigger, three times. Kelley crumpled to the white carpet, his blood staining it red. Jim staggered to a green velvet sectional, and fell back on it.

"Jim! Jim!" Sean shouted.

"Get . . . an ambulance, Sean. He just . . . shot me full . . . of heroin."

22

Jim was back in St. David's South, this time recovering from an extreme overdose of heroin. His family had just gone home, and now Lieutenant Stoker and Major Voitek were with him, taking his final report on the XMD drug case.

"So, Jim, it took you a while, but you did manage to wrap this case up, nice and neatly," Voitek said. "Willard Kenney's dead, and the records we obtained from his home, and the office in San Marcos, gave us enough information to pick up twenty-three more of his cronies, plus the DEA got some more down in Del Rio, and the Mexican authorities rounded up a bunch, too. That's one drug outfit busted up for good."

"Yeah, but another one'll take its place before long, Major."

"Sadly, you're right," Lieutenant Stoker agreed. "I know most of what happened from what you've already given us, but how exactly did you zero in on Willard Kenney?"

"A lot of leg work, and a little luck," Jim said. "I might not have been able to make the case, if Jerry Golden hadn't given me the last piece of the puzzle. I sure hope the courts will drop his and Esther's probation."

393

"It will be dropped if I have anything to say about it," Voitek assured him. "Jerry's one drug distributor who's certainly turned his life around."

"He is," Jim agreed. "By the way, did either of you think on the name Kenney gave his company?"

"You mean XMD Logistics and Distribution?" Stoker said. "No, why?"

"You'll recall why Kenney was arrested the first time, for over prescribing drugs," Jim said. "He lost his medical license for that, plus spent a year in jail. When he got out, he started distributing drugs—this time, illegal ones, all over again. He was an ex-physician, or M. D. So, he came up with XMD."

"Which is something *you'd* come up with, Jim," Voitek said. "Well, thanks to you and Bruce Sherman, two big cases have been cleared off the books. How soon will you be ready to get back to work?"

"Is today too soon?"

"That depends. We've been asked to check into some political kickbacks and bribes in your territory."

"Politicians? I think I'm having a relapse," Jim said.

"Don't worry. The case will be waiting for you," Stoker said. "Now, we'll leave you be. Take care of yourself, and kiss your wife and mother and hug your baby for us."

"That, I can manage," Jim said. "But right now, I do need to get some sleep."

"Not until you get another shot in your butt," Doris, the nurse, said from the doorway.

"Major, Lieutenant. Get me outta here!" Jim pleaded.

"Not on your life, Ranger," Voitek said. "Nurse, he's all yours."

About the Author

Jim Griffin became enamored of the Texas Rangers from watching the TV series, Tales of the Texas Rangers, as a youngster. He grew to be an avid student and collector of Rangers' artifacts, memorabilia and other items. His collection is now housed in the Texas Ranger Hall of Fame and Museum in Waco.

His quest for authenticity in his writing has taken him to the famous Old West towns of Pecos, Deadwood, Cheyenne, Tombstone and numerous others. While Jim's books are fiction, he strives to keep them as accurate as possible within the realm of fiction.

A graduate of Southern Connecticut State University, Jim now lives in Keene, New Hampshire when he isn't travelling around the west.

A devoted and enthusiastic horseman, Jim bought his first horse when he was a junior in college. He has owned several American Paint horses. He is a member of the Connecticut Horse Council Volunteer Horse Patrol, an organization which assists the state park Rangers with patrolling parks and forests.

Jim's books are highly reminiscent of the pulp westerns of yesteryear, the heroes and villains are clearly separated.

Website: www.jamesjgriffin.net

Books are produced in the United States using U.S.-based materials

Books are printed using a revolutionary new process called THINKtech™ that lowers energy usage by 70% and increases overall quality

Books are durable and flexible because of Smyth-sewing

Paper is sourced using environmentally responsible foresting methods and the paper is acid-free